From *Murder a Mile High*

The car swooped around a curve; Emma braced her feet and looked out. It should have been dark by now, but a bright moon was shining high among the clouds, illuminating, as though by daylight, green meadows that stretched away.

Emma looked again. Those weren't meadows; those were the tops of trees—big trees—far, far below! The car swooped again with a screech that must have taken a good two hundred miles off Mr. Weatherbee's tires, and Emma climbed, panicky, to the other side of the car. The view from there was not pleasant either. Jagged rocks that cast black shadows in the moonlight towered high above her—over her, for in some places they seemed to be driving in a half tunnel excavated from the cliff. She didn't blame Chew for hugging the inside track. . . .

She climbed back to the other side of the car and snatched a quick look, then shut her eyes. There was no inside track. They were hurtling down the mountainside at breakneck speed on a single-track road. Even if they made all the turns, which seemed impossible, a single car—just one little old Ford—was all that was necessary to send them off—off over the tops of those gigantic trees, crashing, smashing on a hidden ledge, to broken bits of nothingness.

Emma pounded on the glass in front of her. She yelled, but the head in the stiff black cap did not turn; the pace did not let up. This was Mr. Weatherbee's doing—Emma saw it now—this was a diabolical plan to send her off to be killed, mangled, maimed, there on the lonely mountainside.

Emma Marsh mysteries by
Elizabeth Dean

Murder is a Collector's Item (1939)
Murder is a Serious Business (1940)
Murder a Mile High (1944)

All titles reprinted 1998-2001
by The Rue Morgue Press

Murder a Mile High

An Emma Marsh mystery by
Elizabeth Dean

Introduction by
Tom & Enid Schantz

The Rue Morgue Press
Boulder, Colorado

For Bette and Helen,
H and Don,
Ruey and Bob,
Jerry and Jack,
Jane and karl,
Glen and the Roys

Murder a Mile High
Copyright © 1944, 1970
Reprinted with permission of
the author's estate.

ISBN: 0-915230-39-9

New material © 2001
by The Rue Morgue Press

Central City is a real town, as are many of the
other Colorado towns and cities mentioned in
this narrative, but the author has taken
some geographical liberties and populated
these towns with characters who are solely
the product of the author's imagaination.

Printed by Johnson Printing,
Boulder, Colorado

PRINTED IN THE UNITED STATES OF AMERICA

About Elizabeth Dean

Elizabeth Dean was the wife of a successful Council Bluffs, Iowa, ophthalmologist and her writing was mostly a hobby, although she did contribute articles and stories to many of the high-paying slick magazines of the day like *The Saturday Evening Post*. She used the proceeds from her first Emma Marsh mystery, *Murder is a Collector's Item*, to furnish her Iowa home with antiques, purchased mainly in New England except for one table which had been transported by pioneers in an oxcart to Boulder, Colorado. The proceeds from its sequel, *Murder is a Serious Business*, went to buy purebred Aberdeen Angus cattle to stock her ranch—Buckshot—located near Evergreen, Colorado.

Elizabeth Dean and her husband may have first acquired this summer home to relieve Liz's severe hay fever, but there's little doubt but that she took cattle raising very seriously. In 1951 she finished first in the Jefferson County field trials, with her entry scoring 193 out of a possible 200 points. Although her first two books were set in Boston, where she went to college and later worked in an antiques store, she used her adopted state of Colorado as the colorful setting for the third and final Emma Marsh mystery, *Murder a Mile High*.

Her title is a little misleading because the murders take place not in the mile-high city of Denver but in a semi-fictional version of Central City, located at 8516 feet. Founded in 1859 during the gold rush, Central City was once called "the richest square mile on earth." The Opera House, which is the focus of *Murder A Mile High,* is real (though it has been renovated since the action in that book) and was built in 1878 by Welsh and Cornish miners. Today it boasts the fifth oldest opera company in the United States, founded in 1932, or nine years before the events related in *Murder a Mile High*.

In the original published version of *Murder a Mile High*, Dean calls the town "Golden City," although in one place she accidentally refers to it by its real name. Whether it was the author's choice or her publisher's, it was followed the tradition for books of that period of assigning fictional names to towns in order to avoid possible libel suits. Such subterfuge also allows the author to alter the geography, history and physical characteristics of real places to suit her story. Readers, however, will have no problem recognizing Central City, at least the Central City that existed before limited-stakes gambling turned this once dying city into a boom town during the 1990s, and the Opera House depicted in *Murder a Mile High* is very much as it was at the time of the story, the summer after Pearl Harbor. Dean also works in many stories and legends familiar to tourists who visit the town, from the face on the barroom floor to the paving of the streets in silver bricks to welcome the visit of President Grant in 1873. As with many other mining towns, fire ravished the city on more than one occasion, and as a result builders eventually used more brick than wood in construction, a fact used by Dean to good purpose. *Murder a Mile High* was one of the first detective novels to employ Colorado as a setting. Clyde B. Clason had used a similar mining town in his 1937 Professor Theocritus Lucius Westborough mystery, *Blind Drifts*. Today, of course, scores of mystery writers set their books in Colorado.

In a departure from the first two books in the series, Emma is left to ferret out the killer by herself, although her boss, Jeff Graham, makes an appearance at the beginning of the book, and Emma's boyfriend, private detective, Hank Fairbanks (now off to war), appears at both the beginning and end. If one misses the amusing banter that took place among this trio of hard-drinking sleuths, Emma makes up for it in her relations with several local Central City residents, especially DeLoss Weatherbee, an eccentric elderly man of great wealth and influence, and photographer Shay Horrigan, an old drinking buddy from Boston sent by Hank to keep an eye on her, since Emma does have a tendency to gravitate to dead bodies wherever she goes.

The Emma Marsh books belong to the screwball school of hard-drinking mystery fiction originated by Dashiell Hammett in *The Thin Man* and made popular by writers like Craig Rice and Jonathan Latimer. Award-winning mystery writer Sujata Massey summed it up when she wrote that the books froth "with the same humor as the best Hepburn-Grant movies" of the same period. *The New Yorker* called *Murder is a Collector's Item* "fast and funny," but a *New York Times* reviewer couldn't help but comment in a 1939 review that "Emma drinks more than a nice girl should."

When asked what made her books stand out from the pack, Dean would always cite their spontaneity. She refused to work from either an outline or a synopsis, knowing only the setting, the pivotal incident that sets the plot in movement, and the identity of the murderer. To know more, she said, would take the fun out of writing—and reading—her novels. Her work habits were simple. "I sit down at the typewriter (positioned on a mid-1700 walnut slant desk) and stare at a blank sheet of paper until I write something just to relieve the monotony."

Written on a dare, Dean's first book was published in the spring of 1939. Liz (as her friends called her) wasn't thinking about writing a mystery when she met one day with a group of friends in her Council Bluffs home. One of them suggested as a lark that they each see if they could write 20,000 words of fiction in a month's time. Only Liz met the deadline, at which point her friends challenged her to expand it into an 80,000-word novel. A year later *Murder is a Collector's Item* was completed and accepted by the prestigious Doubleday, Doran Crime Club, whose editors proclaimed it "one of the best stories in the spring. . . .list." It remains today fresh and sparkling, an undated example of the best writing in the field of the period.

For the background of the mystery she drew upon her own experiences. After graduating from Pembroke College (now part of Brown University) and obtaining a masters degree from Radcliffe, Liz worked in the famous Boston antiques shop owned by George McMahon, who provided the model for the irascible but tenderhearted Jeff Graham. Much of the enjoyment in *Murder is a Collector's Item* and *Murder is a Serious Business* lies in her obviously authentic portrait of the day-to-day operations of an antiques shop. Even thousands of miles from home, Emma turns an expert's eye on the "antiques" of Central City, and one of the more enjoyable scenes in *Murder a Mile High* finds Emma scoring a major find in a local antiques shop.

Murder a Mile High was published in 1944, four years after her second book, while Dean was living in Warrington, Florida, near Pensacola, where her husband was stationed during World War II. Her son William said the change in scenery disrupted her writing and though she continued to sell stories and articles to *Colliers* and *The Saturday Evening Post*, she was never able to recapture the spirit needed to create her Emma Marsh mysteries.

Upon her return to Council Bluffs at the end of the war, Dean threw herself into the activities of the local historical society, spearheading a drive to save the historic Squirrel Cage Jail with its revolving cylindrical cellblock. Many of these cylindrical jails were built in the Midwest, only to be phased out when it was discovered that fires could turn them into deathtraps.

Born in New York City in 1901, Dean died in Council Bluffs in 1985 at the age of 84. Her career as a mystery writer was a short one, but she produced three of the most entertaining detective novels of her day and in Emma Marsh gave us a truly original character, a precursor of the independent women sleuths who were to come into their own during the last two decades of the 20th century.

Tom & Enid Schantz
Boulder, Colorado
April, 2001

PROGRAM

ARMY-NAVY RELIEF BENEFIT

July 5-25

CENTRAL CITY

ANNUAL

PLAY FESTIVAL

Auspices of the Pioneer Historical Society
Presenting

THE STOLEN BRIDE

A light opera by Prusha

With

HORSACK, *the famous Czech tenor*

MISS ALLEGRETA PINZI, *and*
a brilliant group of Metropolitan singers

Ride the famous narrow-gauge railroad up Cold Water Canyon
to Central City. Two trips daily.

CHAPTER ONE

MISS EMMA MARSH, having devoted the major part of her twenty-seven years to the care and feeding of J. Graham, Antiques, had almost decided to transfer her affections to Mr. Henry Fairbanks, periodic investigator of crime, when the Navy, in a manner of speaking, beat her to it.

It was hot in Boston; it was hot in the shop, but Emma was cold with apprehension as she talked to Hank on the phone.

"But why do you have to go so soon? . . ."

"But I couldn't possibly go with you. What would Jeff do?"

Mr. Jefferson Graham, who had his thumbs on the morning mail but his ear on the conversation, said that he'd do all right.

"You know I can't marry you," Emma wailed. "I haven't anything to wear." She hung up the phone and turned to Jeff. "Hank's got his commission. In the Intelligence."

"The Navy," said Jeff, "must be in a tough spot—"

"How can you talk that way? He has to go tonight."

"—and in a hurry."

"Tonight." Emma wiped the corner of one eye surreptitiously. "To California."

"You got a letter."

"And he wants me to go with him."

"Why don't you? It's from Mary."

"The blessed lamb! But how could I?"

"Why not? What's Mary doing in Colorado?"

"Why don't you read it and find out?" Emma blew her nose.

"Okay." Jeff slit the letter and drew out a single sheet. " 'Central City, July 11'—for Pete's sake, where's that?"

"In Colorado," Emma snapped. "They have some kind of a Play Festival," she relented. "She's singing, naturally."

9

" 'My dearest darling,' " Jeff read, " 'It is perfectly marvelous here, and the opera is really good. I wish you could come out. See if you can't persuade that wretch that you work for—' "

Emma reached for the letter, but Jeff held it out of her way.

" '—to give you a vacation. Darling, I am in love—' "

Emma groaned, "Again!"

" '—and this time it is the real thing. He is utterly marvelous—and a superb tenor—' "

"He's a heel," Emma interrupted. "They always are. She has the worst taste in men. A tenor!"

" '—but things are complicated—' "

"I bet!"

" '—and I really wish you would come. And bring Hank. I may need him professionally. All my love. Remember me to Jeff.' I remember her," Jeff snorted. "She went around with Finny Goldstein, and he got sent to the pen."

"You introduced them," Emma reminded him.

"She's crazy," said Jeff. "But she sure can sing."

"She's a swell person," Emma defended stoutly. "She's just unlucky about men. She went with Ben Harris in school. He was captain of the football team until he stole some examination papers. But don't say anything about her needing him professionally to Hank. He can't go, and it would bother him if he thought I might get mixed up in something."

"Oh," said Jeff, "I thought you weren't going."

"I could go with Hank"—Emma put away her handkerchief—"as far as Chicago—or maybe it's Denver—and then go to see Mary. There'll be lots of admirals and things," she added, "to take care of Hank, but Mary sounds as though she needs me."

And so it was in the Denver station that Emma said good-by to Hank. Hank had an hour to wait for his train, but the narrow gauge that clattered and climbed up Cold Water Canyon left immediately.

"Good-by," Hank had said, "and behave yourself."

And Emma had nodded because there was a lump in her throat, and she was afraid she would cry. She hated to cry in public. The lump was still in her throat as the narrow gauge rattled over the plain to the foothills. The cars were filled with pleasant, chattering people, also bound for Central City, but Emma did not notice them. She was telling herself not to spoil the coming visit with her own trouble. Mary would have enough troubles for both of them. Poor old Mary! Always in love with the wrong men. Good old Mary. Always glad to see you, always the same hectic, enthusiastic person. It was funny about Mary. Men said that women couldn't have friendships, long ones, that withstood the test of years without the exchange of biographical letters; men said—and by men Emma meant Hank—that women couldn't put a friendship down and pick it up after a lapse without going over each other's past with a fine-tooth comb, but even Hank had to admit that Mary was different.

Mary could come back from Italy or Hollywood or a night club in Passaic and say, "Hello, darling," and tell a funny story and slip back into your life as though she had never been away. Jeff said it was because she could listen to other people's experiences and didn't bother to enlarge upon her own; Hank said that she was another person for Emma to mother and pick up after; Emma didn't try to explain her feeling for Mary; it was made up of having gone to school together, of wearing each other's clothes, of copying each other's papers, of double dates and pet peeves, of a zest for people and places, and a relish for the ridiculous. Emma would simply have said that Mary was her friend, and because Emma was a very loyal person that was enough.

Since Mary had left school to go on with her music, as the phrase went, they saw each other sporadically but always with renewed pleasure. Once Mary had spent several weeks in Boston singing a minor role in a touring opera company. She had lived at Emma's apartment, and it had been fun, except for the Finny Goldstein episode, which was all Jeff's fault. The last time, Emma stopped to think, had been two—no, nearly three—years ago. Mary had come back from Italy just before the war, rather thin and pale, with just the merest trace of an accent about which they kidded her. Then she had gone off almost at once to South America. She had sent Emma a post card from Lima, a picture of mountains. . . .

Emma had seen the mountains that morning, rising ghostlike from the plain. Now suddenly she was in them. She looked out the window, out and down, down far below to rushing water, and up, high above to black, lowering cliffs. Mountains were pretty to look at but, close to, they were a little overwhelming. It was so far to the top that there was no sun in the canyon, and so far down . . . .

Emma told herself not to be silly, but she moved cautiously across the aisle to an inside seat. It was a *very* small train, and her weight might be just enough to send it toppling over the edge. The train kept on climbing.

Mary, warned by wire, was on the crowded platform to meet her, blue eyes sparkling, tanned face shining and eager.

"Darling," Mary said, "my sainted darling, this is utterly marvelous. It has been much too long. . . .Don't you love the train? How is Hank? How is Jeff?"

"Angel," said Emma, "everyone is swell, almost, but what about you? I gathered from your letter—"

She broke off because Mary was making faces at her to shut up and was dragging forward a tall blond man. . . .

"Darling, this is Robert Sauer."

He was very fair; his pale hair was cut *en brosse* . . . .

"Rho, this is Emma."

He was broad-shouldered and thin-hipped. . . .

"How do you do?"

There was a heel-clicking precision about his greeting. . . .

This, Emma thought to herself with a sinking heart, this, this *Aryan,* was Mary's tenor. He was strong; he was young; what was he doing here? Why wasn't he in the Army or the Navy? She was being irrational and knew it. Because the man looked like a German was no reason to dislike him. He was probably a fine fellow; it was probably just that Mary had always picked somebody queer. . . .

Emma became conscious of an obvious silence. "My bags," she said. "I've got three bags. . . ."

"Rho'll take them. I said 'take them'!"

"Oh yes. Of course." Robert Sauer picked up the bags awkwardly, his face flushing.

What was the matter with him? Too good to carry bags? Emma pulled herself up short. This was no way to act. It was only that she was tired. What would Mary think of her? She looked at Mary, who was looking at Sauer and looked away, looked about her.

Central City sprawled up the side of a gulch, a hodgepodge of decayed and dilapidated buildings. Old warehouses, freight depots, and machine shops clustered around the station, while higher up, on top of the ridge, were the spires of several churches and houses that still bore traces of care and habitation. The air was thin and clear, and the sun burned hotly through it. It was good to be out in the sun after the darkness of the canyon.

"What an amazing place," said Emma.

"Could you imagine living here?"

"Heavens, no!"

"Don't hurry, or the altitude will get you."

"It's not the heat; it's the altitude."

It wasn't a very good joke, but they were getting back, back to the pleasure of seeing one another, as they walked up the narrow street, Sauer behind them with the bags. Mary stopped at a small restaurant.

"There'll be so many people at the hotel," she explained. "And I only have time for a sandwich because I have to introduce you to our landlady. You'll die at the house. Very General-Grant-slept-hereish." She turned to Sauer.

"If you will excuse me"—Sauer spoke stiffly—"I will continue with the bags. You will want to renew your acquaintanceship." He bowed to Emma. "So glad to have met you."

"Run along," Mary interrupted Emma's nod, but her voice was gentle. "I'll see you later."

Feeling that she had been rude to the point of boorishness, Emma followed Mary into the restaurant. She ought to say something. To apologize.

"Hello, Miss Pinzi," said the waitress, looking Emma over curiously.

"This is Miss Marsh," said Mary.

"Hello," said the waitress. "You come up for the opera?"

Emma said yes and gave her order primly, knowing that Mary was laughing at her primness.

"This isn't Boston, my dear. Up here everyone works during the tourist season. They feel that they're doing the tourists a favor, and in return they expect to be favored with your friendship. You might as well give in; they'll know all about you eventually." There was a trace of bitterness, Emma thought, in her last words.

"How's Hank?" Mary changed the subject.

Emma told her about Hank, and then, because Mary was quick and warm with her sympathy, Emma added:

"I'm sorry if I was rude to Sauer. I don't know what got into me."

"Skip it," said Mary.

"He's so—so *Prussian*," Emma blundered on.

"He knows it. He won't bother us. Good-mercy-me, we have to hurry."

They left quickly, and Mary led the way through gathering crowds of people now overflowing from the sidewalks into the narrow street.

"That's the Teller House." Mary pointed out an ornate four-story structure of weathered brick. "It's sort of the center of things. It used to be a famous hotel in the boom days. The sidewalk was paved with silver in front of it in honor of Lincoln or Grant or Sherman or somebody."

"I bet," said Emma.

"And behold!" Mary gestured grandly. "The opera house! Booth, Kean, Jefferson, and Modjeska! And now me!"

She was leading Emma across the garden that separated the opera house from the hotel. There were knots of people standing or walking about, waiting for the afternoon performance. One group was centered about a man in Tyrolean costume: leather shorts, embroidered suspenders, and velours hat, who laughed and postured and gestured with an alpine stock.

Mary's chatter stopped short, and Emma could hear her catch her breath.

"And that," Mary went on in a tight voice, "is Horsack. Horsack, the great Czech tenor, appearing in the Czech opera, *The Stolen Bride.*"

"Tenor?" asked Emma.

"Check," said Mary, "and double check."

"But I thought—" Emma had to pause to catch her breath in the middle of a flight of wooden steps. She had been going to say that she thought Sauer was Mary's tenor. But Mary hadn't said Sauer was the tenor, and here was a tenor, and Mary's voice was queer when she spoke of him. Emma had made a mistake, and this, then, was Mary's love, not the blond Nordic. Emma wished she had settled for Sauer, because this man was worse, much worse. He was short, almost stocky; his face was dark and alive and arrogantly dominating, and he had been showing off before the people he was with. He hadn't gone to the train with Mary because he obviously wasn't the kind to meet trains and carry bags.

"Take it easy," Mary called back to her, "but keep moving!"

Emma plodded to the top, trying to drag the thin air into her lungs, and gave only a shuddering glance at the Victorian monstrosity that was Mary's rooming house. The Estis Mansion, Mary called it.

They went in at the side door, through a tiled entry, and into a dark hall. Emma passed the inspection of the Victorian landlady, registered, and was hurried upstairs to wash, and hurried down again because it was almost curtain time.

Emma suffered herself to be pushed and led and only half listened to Mary's running commentary on the town, the scenery, the opera, and the past winter in South America. Emma was getting tireder every minute. Possibly it was the altitude; possibly the fact that she and Hank had spent the last night of their trip in a crowded day coach had something to do with it.

CHAPTER TWO

SOMETIME in the middle of the last act Emma woke from a comfortable snooze and looked around guiltily. Opera always did it to her; tired or not, she could sleep through the best of them. It made no difference that Mary was singing the leading role and would expect her to say, "My dear, you were superb in the Maypole scene."

Was there a Maypole scene, Emma wondered, or had she dreamed it? Anyhow, she felt better. She glanced at her neighbors quickly, covertly, to see whether or not they had caught her at her nap, and was aware that something was wrong. The polite, musically minded tourists gathered in the old opera house were buzzing impolitely. On the stage the chorus of gypsies, Tyrolean lads, and village maidens, beer mugs pointed upstage, were waiting for a carefully built-up entrance. But no one entered. The orchestra, which had been tum-tumming along, took up the chorus again; the company followed, and this time, on a swoop of song, the tenor entered.

Where had he been? Emma wondered. Over to the hotel for a small beer? He'd catch his.

Emma blinked. Had she slept through into another opera? This was another tenor. This man was tall and big and blond, while Horsack was dark and heavy-set. The blond lad was all right though; he was singing like crazy. Emma sat up straight. Though he was considerably darkened by his makeup, Emma recognized the blond man. He was Sauer. Sauer was a tenor. That made two tenors for Mary to be in love with! Where was Horsack? Mary was lucky to have a spare tenor to fall back on.

Now Mary was coming on, to be reunited, after many operatic vicissitudes, with the tenor. Mary seemed a little wobbly, both as to voice and knees.

Sauer crossed right and put his arm around Mary's shoulder. The chorus crowded back, jostling each other, as though this bit of business were premature, but it helped Mary. She straightened up, and her smooth contralto swelled out in the final duet.

In a few minutes the opera was over; the lights went up, and the audience, done with its applause, started to leave. Emma, pushed along by the crowd, took in the names carved on the backs of the seats—for a hundred dollars and up, Mary had told her, you could have a name chiseled in for posterity. Any name? Petroleum V. Nasby? Donald Duck? If she had a hundred dollars she would have Jeff's name put on a chair, though he would probably sniff at the opera house. It wasn't anywhere near old enough to interest him, and its Victorian murals came perilously close to being quaint. The chandelier wasn't bad though; it really wasn't bad at all.

Emma was gazing up at the elaborate mass of crystal above, not looking where she was going, half conscious of the conversation around her.

"Better than Horsack . . ."

"Superb . . ."

"Not so good . . ."

"Party last night too much for Horsack?"

Someone trod on Emma's toes, and her gaze came earthward as she uttered a sharp "Ouch." A small old man in a black serge suit was crowded up against her, muttering.

"I beg your pardon." Emma tried to sound sarcastic, but her efforts were lost. A surge of the crowd separated her from the old man and bore her along, irresistibly, to the balcony exit.

Emma paused there, leaning on the rail to rub her foot and to look at the people milling about below. The garden was bright with flowers and the summer dresses of the women. The sky was blue; the sun sparkled. The mellow brick of the hotel, the cobblestones of the narrow street, the archway of an old livery stable were all a pleasant continuation of the operatic setting. Had one of the crowd jumped upon a garden table and burst into song, the act would have been perfectly in keeping.

Instead a voice said, "Stick around for a while. All hell's liable to break loose."

Emma whirled about, but the words were not addressed to her. The old man in the black suit was speaking to a Chinese in the livery of a chauffeur.

"Where's Susan?" he wanted to know.

The chauffeur said that she was at the hotel.

"If you mean bar, say so," the old man snapped and moved off down the stairs.

Hell, Emma decided, was going to break on Susan's head. She stayed where she was for a moment, looking away from the bright scene below her to the barren, scarred mountainsides that surrounded the town.

There were few trees; they had been cut down to make timbers for the mines in the days when Central City had been the heart of "the richest square mile on earth." There were rocks and broken machinery and slopes of discolored yellowish earth, tailings from the now-abandoned mines.

From the little that she knew of mines and mining, Emma tried to imagine what Central City had been like, tried to imagine the gulch teeming with prospectors, the streets filled with miners, donkeys, freight trains, bankers, and gamblers. All that was gone now; Central City was what was called a ghost town, with only the opera house and the hotel to proclaim its former grandeur.

And the Estis Mansion. She should be getting back there now to meet Mary. She was mildly anxious to find out what had gone on backstage, and Mary's account would not belittle its source material. Mary had a tendency toward overstatement, but Emma could imagine that changing tenors in midstream might be something of an operatic feat.

"My dear," Emma could hear her saying, "I was that nervous I was trembling like a leaf. . ."

But that was no exaggeration. She had been. Having the lead in this opera was a big thing for Mary. Mary had studied and worked long and hard and sincerely; since she had gone to school with Emma she had sung in musicals and night clubs to make money for study in Italy. This opera, according to Mary, was one of the few written with a contralto lead. Composers, it seemed, as well as producers, always gave sopranos the breaks. Mary had some wild tales to tell of producers and sopranos, funny ones too. She was still the same old girl so far as her sense of humor went.

Emma went down the stairs from the balcony and edged her way past a group of plump women thumbing through guidebooks, around to the rear of the opera house. Mary had pointed out how handy the stage door was to the side entrance of the rooming house—beg pardon, Estis Mansion. Up the steep flight of steps, and there you were.

Emma walked past a group standing by the stage door—members of the company, she guessed. They looked like opera singers, and, to make the guess easier, some of them were still in costume. One of the men glanced at Emma and nudged his neighbor. The rest fell silent, and Emma climbed the steps stiffly, conscious of their attention.

Anyone would have thought she was the one in costume! There was nothing the matter with her. She looked all right, or at least as good as she ever did. She forgot her irritation as she paused for a good look at the Estis Mansion and realized what a be-bayed and be-turreted monstrosity it was. If it was a sample of what the local mining barons did with their money, it served them right to go broke.

Nothing had been spared—tortured brick, pierced by narrow windows, angled and bulged its way upward for two tall stories, until it was halted by a cupolaed mansard roof. A jigsaw-fretted veranda swept around the front of the house, partially concealing but not improving the stained-glass tops of the windows, the bulging bays, and the ornate woodwork of the doors. That the doors were solid walnut and their knobs reported by Mary to be of solid silver helped not at all. The veranda extended halfway down the side next to the opera house, covering the side entry that was used by the roomers. The double-doored front entrance was reserved for those who paid a quarter to view the glories of the house and tried to get their money's worth by filching knickknacks and breaking fingers from statuary in the time-honored manner of tourists.

As Emma approached from the side a group of tourists was even then leaving from the front of the house, a gay, frolicsome group that seemed to have been amused, rather than impressed, by what they had just seen. They scattered from the walk and gathered in bunches on the lawn. A man in a bright tweed jacket pointed a camera at Emma, who smiled and waved because they seemed nice, friendly people who felt as she did about the house.

Then Emma went up the side steps and into the side entry. The entry was lit by a colored-glass window high to the left, but it was dark after the glare outside. Emma shut the door behind her, blinked, and heard a burr—

click, click at insistent intervals. She saw the telephone before she saw the body. She almost stepped on the body as she started forward to hang up the dangling receiver—almost stepped on the body of a man in Tyrolean costume, complete with leather shorts, embroidered suspenders, velours hat—even the alpine stock. Emma looked at the man's face and in spite of the half-light knew that she had found the absent tenor.

Emma leaned over and felt the bare, hairy knee that was exposed below the shorts. Cold as a clam.

Burr—click, click.

Horsack had come over to telephone.

Burr—click, click.

And had been hit on the head. Because now that the glare was out of her eyes Emma could see that the head lay in a pool of blood, a lot of blood, coagulated now by the cool tile floor.

Burr—click, click.

Damn the thing. Emma reached across the body and hung up the receiver.

What was it Hank had told her? Head injuries always bled a lot, sometimes all out of proportion to the damage done.

Maybe Horsack wasn't dead. Emma felt for the pulse. There was none. She opened her bag and held its mirror over the gaping mouth. No moisture.

All right, the man was dead.

Emma straightened up and rested her hand against the wall because the entry was dark again. Emma told herself not to be silly; it was only that standing up suddenly had made her faint. This man didn't mean a thing to her. She didn't even know him. He was just a body. A body that was no business of hers. All she had to do was walk out of the entry and leave him for someone else to find. Emma's stomach, always unreliable in times of crisis, gave a warning lurch, and she went out the door rather more quickly than she had intended, to lean against an elaborately turned pillar. When the blackness had cleared from her eyes she looked around for someone, anyone, but the yard was empty; the gay tourists had vanished. Where was the landlady, Mrs. Danforth? Where was Mary?

Where was Mary?

The tenor that Mary had been in love with was dead. Or was she in love with the other tenor?

The sick feeling returned to the pit of Emma's stomach. Mary had written that she was in love with a tenor and might need Hank professionally, and now a tenor was dead. Emma told herself that she was being absurd; the thing to do was to telephone the police.

Emma remembered where the telephone was and decided to hunt for another. She started down the steps, saw a dark, swarthy woman leaving the stage door of the opera house, and hailed her. But she didn't ask about a telephone.

"Is Mary in there? Mary Dolan—I mean Miss Pinzi?"

The woman's expression was cool and hard; it was not improved by a mole on her chin.

"She iss not here. She iss probably in the hotel." The voice hissed disapproval.

And why shouldn't Mary be in the hotel? Emma wondered. Mary had said that it was the center of things. It would have a telephone too. That was probably where everyone went after the performance.

CHAPTER THREE

THERE WERE so many people in the hotel that Emma had to edge her way into the lobby and, once inside, found further progress blocked by a firmly occupied chair placed in the lee of a rubber plant. Seated in the chair with his back to Emma was the old man in the black suit

His words came suddenly back to her: "All hell's liable to break loose."

Well, it had, in a sort of local way. But had he known? Why, perhaps this was what he had meant!

At Emma's half-smothered exclamation the old man jumped in his chair and pulled himself up to face her. For a second they stared at each other in mutual, if dissimilar, astonishment; then the old man laughed.

"Don't do that," he said. "To this day it makes me kinda nervous to feel somebody back of me."

So, Emma was thinking rapidly, trying to laugh it off, was he? But he jumped as though he thought she'd been after him with a gun. He looked like an old-timer. Used to killings. And gifted with a singularly accurate gift of prophecy.

Emma forgot for the moment that her only concern was to get in touch with the police; she forgot that, if her insatiable curiosity got the better of her and she got into trouble, Hank wouldn't be there to help her out. Her mind, which a moment before had rejoiced that this murder was none of its concern, was now busily hopping to and fro, connecting this old man with the dead body in the entry. Why, he'd practically as good as admitted he knew it was going to happen, and there he stood, smiling at her and looking as though butter wouldn't melt in his mouth. She could pretend too.

"Tell me," she said casually, "what do you do up here with a body?" After it was out she realized she should have said, "when you find a body."

The way she had said it sounded as though she had a body to get rid of, but the old man wasn't fazed.

"Mostly," he said, "we bury 'em."

Why, the old smarty. Emma almost giggled; then she reminded herself that he should have immediately suggested calling the police. Anybody knew that. He was just stalling; she would stall along too.

"Even," she continued, "if it's sort of newly dead—and bashed in?"

"Is it a large body?" the old man wanted to know. "If it isn't you could put it in a trunk; if it is, I'm afraid we'll have to cut it up."

Emma's eyes grew wide and round. The man was crazy. She started to back away, but the old man followed her, saying:

"Come outside. We can talk it over better out there."

It was absurd to scream, Emma thought; she was perfectly safe with all the people around. The crazy old man had probably killed Horsack, and he'd confess it in a minute if he kept on the way he was going. All she had to do was keep on baiting him, but she wished Mary would come.

"In summer," the old man was saying, "the ground is soft, but if you don't get around to taking care of 'em—" He wrinkled his nose. "Whereas in winter they keep better, but the ground is so danged hard . . . . Where is this body?"

The question was so sudden that Emma pointed, licking dry lips before she said, "Up there in the entry."

"Well, blast the diggings and call it mine," the old man cackled. "Lizzie Danforth's. Anybody you know?"

"Of course not. I mean I know who it is. Horsack, the opera singer. You remember, you heard him this afternoon." She was trying to establish some point of contact with the wandering mind in front of her. If she could just get him on the right track he'd probably tell her the whole story. "He sang the first part of the opera," she went on gently, leadingly, "and then he didn't come back. Didn't you like him?"

"Nope. Who are you?"

"I just got here this noon," Emma told him. "I'm a friend of Mary Dolan's—Miss Pinzi's. She's one of the opera singers too."

"And I'm DeLoss Weatherbee," said the old man.

Emma gave up. The crowd in the garden was thinning out, and there was still no sign of Mary. "I'm glad to have met you," she laid politely, "and now I must be going."

But the old man was too crafty for her. "I know what you're thinking," he said, "but don't do it. Only as a very last resort should you call the police. I know a man that can help us."

He took her by the arm, and his fingers were strong, for all they looked so old and skinny. He led her around to the sidewalk in front of the hotel, where there were more people again and where Emma felt it was safe to humor him. He might say something; something might break just right, and she'd have the case all solved before Hank—Hank wouldn't, Emma reminded herself, hear of this case for many a long day.

"Silver, my eye," said the old man.

"What?" asked Emma. She looked down and saw at her feet aluminum-painted oblongs on the limestone slabs in front of the hotel.

"Is it supposed to be silver?" Emma asked, not much caring.

The old man smiled a satisfied smile. "When'd you say you got here?"

"About one. A little before."

"And ain't nobody told you the story about how when U.S. Grant was here in '73 the street was paved with silver?"

Emma nodded. What might have happened in 1873 seemed to have no bearing on the present problem. What she ought to do was walk away from this silly old man and find a telephone. Instead she said politely, "Yes, I heard that. Is it true?"

The old man chuckled. "That's what they say." He passed the bar entrance with an incoherent mutter and led Emma over the worn doorsill of a dusty shop or office whose window was lined with queer-looking flowerpots. The office was empty, except for a battered table, a couple of chairs, and a counter on which were three small bags, tied and labeled. There was a hot metallic smell in the air.

Furnaces, Emma couldn't help thinking, and bodies. She told herself that she was crazy too.

"Sol!" yelled the old man.

Another man came in from a back room. He was bespectacled and not so old as Mr. Weatherbee, but he wore a similar dusty black coat that sagged open, revealing a similarly sagging vest. "Well," he said, "if it ain't Napoleon back again."

There—Emma almost sighed with relief—he knew the old man was crazy.

"Sol," Mr. Weatherbee's voice was reproving, "make you acquainted with Miss Marsh. Mr. Faber."

Emma's words were sincere: "I'm glad to meet you."

"Likewise," said Mr. Faber.

"Give us a drink, Sol," said Mr. Weatherbee. "We got a problem."

Emma tried to catch Mr. Faber's eye, but he was reaching under the counter, whence he produced a couple of glasses that had seen previous service.

"What's the matter?" he wanted to know. "Won't they let you in the hotel any more?" He seemed to think it was a joke.

Mr. Weatherbee, who had been reading the label on one of the little bags, threw it down with a sniff.

"Too many blame people around drinking cocktails," he stated. Then: "Alice B. Simms—she didn't amount to much, did she?"

"Two dollars to the ton ain't so bad."

But the old man had lost interest in whatever it was that they were talking about. He handed one glass to Emma and took the other himself.

"Well," he said, "here's to crime."

Mr. Faber took a swig from the bottle and wiped his mouth on the back of his hand. Mr. Weatherbee downed his drink in a casual gulp. Emma, not to be outdone, attempted to follow suit, choked on the raw whiskey, and set down her glass, fighting for air.

"You from the East?" Mr. Faber asked politely when Emma's coughs had subsided.

Emma nodded.

She supposed Mr. Faber knew the old man and was trying to humor him, and she was grateful for Mr. Faber's unwitting protection, but that wasn't helping her with her problem of getting to the police. Perhaps she could get a word with Mr. Faber alone. Failing that, she would walk firmly to the telephone that she had spotted on the wall.

"Mr. Faber," she began, but Mr. Weatherbee cut in ahead of her.

"Sol," he said, "we got a little problem."

"So?" Sol looked at the old man.

"Yep. The little lady here"—Mr. Weatherbee lowered his voice—"has got a carcass."

"Mm. . . ." Mr. Faber appeared to give the matter serious consideration.

He was probably wondering, Emma thought, what the old man was up to and how to talk him out of it. He was probably familiar with the old man's delusions and knew that he had lured her there with some story—unless, good gracious, he thought she was crazy too!

Mr. Faber looked at Emma, and there was a gleam in his eye that made her uneasy. "The rendering works," he said, "is your best bet. They'll even pay you for it."

Emma held onto her good sense firmly with both hands. Mr. Faber had misunderstood, and small wonder. He thought she had a dead horse or a cow to dispose of.

"I'm afraid—" she began.

But again Mr. Weatherbee was ahead of her. "The rendering works don't like 'em if the hide is damaged."

Mr. Faber turned to Emma. "How about it? Good condition?"

"Yes," Emma shouted, "all except the head. The head's bashed in. You don't understand. I'm not talking about an animal. It's a man."

"Dear, dear me"—Mr. Faber shook his head sadly—"you shouldn't do things like that; you really shouldn't. It's lucky I've got a good fire in the furnace today so's I can take care of it for you."

"Old Sol," said Mr. Weatherbee proudly, "he always comes through."

Emma looked from one to the other in horror and despair. They were both crazy, stark-staring mad. They probably would destroy a body. Why, what was in those little sacks, concentrated, of course? That was the way she would end up if she wasn't careful. She had to get out. She looked toward the door, but Mr. Weatherbee stood directly in front of it, and she remembered the strength of his fingers. She could make a dash for the telephone, but Mr. Faber could stop her. It would be better to scream.,

She had her mouth all open when the long, shiny nose of a black car crept past the window, a door slammed, and a very pretty girl rushed into the shop. She was young, not more than eighteen, with blond curly hair, a golden-tan skin, and a figure that was fresh, firm, and upright. She looked like an angel from heaven to Emma in spite of the impatient scowl on her face.

"Grandpa," the girl said accusingly, "Chew saw you come in here."

Mr. Weatherbee held up his hand. "My granddaughter, Susan," he said. "Miss Marsh."

"I'm very glad to see you." Emma felt that the conventional how-de-do was again inadequate.

Susan gave a perfunctory nod that Emma understood perfectly. The girl and the chauffeur were supposed to be looking after the old man, and he had given them the slip. They were probably rich. That explained the car and the chauffeur and the fact that the old man was running around loose. She wondered who was supposed to look after Mr. Faber.

"Grandpa," said the girl, "it's after five o'clock and Paul hasn't shown up and we'll never get down the mountain to the party and back for the performance if we don't start now."

"Maybe," Mr. Weatherbee said calmly, "you better run along. I'm busy right now."

Susan stamped her foot. "The party's for him, and he's not in his room, and you've got to come."

That was no way to handle him, Emma thought. You had to cajole and coax and humor. "He isn't busy any more," she said. "He's been showing me around, and I really must be going." She started toward the door. "Thank you so much." She turned to nod a bright good-by and found herself looking at a shiny gun barrel poked through a hole in Mr. Faber's right-hand coat pocket. One of Mr. Faber's fingers was at his lips, and Emma quickly grasped the idea that he meant her to be silent.

Mr. Weatherbee was advancing on his granddaughter. "Chew," he was saying, "will take you home."

"But, Grandpa—"

"Susan!" Mr. Weatherbee's voice was no louder, but it cracked like a whiplash. "Get in that car."

The cloth around the hole in Mr. Faber's pocket was frayed and worn. From use. They had done this before. Crazy. Crooks. She had happened on one of their bodies before they got a chance to burn it in the furnace. They'd burn her. Murder ring. Girl sleuth uncovers crime wave. Paul. Alice B. Simms. She heard the sound of the departing car and the closing of the office door. She stood still, expecting Mr. Weatherbee to leap at her from behind with a short length of cord or a pad of chloroform.

"Sol," said Mr. Weatherbee, "now that you've spoiled the fun with that gun, maybe you better show the young lady your badge."

The shiny barrel receded into Mr. Faber's pocket, and the other side of his coat went back, revealing an equally shiny badge. Mr. Faber was standing very close to Emma, but he shoved his vest forward so that she could not fail to see that S-H-E-R-I-F-F was printed plainly on the badge, but even so it took a moment before Emma could read it and another moment for her to realize that she had been utterly and gloriously had.

Mr. Weatherbee wasn't crazy. He had brought her directly to the sheriff, who was now doubled up with convulsive glee and being pounded delightedly on the back.

Emma sat down in a chair, thoroughly abashed and still feeling a little green around the gills.

Mr. Faber laughed until he bent over so far that the gun barrel again poked its nose through the frayed hole. Mr. Weatherbee laughed until he got to coughing and had to be restored with a shot of Mr. Faber's preservative.

"Jesus-menders," said Mr. Weatherbee, revived, "I haven't had so much fun since we tied the two Chinamen over the corral gate by their pigtails."

"You old devils," said Emma.

Mr. Weatherbee looked at her, observed the color of her face, and became instantly apologetic. He poured a drink, which Emma drank, splutter and all, and felt the better for.

"You scared her, you big dummy, pulling that gun."

"I had to keep her here somehow," Mr. Faber bristled, "while you got rid of the kid."

An odd expression crossed Mr. Weatherbee's face. He looked as though he expected Emma to speak, so she said, "She's awfully pretty, isn't she? I should have caught on that you were joking. I guess finding the body upset me more than I realized."

"Oh." Mr. Faber looked suspiciously from Emma to Mr. Weatherbee, suspecting a fresh joke. "A body."

"She found it." Mr. Weatherbee waved his hand at Emma, disclaiming any personal interest.

"This is the truth," Emma began. She meant that she was not going to decoy the sheriff away to look at a nonexistent body in retaliation for the trick played on her, but as she spoke the words Hank's oft-repeated advice came back to her: "Tell the truth to the cops; they'll find out anyway." Well, this was one time that she could follow his advice in letter and spirit. She didn't know the man whose body she had found; he meant nothing to her. She had nothing to conceal, and for once full cooperation with the law was going to be a cinch. She told her story of the finding of Horsack's body as briefly and accurately as she could, adding the details of her arrival and her lunch with Mary because she knew she would be asked about them.

"That's how I knew who it was," she explained. "Mary—Miss Pinzi—pointed him out to me."

"Why?" Faber wanted to know.

"Why? Why, because he's famous, for one thing."

"Did she say anything about him?"

"No. As I remember, she said, 'There's Horsack, the great Czech tenor. Check and double check.' That's sort of a bad joke," Emma felt obliged to explain. "You see, the composer of the opera is a Czech—"

"I get it," said Mr. Faber. "That all?"

"All about him. I was telling her about Hank—a friend of ours who's in the service—and then she took me over to get a room, and then it was time for the opera." Emma leaned forward in her chair, forgetting that this murder was nothing to her. "You know," she went on, "Horsack must have been killed while the opera was going on, because he didn't come back for the final scene and they had to put in an understudy. All you have to do is to check up on where people were during that time, and if there's anybody that wanted to kill him, why, that's when they did it."

Faber shook his head a little dizzily, being unused to Emma's whirlwind summaries. "Supposing we had a suspect. What time would we check him for? When was Horsack last on the stage?"

"Why, when—" Emma began and stopped, realizing that a good bit of what went on in the last act of the opera was unknown to her and that her excuse was going to sound very, very fishy. "I can't tell you," she admitted. "I was asleep."

There was a quiet pause in the office. Mr. Faber's eyebrows were up interrogatively, and Mr. Weatherbee seemed extremely interested in the toe of his high-heeled gaiters.

"I was asleep," Emma repeated. "I really was. I've been on the train for days, and I just dozed off. You can tell him when it was," she appealed to Mr. Weatherbee. "You were at the opera. I saw you."

She didn't mean her words as a threat, but it came to her that she had also heard Mr. Weatherbee and that he had not yet given any explanation for his peculiar prophecy.

The old man nodded. "Right after the place that goes ta-ta-ta-tum. In the palace garden. And she was asleep," he added gently. "I sat behind her."

Emma gave him a grateful glace and was dumfounded to observe that Mr. Weatherbee's left eyelid, the one away from the sheriff, was closing over his mild blue eye in a very obvious wink. She said nothing, but she doubted very much that Mr. Weatherbee had been seated behind her. She looked Mr. Weatherbee over again, from the top of his respectable gray head to his peculiar shoes that resembled house slippers except for their three-inch slanting heels. It occurred to her to wonder which end of Mr. Weatherbee was indicative of his character. She told herself not to be silly. Mr. Weatherbee was a harmless old man who had played a joke on her because she had startled him out of a nap; now he was making it up to her by corroborating her story. He wasn't crazy, and he had acted correctly in bringing her to the local police, if she had had wits enough to know it.

"I suppose," Mr. Faber was saying, "we might better go have a look at this body."

He spoke tentatively, as though waiting for the old man's approval. Mr. Weatherbee nodded and pulled out a fat silver watch.

"You seen Dominic around?" he asked.

"Not since the show let out. He goes down the canyon to see that the tourists that still have tires don't fall off. He won't be back until time for the show tonight. Unless I call him."

Mr. Weatherbee appeared to turn the matter over in his mind. "Maybe you better," he announced finally. "Dominic's the cop," he explained to Emma, "the state police."

Mr. Faber sighed. "Being sheriff of Gilpin County ain't the job it used to be. We ain't had a killing up here for a long time. I kinda figured I'd like to handle this myself. But I guess you're right. This Paul Horsack is kind of well known, they tell me, and folks'll be expecting fingerprints and blood analyses and all that hanky-pank before we arrest somebody."

"Paul!" Emma spoke accusingly. "I didn't know his name was Paul."

"My, my." Mr. Weatherbee seemed surprised. "I guess you don't get to operas much."

Paul was the man with whom Mr. Weatherbee's granddaughter had

had a date. Emma's mind, its confidence now almost fully restored, was busy seeing recent events in a new light. The old man had been expecting something. She had brought the news of that happening directly to him. That was chance, of course, a lucky chance, and while he had seemed to take her directly to the police, he must have known that the state officials would have to be called in. He had delayed that by making the sheriff party to his joke until his granddaughter had time to get away. She'd tell the sheriff— No, the two of them seemed pretty clubby, but she'd have a word to say to this Dominic when he got there.

"I suppose"—the old man's voice was mild and sad— "you're wondering why I didn't send her to Cheyenne. "

Emma looked blank.

"It's across the state line."

"Oh." Emma was not used to having her mind picked by anyone but Hank and surveyed Mr. Weatherbee with surprise and a new respect.

"Chaperoning an eighteen-year-old," the old man went on, "is an awful job."

Emma wondered if his granddaughter frequently got involved in murders, but she said nothing, not having thought up anything new to say.

"I'm sorry she busted in here—"

Emma could well imagine.

"—giving you wrong ideas. . ."

Oh yeah?

"I kind of figured we'd come down here and talk this thing over with Sol."

Still Emma said nothing. Let him talk. It was his murder now, not hers. All she was going to do was to tell the police everything.

"And the more I think about it, the surer I am it was a good idea, because it appears to me that we're both caught in the same stampede."

"Don't be absurd." Emma was thoroughly disdainful. "I simply happened to find the body. I'm not in this thing at all. And, besides"—Emma threw caution to the winds in her new zeal for honesty—"I intend to tell everything I know."

"Sol," said Mr. Weatherbee, "give me another drink. I ain't as young as I once was, and my mouth gets awful dry talking."

He stretched out his thin legs, downed his drink, and closed his eyes for a moment.

"The similarity of our predicaments," he announced after a pause, "is as easy to see as a twenty-dollar nugget. I got a dad-blamed granddaughter. You've got a friend name Pinzi—or Dolan. Just the fact that she's got two names is against her."

Emma stared at him in amazement, forgetting that for a moment she, too, had wondered about Mary. It was ridiculous; it was fantastic. The old man was just making it up to protect his granddaughter.

"Why, you can't do that," she burst out. "Try to pin it on her, I mean. Why, I've known her for years and years; I went to school with her. We were on the same hockey team and borrowed each other's clothes. I know she wouldn't do a murder. And, besides, she couldn't; she was on the stage. Furthermore," Emma added the last reasonable touch to her logical defense, "opera singers always take fancy names."

"Like crooks." Mr. Weatherbee held up his hand to forestall interruption. "I'm not saying she did it. It just happens that I've seen that show seven times, thanks to my granddaughter, and your Mary isn't on the stage from the Maypole scene to the finale. Horsack goes off in the Maypole scene and comes back just before Pinzi. He had plenty of time to go and get himself killed."

"If you're implying she had time to kill him"—Emma was angry— "it would be just as sensible to say that I sneaked off while I said I was asleep and did it myself."

"Maybe you did," Mr. Weatherbee said placidly. "I'm not so sure it was you I saw."

This bald-faced denial of his previous statement left Emma completely bewildered, more uncertain than ever what Mr. Weatherbee was up to, except, probably, no good. The opening of the office door gave her a moment's respite in which to collect her thoughts. A tall, grizzled man came in, caked with mud, from the lantern in his peaked cap to his high boots. He was after the remains of Alice B. Simms, which turned out to be samplings of ore in which he thought Mr. Weatherbee ought to be interested. While Mr. Weatherbee elaborated on the unlikelihood of his being interested in anything so picayune as two dollars a ton, Emma reestimated Mr. Weatherbee. His appearance—his gray hair, his mild blue eyes, and his shiny serge suit suggested a rather poor but pleasant elderly man, a touch eccentric, as witness the curious high-heeled, side-elastic boots. A retired something-or-another. Businessman? Banker? Farmer? No, rancher, Emma decided, recalling the heels of cowboy boots. But on the other hand, the shiny car, the chauffeur, the granddaughter belied the note of poverty, as did a certain assurance in Mr. Weatherbee's manner. Emma had seen his blue eyes snap, had heard the rasp in his voice, and had noted that his granddaughter obeyed him. The sheriff had obeyed him too. Now he was talking to the strange man as though he knew all about mines and mining. Emma decided that all she knew about Mr. Weatherbee was that he was an old man with a perverted sense of humor, who was not above playing both ends against the middle to get what he wanted. And who seemed to be in a position to do the last successfully. That was the point.

His granddaughter was in some way connected with the murder, at least with Horsack. The old man was rich and, therefore, influential; he was in cahoots with the sheriff—and probably the state police as well. He would undoubtedly use every bit of his prestige to keep his granddaughter out of the trouble that loomed ahead, and yet he had, Emma realized, in his own fantastic way, tried to help her. At least he had believed her story and taken her to the sheriff; no, it was more than that—it was as though he were offering her a help that she did not need or understand in return for a certain protection for his granddaughter. She, Emma, didn't need help. But both Mr. Faber and the old man seemed to think Mary would. Maybe they knew something she didn't know. Or thought they did.

Emma repudiated the idea that they could actually know anything bad about Mary, but she couldn't see that it would do any harm to ally herself with the side of law and power. The power might corrupt the law, but if she were on that side— Emma refused to admit that she would be party to corruption or derive benefit therefrom and gave up a too-careful scrutiny of her motive in deciding to play along with Mr. Weatherbee. She told herself that she rather liked him. He was amusing—if his jokes had been played on someone else she would have thought it hilariously funny—he was loyal, a quality that Emma prized, and under his placid manner there was a dominating quality that reminded her of Jeff. She looked at him now, chair tipped back, his hands cozily cuddling the empty glass against his chest.

"When you find another Thunderbolt," he was saying, "come and see me."

If Alice B. Simms was the name of a mine, so, probably, was Thunderbolt. Emma decided that Mr. Weatherbee was cute.

"Sol"—Mr. Weatherbee made the transition from mines to murder on the heels of the locator of the Alice B. Simms—"the opera lets out about four-thirty, four thirty-five today on account of the little hitch in the performance. It is now"—again he consulted his silver watch—"exactly thirty-one minutes past five. Does it strike you as peculiar that there ain't nobody else found this body and called you about it?"

Mr. Faber pondered the suggestion. "Could be. Though Lizzie Danforth herds the tourists in the front door and has the roomers use the side one."

"Who's she got staying there now?"

"Miss Pinzi and Professor Burkhardt. He won't be coming back until it gets dark."

"And me," Emma said meekly.

"Anyhow"—Mr. Weatherbee stood up and reached for his hat—"it'll be interesting to see if things is just as Miss Marsh left them."

"I'm not sure," Emma spoke hastily, "that I want to go in there again."

"I got good eyesight," said Mr. Weatherbee, "and Sol ain't blind yet. You told us how things was; we'll compare notes afterward."

Although Emma had not spoken of it, he seemed to sense her tacit agreement of his generalship. Sol put in a call for Dominic, and they left the office, planning like conspirators. Emma would return to her room and stay put until Mr. Weatherbee and the sheriff had seen the body. Mr. Weatherbee would break the news to Mrs. Danforth. By that time Dominic might be there, if he hurried. No further word was said about Mary.

They picked their way up the street between the people who had seen the square dancing and were going to the bar and those who were reversing the process. The scene was still bright and gay; not for another hour would the sun go down behind the mountains.

As they passed the gardens a man whom Emma thought she recognized as the tall blond tenor saw them and started forward; then he stopped, looked at the sheriff, and turned away. Mr. Weatherbee, who was at that very moment explaining to the unoperatically inclined Sol what had happened when Horsack failed to take his cue, did not notice the blond tenor. Pretended not to notice him? Emma wasn't sure which. Mr. Weatherbee had a casual way of ignoring certain things or remarks, but he picked others up fast enough. He was old and he might be deaf, but he wasn't dumb. Emma was sure of that. Probably the blond tenor had killed Horsack so that he could sing his role. Opera singers were supposed to be jealous and temperamental. But not Mary. Where on earth was Mary?

They passed the opera house and ascended the steeper slope of Mrs. Danforth's sidewalk.

"Old Bert," said Mr. Weatherbee, gazing at a cast-iron stag but probably not referring to it, "he was a son of a gun."

"Lizzie," said Sol, "kind of takes after him."

Mr. Weatherbee sniffed. "You wasn't dry between—" He looked at Emma and amended his speech, "—behind the ears when old Bert died. Bertram Estis was Mrs. Danforth's father," he explained to Emma. "Him and me had a stake in the Thunderbolt."

"Only his son-in-law"—Sol waited for Mr. Weatherbee to make the turn up the brick steps of the walk to the house—"blew the money on dead Indians."

"De mortuis nil nisi bonum," said Mr. Weatherbee surprisingly. "You can't blame him for giving his collection to Chicago when we wouldn't buy it. He was just ahead of his time. You ever been to Mesa Verde?"

"Well, Alf Danforth was there when nobody would believe that mummies came anywhere but from Egypt. He was kinda like some people is about antiques."

"Mmm," said Emma.

"You wouldn't believe it," Mr. Weatherbee went on, "but there's people up here collecting old oxshoes and barbed wire."

"Anyhow"—Sol apparently felt the conversation had been straying—"old Bert built a mighty fine house."

The Estis Mansion rose before them, the complexities of its horrid pile more apparent from the front. Its turrets climbed skyward; its plate glass gleamed; half of its silver-handled outer front door stood open.

"You go right in," said Mr. Weatherbee, "and go on upstairs. Sol and I'll sort of mosey around to the side."

He spoke as though they were planning nothing more serious than a raid on the kitchen cookie jar, and Emma, who had begun to worry a little about Mary, felt better and smiled and nodded. The whole thing was farcical: the operatic setting, the two old men, the beautiful granddaughter, even the body in its remembered absurd costume. The ridiculous house, the man who collected Indian relics were all so far removed from reality that Emma saluted them jauntily as she walked in the door.

Emma had not yet been in the front hall, and as she opened the inner door she paused before the array of bristling antlers that gloomed down at her. Elk, sheep, bison, and the lesser horned species lined the walls with their decapitated heads and offered their hoofs as sharp supports for hats and sticks. The effect was distinctly grim.

A man's voice came from the dining room and Mrs. Danforth's, genteelly but firmly directing the signing of her guest book. Mrs. Danforth stepped into the hall to say good evening, but Emma only nodded and marched straight ahead—not daring to glance down the dark corridor that branched off to the side entrance—up the stairs, past the bronze girl who partially lessened the gloom with a bunch of electrically lighted flowers, past the steel engravings of dogs, stags, and Highland cattle, all along the upper hall, her feet light on the rubber matting.

Not until she reached her own door did she realize that she had been holding her breath. She let it out with a loud sigh and felt her scalp prickle as she heard a rustle from the other side of the dark panels. It might be well to exercise a little caution; after all, murder had been done in that house, and she hadn't taken the key to her door. Nobody did, Mary had told her. Emma bet they would from now on. The other closed doors of the hall were suddenly as menacing as the closed door to the side entry. Emma felt a great desire to be behind her own door and to have it locked. She tried the knob, but it did not turn, and for a moment she was aghast. This was her door. Or was it? She hated the thought of trying those closed doors. Then there was movement, and a voice whispered: "Who is it?"

"Me," said Emma, also whispering.

The door swung inward. Mary stood by it; her face was ashen, and in the fireplace grate a thin wisp of smoke still ascended from burned paper.

"Holy saints," said Mary, "where have you been? You didn't come in the side way?" she went on without waiting for an answer. "You couldn't have."

"No." Emma didn't explain. "I came in the front door."

"Praises be. I was afraid you'd come back the way we went out. I wanted to find you to warn you. Oh, something awful has happened. He expected it—anyhow, he was afraid of it. Paul"—her voice broke—"has been killed, and I've waited and waited for someone to go into that terrible place, but nobody does, and I've got to call the police myself."

At first all Emma could think of was that Mary had been in the house all the time, that if she, too, had only come in she would have found Mary and would have been spared the harrowing entanglement with Mr. Weatherbee. Then she realized that it was Mary who had discovered Horsack's body. But why, she wondered, hadn't Mary called Mrs. Danforth or notified someone immediately? Well, why hadn't she herself, for that matter? Rather than explain that, she said quietly, "You don't have to tell the police; I've done it."

Mary crumpled up on the floor, but she did not faint. Her shoulders shook with sobs as she lay there.

"Don't," said Emma, and then tentatively, because she wanted to get the tenors straightened out, "Were you," she asked, "fond of him?"

Mary sat up quickly, her eyes sparkling with tears, but more with anger. "I hated him. I loathed and despised him. It's only—only that the floor of the entry was so cold."

Her sobs broke forth again, and she buried her face in the magenta roses of the carpet. Emma, more confused than ever, knelt beside her and patted her awkwardly on the back.

"Please don't, Sticky," she said.

"Oh-h." Mary sobbed harder. "Nobody's called me that in years. I'm so unhappy. I'm so unhappy I could die."

Emma was sorry for her. Finding a body was no joke, not if it was someone you knew, someone you were fond of. But Mary had said that she hated Horsack, and yet her grief seemed out of proportion for grief at the death of someone she disliked. Mary always dramatized and exaggerated things; she probably didn't hate Horsack at all, and yet her emotion seemed real. It all went around in circles to Emma, but she knew that she had to get Mary straightened out before the arrival of Mr. Weatherbee and the sheriff. What those two hardened old reprobates would make of Mary's actions she could too easily guess. She'd have to take care of Mary.

The weight of the world settled again on Emma's shoulders. She had thought this murder meant nothing more to her than the answering of a few routine questions. She had hoped that it would interrupt her visit with Mary no more than Horsack's absence had interrupted the flow of the opera. The police would take over, just as the blond tenor had taken on Horsack's part. But Mr. Weatherbee had disturbed her with his hints, and now Mary was acting in an overwrought fashion that presaged no good, though it was perfectly natural if Mary had been in love with Horsack. But Mary said she hated Horsack.

"Please." She patted Mary's shoulder again. "The sheriff and Mr. Weatherbee will be here in a minute. You don't want them to see you that way."

Her words were magical. Mary sat up straight. "The sheriff and who?"

"Mr. Weatherbee. An old man. I asked him how to find the police, and I thought he was crazy, but he seems to be sort of in the know."

"Sort of!" Mary's voice was angry. "He only owns half the state and most of the mint. He supports the Art Center and this Play Festival. He's so old it's unnatural and so rich it's immoral. And he's got four sons and a granddaughter that is an underhanded, sneaking, thieving, brazen witch, who thinks that just because she's young and blond and a Weatherbee she can have any man she wants. She can too"—her voice changed from anger to bitterness—"any man like Paul."

Emma began to see a faint gleam of light. "I didn't know," she said meekly.

"No," Mary's tone was resigned, "I don't suppose you did. You probably barged up to the first person you saw and said, `I've just seen a murder; where's the cops?'"

"Well," Emma admitted, "it wasn't exactly like that. . . ."

"Holy saints!" With the Weatherbees put in their place, the import of Emma's words came home to Mary. "Did you call the police? Then you must have found him. How awful, how dreadful for you. I've been a perfect beast, sitting here wailing, not realizing what you've been saying . . . ."

Now Mary was being herself, Emma thought.

"You poor little thing. I didn't think it would be like this; truly I didn't. I thought he was making it up, but I thought you could tell us what we ought to do. On account of Hank, you know."

"Making what up? Tell who what to do about what?" Emma was interrupted by the sound of feet and doors below and a piercing, shivering cry.

"And that," said Mary prosaically, "will be Aggie, poor soul."

Emma had the feeling that she had to begin somewhere, had to put her finger on one simple thing of fact, before she lost her footing entirely and was swept away by the tide of events.

"Darling," she said, "I'm so mixed up I don't know—what I don't know. Just start at the end and tell me, who is Aggie?"

"Agatha Estis. She's Mrs. Danforth's aunt, and she's an old maid, and she's feebleminded, and she draws pictures. Wait till you see them."

"Okay." There were other things more important to Emma than Miss Estis' pictures. The questions. There were always questions. The same questions asked over and over again until someone gave the wrong answer. In a few minutes a strange policeman named Dominic was going to start asking her questions, and, while she was still firm in her determination to tell the whole truth, there were a few things she wanted to get straight.

"About the motive," she began, "they always think there has to be a motive."

"You mean"—Mary looked up, and Emma's heart sank, because there was fear in Mary's eyes—"you mean would anyone special have a special reason for killing him? No one but me."

At Emma's horrified exclamation she seemed to pull herself together and rushed on:

"I don't really mean that. Everybody hated him. He was mean and hateful. He had a thousand tricks of stealing the show, of making you miss your lines."

Emma could hear voices. In a minute Mr. Weatherbee would be there, and this strange Dominic. She had to get some kind of sense into Mary.

"Look here," she said, "you don't have to tell the police how you feel or what you think. Only what you know. About his being afraid of something and how you came right over here after the performance and found the body—"

"Oh, but I didn't."

"But that's what you just said."

"I didn't say anything of the kind, and don't you be saying I did."

There were footsteps outside the door and a knock. Thoroughly bewildered and no little uneasy, Emma got up slowly. If she had to skip things in her story she'd get mixed up and make things worse for Mary, who would undoubtedly make things bad enough for herself if she went on to the police the way she had been talking to Emma. .

Emma opened the door. There was the sheriff and Mr. Weatherbee, looking particularly small beside a large red-faced officer in the uniform of the state police.

Mr. Weatherbee said politely: "Miss Marsh, make you acquainted with Officer Dominic Nitti."

"How do you do?" Emma stepped aside to let them enter and turned to include Mary in the introductions. No Mary. Not visible. Emma's eyes fell on the double doors. They were closed now, but they had been open when she came in. And Mary was nobody's dummy. All she had to do was to stick her ear to the crack to hear all that was said.

"Do sit down," Emma said graciously. "Officer, do you care for a cigarette?"

Nitti started to take one, looked at Mr. Weatherbee, and shook his head.

So, Emma thought, he was playing the old man's game too, was he? She took a cigarette and passed them to the others, who both accepted. After all, Emma decided, Nitti probably needed both hands and an ear to hold notebook and pencil.

"All right." Nitti was anxious to get started, to give a good impression. "What do you know about this?"

Emma felt right at home. All cops were so comfortably alike. Was it their training that did it, or did just the same kind of men grow up to be cops? She must remember to ask Hank about that.

"I found Mr. Horsack," Emma said simply, "and then I found Mr. Weatherbee. He wasn't dead—Mr. Weatherbee, I mean. He was very helpful. He said we must notify the police." She looked at Mr. Weatherbee sweetly as she said it. She'd give him a break because she might need one from him sometime.

"Your name is—?" Nitti remembered and wrote it down. "Where you from?"

"Boston." Emma said it proudly.

"What are you doing here?"

"Visiting. Visiting Miss Dolan." The name had to come out.

"Same as Pinzi," Mr. Weatherbee put in. "I told you."

Was he warning her, Emma wondered, to stick to the story she had told him? But the old man leaned against the tufted back of the teeter-totter chair and teeter-tottered gently, his eyes vacantly roving the room.

"What time did you leave the opera house?"

"Why, I don't know. Mr. Weatherbee said it was four thirty-five." Mr. Weatherbee gave Emma a pained look, and she could have hung her head in shame. Hank had told her often enough never to involve anyone else in her statements. She hadn't said anything particularly damaging, but she was glad to get Mr. Weatherbee's warning, and she had almost immediate opportunity to make restitution.

"What did you do then?"

"Stood on the balcony for a few moments watching the crowd."

"Did you see anything unusual?"

"No."

Emma spoke without hesitation. If Nitti had said "heard" her answer might have been different, though she wasn't sure, considering it afterward, whether or not she would have repeated Mr. Weatherbee's remark. But her "No" was out, and it was too late to change it, for Emma had caught the triumphant gleam in the old man's eyes. She went on rather quickly to say that she had returned to Mrs. Danforth's and described again the finding of the body in the entry.

"Then?"

"Why, then I went over to the hotel and found Mr. Weatherbee."

Nitti interrupted her: "You came back here, but after you found the body you went to the hotel. Why was that?"

Emma didn't say, because her first impulse had been to find Mary. She said, "To telephone the police."

"There's a telephone in the entry."

"I didn't feel so good." This was the truth. "And I went outside, and I didn't want to go back—in there, you know."

"All this took up a lot of time?"

"Why, no." Emma fell bodily into the trap. "It didn't take but a few minutes."

"All right." There was an aha quality in Nitti's tone. "You got away from the opera at four thirty-five. Say you found the body at quarter of. How do you account for the fact that I wasn't called until five-thirty?"

Emma could account for it fast enough, but to do so seemed to involve a great many people. She looked helplessly at Mr. Weatherbee, and Mr. Weatherbee stepped nobly into the breach.

"You heard her say she didn't feel so good. Who would? Bodies ain't a nice sight for a lady. When she got to me I thought she was going to faint, and I had to get her out of that danged crowd in the hotel. And then she got hy-sterical; I say she got hy-sterical"—Mr. Weatherbee looked sternly at Emma, who moved her hands about, trying to act the part of a nervous, fidgety female—"and I couldn't get nothing out of her for a while, and then I took her down to Sol here to tell her story, and then my granddaughter come busting in, wanting me to go to Denver with her, and I had to get rid of her, and then Sol called you. Only I guess," he finished blandly, "all that took longer than we thought."

It was true, Emma had to admit, except for the degree of her hysteria, all true, and yet there was deception in every word of it—deliberate motive concealing deception. In that it protected Mary, Emma was grateful, but she made instant decision to play along with Mr. Weatherbee because, she decided, Mr. Weatherbee would bear watching.

His story told, Mr. Weatherbee got up and ambled around the room, fingering the lace curtains, the Dresden set on the commode, and looking, with a twinkle in his eyes, from the carved lovebirds atop the walnut bed to Emma. But there was no twinkle in his eyes as he paused in front of the grate and looked at the blackened papers. There was no smoke rising from them now, but Emma knew that if he touched them they would still be warm.

Nitti snapped an elastic band around his notebook and stood up, pulling down his tunic in the immemorial manner of cops. Emma, thinking the interview was over and that she had done rather well, was about to relax, when Nitti spoke again.

"What made you think this Horsack had been murdered?"

It took Emma a moment to get her mouth closed. "Why," she stuttered, "his head. And the blood . . ."

Nitti's smile was as condescending and as unbelieving as though she had been an old maid trying to convince him that there was a man under her bed.

"Don't let a little blood upset you. I seen a lot more blood in accidents, like when a driver goes through a windshield. You didn't see any weapon?"

Emma admitted that she had not.

"Because he fell or fainted and hit his head on the doorknob. Blood all over it."

Relief, disbelief, and chagrin crowded Emma's thoughts.

"He was kind of a hefty man," Mr. Faber put in, "and he probably run up them steps. He mighta had a heart attack."

He might have, Emma thought, done just that very thing. The medical examination would prove or disprove it. People did die from whacking their heads on something instead of being killed by the reverse. She had walked in on a body and had assumed foul play, probably from past experience. Hank would howl when he heard about it; Hank would howl when he heard what Mr. Weatherbee had done to her.

The silence was broken by the sound of a knock and voices in the next room.

". . . dreadful, dreadful accident," someone was saying excitedly, "but the performance will go on as usual."

And Mary's voice, "Of course."

"Hear pretty plain through them doors." Mr. Weatherbee made it a statement. "Sounds like Alvarado, the director. The show must go on, or the Historical Society will have a fit."

He leaned over and picked up a piece of paper that had fallen from the grate. "Been having a fire?"

"No," said Emma. Not she. So help her.

"You could have," Mr. Weatherbee pointed out, "just as easy as not.

It gets right nippy up here as soon as the sun goes down."

Emma couldn't help feeling that Mr. Weatherbee had looked upon her ingenuity and found it wanting. And why in the name of darn hadn't she said yes? There had been a fire, and Mr. Weatherbee knew it, and what difference did it make, if Horsack's death had been accidental? Of course it hadn't been her fire, so she wasn't really lying any more than Mr. Weatherbee had been lying about the delay in calling the police. Mr. Weatherbee probably understood that; he had merely been pointing out that she could have told a better story if she had put her mind to it. Mr. Weatherbee had been right. They had both been in the same boat—the two of them; he with a granddaughter who had a crush on Horsack, and she with Mary, who appeared to feel just the reverse, and whether Horsack's death had been murder, as she had hastily surmised—or accident—was not determined. It was just as well not to let gossip get started.

"Good-by, Mr. Weatherbee," said Emma sincerely, "and thank you."

"Good-by," said Mr. Weatherbee. "Everything all right now?"

"Sure." Emma smiled at him. "I'm going to have a swell visit."

Mr. Weatherbee, unaccountably, looked disappointed. "Lizzie," he continued, "says she didn't hear anything. She was busy all afternoon with a bunch of tourists that didn't care for the opera. Aggie's been picking wild flowers." He sighed and led the way out.

CHAPTER FOUR

EMMA could hardly wait for them to leave, so anxious was she to talk to Mary, but there were still voices coming from Mary's room, so she fretted about, taking things out of her bag, smoking a cigarette, and admiring the set on the washstand. It really was Dresden; she looked at the bottom of the toothbrush mug to make sure, opened the door of the compartment below, and giggled at the chamber mug with the crocheted silencer on its cover. Jeff would get a kick out of that.

She turned around quickly because she thought she heard a noise. It came again, a faint tap on her door.

"Come in," Emma called, wondering who.

There was a pause, and then the door opened softly, slowly, and a weird figure sidled in. For a second, from the fantastic costume, Emma thought it was someone from the cast to see Mary. Then she saw the towels over the purple-clad arm, the gray hair, the reddened eyes, and the wavering mouth in the smooth, pink face and remembered what Mary had said about Agatha Estis: "She's feebleminded, and she draws pictures." After her experience with Mr. Weatherbee, Emma shied away from implying mental derangement on anyone, and except for the towels, the artist getup was perfect from beads to sandals. There was even a smudge of paint on the front of the smock.

"Come in," Emma repeated gently, because the old creature looked ready to fly at a harsh word.

"She told me to bring these." The towels were extended..

"Thank you."

"My name is Agatha," the woman said, "Agatha Estis. Please don't call me Aggie." Her reddened eyes were soft and pleading like those of a scolded dog.

"Why, of course," Emma agreed. "Agatha is such a pretty name."

Then the double doors opened and Mary burst into the room.

"Darling— Oh, hello, Aggie."

Agatha Estis' mouth trembled and her face puckered up, but she did not cry. She pointed to the towels in Emma's hands.

"She told me to bring them," she said, but as she spoke her eyes followed Mary's to the rack beside the commode. It was already amply stocked with towels, and with a little moan Agatha fled from the room.

"Just nuts," said Mary cheerfully. "And snoopy. She's forever popping up with something she claims Mrs. D. told her to do that's already been done. Did she bring you a picture?"

Emma shook her head, marveling in the change in Mary. A few moments before she had been in apparent distress at Horsack's death; now she was almost indecently happy.

"No," said Emma, "she didn't."

"She will. She gives them to everyone. There were some in Paul's room. . ." Her brows came together for a moment. "I suppose they told you? That Paul's death was an accident?"

Emma nodded. "I feel as though I had made a complete fool of myself."

Mary nodded. "Going around with Hank, I guess, sort of keeps the idea of foul play in the mind. But I don't blame you. I thought somebody had done him in too. You didn't know him, but he was so healthy, so alive, so—so vital, that somehow it never occurred to me that he had a weak heart or could have fallen down and bumped his head. He would have hated it—it's such an undignified way to die—but since it had to happen I'm so glad it's over I could scream!"

Emma looked at her in horrified amazement.

"Darling, you think I'm dreadful, don't you, but have you ever been in love with someone that you loathed and despised and hated and loved just the same?"

Emma was too astonished to shake her head, but Mary was going on, her words crowding each other in their eagerness to get said.

"He had the voice of an angel and the disposition of the devil. He was horrible to work with and rude to everyone, and he made a play for every woman in the company when he couldn't get his hands on somebody with money, but for six months I was miserable when he was out of my sight and all jelly inside when I was with him and disgusted with myself all the time for being such a fool. And later, even up here, he wouldn't let me alone—"

Emma interrupted her, "But you couldn't possibly love any—"

"That's what you think. But I did. He could be awfully sweet when he wanted to be, and there was something about him—even when he looked at you and said, 'God, you're an ugly wench'—that made you turn over inside. I don't suppose you understand; it's an experience you have to have had to know about, but now I know that, I know he can't bother us any more—the whole company, I mean—it's like waking from a nightmare. It's like being let out of jail." She paused and looked at Emma. "Darling, do you think I'm horrible?"

"Don't be a dope," said Emma. She could understand now why Mary had said she had a motive for murdering Horsack. "You just pick horrible men. You know," she added, "when I first got here I thought—I assumed—that Sauer was your tenor."

"Did you?"

"I suppose Horsack was worse," Emma went on, "but I'm glad it's not Sauer."

Mary didn't say anything, and Emma finished blithely, "All he needs is a monocle to look like a younger Von Stroheim."

"Come on," said Mary, "rules to the contrary, what we need is a drink."

She threw open the door, and as she did so Emma saw the door on the opposite side of the hall close quickly. Mary saw it too.

"Damn," she said without lowering her voice, "I forgot about Aggie. She probably had her ear glued to the keyhole." She took Emma's arm and when they had reached the stairs said in a lowered tone, "She was one of his conquests too, poor thing. He led her on and praised her pictures and then made fun of her. He was a first-class worm, that one."

Emma agreed thoroughly, but she did not answer because Mrs. Danforth was standing at the foot of the stairs, waiting for them. She was dignified and calm, but her face was tired, and when she spoke her voice was husky. She held out a key.

"To the front door," she said, "because I wouldn't expect you to use the side one. I'm going to lock up early." Her voice cracked. "I've talked too much today."

She smiled a quick smile, and Emma realized that Mrs. Danforth had been a handsome woman.

Mary put her hand on Mrs. Danforth's arm impulsively. "Thank you," she said. "You're always thinking of nice things, and it's a shame this— this had to happen in your house."

"I am only grateful that he was not staying here. If he had been I should have known him better, and to those who knew him well this must have been a great shock."

"Yes," said Mary.

She put the key in her bag and left rather hurriedly. Outside the door she spoke angrily to Emma. "What business is it of hers how I feel?"

"None at all. I don't think she meant to imply that."

"Oh yes, she did. She knew what was going on. Paul wanted to stay there. She even let him register, but he made some crack about hoping our rooms would be as close together as our signatures were in the book, and she said she had misunderstood, that there was only one room available. It was just as well."

"You mustn't be hypersensitive."

"About having been a fool, you mean? I'm going to forget it just as fast as I can."

As they went through the hotel lobby Emma was a little surprised to see Mr. Weatherbee dozing in his chair by the rubber plant. She had imagined that he would have gone home, and then she remembered that he had sent his car to Denver. He was rather a sweet old duck in his anxiety to take care of his granddaughter. If Emma was any judge of persons, she imagined that Mr. Weatherbee had realized what Horsack liked about his granddaughter and had disliked him cordially. Now if Horsack had really been murdered—but no, Mr. Weatherbee had been at the opera—or had he? He could have slipped out too. It was almost a pleasure to speculate about the murder of such an unpleasant person as Horsack had undoubtedly been, and Emma relinquished the idea reluctantly as they climbed up to the bar.

It was early for dinner, and the crowd had thinned out; those who had come up for the matinee had gone home, and those who would attend the evening performance had not yet come. They had the bar practically to themselves, and Emma had ample opportunity to take in the ornate mirror, the stuffed owl, and the faded, framed clippings announcing stagecoach runs, the visits of celebrities, and suchlike.

"You wonder where it all comes from," she said sadly.

"What do you mean—the licker?"

"No, the black walnut."

"I thought it came from trees."

"You're thinking of maple sugar."

"Sure an' I am. What do you want to drink?"

"What's a Gregory Gulch Special?" Emma was reading from the list soaped on the mirror.

"Bourbon," the bartender replied, "and champagne with a dash of grenadine."

Emma shuddered. "It sounds horrible. I'll have one."

"Eggnog," said Mary. "And not too much brandy."

"Pretty sad about Mr. Horsack," said the bartender, working gently on the champagne cork.

"Very sad," said Mary.

"Lucky you've got Sauer. They say he was fine this afternoon."

"Sauer's fine," Mary agreed.

The cork popped, and the bartender moved away from them, selecting other ingredients for his devil's broth.

"You can't get away from it, can you?" Mary muttered.

"Horsack?"

"Yes. Why do they have to keep talking about him? Why can't they let it go?"

Emma thought that any local interest in Horsack's death was only natural, but she didn't see that saying so would help Mary. What Mary needed was distraction, preferably in the form of some other male. A nice male, one who would be kind and considerate—a change from Mary's usual run.

"Here you are, ladies." The bartender did not linger; other people were coming now, or he might have sensed Mary's unwillingness to talk.

Emma sipped, rolling the drink around experimentally.

"Not bad," she pronounced. "Really not bad at all."

"You better tie weights to your feet." Mary was skeptical.

"It's good. Being here with you, I mean."

"Don't think I'm not glad you are here."

"Remember the chocolate malteds we used to have in the middle of the mornings?"

"And the sugar doughnuts?"

"You mean crullers."

"I mean doughnuts."

"Here we go again."

Suddenly a voice behind Emma said, "Don't turn around. Break it to me gently—this can't be Daddy's little girl."

"Shay!" Emma exclaimed. "Shay Horrigan."

Hands held her head still, but in the mirror she could see the familiar tousled form of Hank's photographer friend, last heard from in China.

His hair was rumpled; his suit was unpressed, but except that he was thinner, he looked very natural and was very welcome.

"Have you got a kiss for Daddy?"

"Don't be absurd. Shay, you idiot, let go of me."

"Not until you introduce me to the cute little beetle."

"Miss Dolan. Mr. Horrigan." Emma pointed them out to each other in the mirror.

"Irish, too." Shay positively purred. "Ain't I the lucky one? Stop me if you've heard this. Once there were two Irishmen."

"I know," said Emma. "Now there are millions of them."

Shay tweaked her ear. "You know everything. Where's Hank?"

"San Diego and points east."

"So I heard—so I heard." He left Emma abruptly and pulled up a stool beside Mary. "Tell me about yourself," he commanded.

"Do you know this person well?" Mary asked of Emma.

"Too well to believe a word he says."

Shay gave Emma a dark look. "That's no way to creep into my heart. If we're going to get personal, where's the body? There has to be a body with you around."

Beyond Shay someone set a glass down on the bar sharply; it was the dark woman with the mole. Mary turned a little white, but Emma only looked annoyed.

"We'll discuss this after the hand," she said pointedly.

Shay pursed his lips and looked wise. "Tell me just one thing. Is it anybody I know?"

"No," said Emma. "Absolutely no!"

Mary got down from the stool. "I'm going to order a sandwich. Come on back when you've finished."

"Okay."

Shay watched her walk away and then looked at Emma. "What's the angle?"

Emma, who by now had decided that Shay was just what Mary needed, did not feel that it was necessary to tell everything.

"A member of the company," she said primly, "met with a fatal accident this afternoon. It is naturally upsetting."

"You don't tell me." Shay mimicked her tone. "Might I inquire the name?"

"Paul Horsack, the tenor. Mary's the female lead—"

"Horsack," said Shay. "That's too bad."

"Did you know him?" Emma was only mildly surprised, because Shay knew a lot of people. "He sounded like a heel."

"Sure he's a heel, but he used to be Beneš' secretary, and he's all tied up in the Free Czech business."

"Oh," said Emma, "then it's too bad. But we ought to go back to Mary, and you haven't told me what you're doing up here or where you've been or anything."

"Okay. This guy just happened to die, and he meant nothing at all to the little beetle, but we won't discuss it. I'm up here to get pictures of this historic spot and the brilliant opera company here assembled, as you could have guessed if you'd given it a moment's thought. I came back from China via Burma and Africa and won't discuss that either, if you please. Where has the little beetle hidden herself?"

They went out into a space between the wings of the building that was now called a patio and was used as an open-air dining room. Mary was seated at a table, but she was not eating. She was talking earnestly with the blond tenor, Sauer. It was perfectly natural that they should be talking; in fact, since Sauer was presumably taking Horsack's role, it was almost surprising that they had not already had some kind of conference, but for no reason that she knew of Emma was uneasy at seeing them together.

Sauer saw Emma and Shay and stood up, and Emma could feel Shay stiffen even as she did herself. Sauer was young and tall and broad, as Emma had remembered him, but without his costume and makeup the solid squareness of his head and neck was more apparent. If there were such a thing as a perfect Aryan, Sauer was it, and there was an unheard click to the precision with which he arose.

Mary looked up blankly, as though her mind had been far away, then remembered her manners and made the introduction. Sauer bowed to Emma, a deep bow from the waist. He extended his hand to Shay and said, "Hello, I'm glad to meet you."

Shay shook hands and sat down beside Mary. Emma, feeling her bristles relax, sat down too. A man didn't necessarily have to be a German just because he looked like one. Sauer probably wasn't his real name anyway. Look at Mary; she had taken an Italianate name in the days when it was fashionable to do so, and she wasn't above putting on displays of operatic temperament when the occasion demanded.

"Did you come for the opera?" Sauer was asking of Shay.

"More or less." Shay's tone wasn't exactly curt, but it was far from sociable.

"It is good." Sauer's face lit up. "It really is good. And tonight—" he turned to Mary—"it will be superb."

"Listen to him," said Mary. "He thinks he's good."

Sauer's face fell.

"Poor Rho," Mary went on, "he's so happy to be singing the part of the count that he forgets to be sorry about Paul."

Emma could see the muscles along Sauer's jaw tighten. "He was a very fine singer," he said stiffly.

"He was a Czech, wasn't he?" Shay asked, though why he had to bring it up wasn't clear to Emma. She knew that Shay knew Horsack was a Czech.

"I like the Czechs." Mary was speaking deliberately to Sauer. "Why is it that you people don't like them?"

The look in Sauer's eyes as he answered surprised Emma; it was that of a dog being tormented by his master. A look both pleading and patient. "It was not his nationality that I objected to," he said.

They were interrupted by the sudden appearance of a short, fat, out-of-breath man who was calling for Miss Pinzi. He ignored Emma and Shay and waved aside attempted introductions. He had been looking everywhere for Mary, he said, and now that he had found her she must come with him at once. And why was she eating? She should not eat. Look at Sauer; he was not eating; he knew better.

Mary said that she was eating because she was hungry and finished the last bite of her sandwich before she stood up.

Were Emma and Shay coming to the performance?

Shay definitely was not and reminded Emma that they had not eaten. Emma thought maybe she would eat and go to bed, but there was the matter of the key. It was finally arranged that they would meet later at the hotel, because Mary wanted a meal then. Shay said that they would be in the bar.

Mary was leaving, followed by Sauer, when a busboy, navigating the now-crowded patio with a tray of dishes, bumped into Sauer.

"Stay out of my way, you goddamned Nazi."

It was only a mutter, but Emma and Shay heard. Sauer heard it, too, because his face went scarlet.

"The whole thing," said Shay, "stinks. And what hurts me most is that the first cute beetle I've seen since last week is mixed up in it."

Emma knew that he didn't mean her. And while Shay's intentions had never been serious yet, they were always fervid enough to be diverting. And diversion, Emma decided, would be good for Mary.

"Mary isn't mixed up in anything," she said, "and I don't think there's anything for her to be mixed up in."

Shay reached for the menu, found the place that said steak, and pointed it out to the waitress before he answered. "I'm surprised at you," he said. "I deplore your lack of imagination. Here's a beautiful girl who goes all funny when a dead Czech is mentioned, mixed up with a fellow who obviously hated the guts of the aforementioned corpse and who is

German to boot. I'm not a reporter; I just take the pictures, but even I can smell a story in that. And you're here, my little friend, and don't forget that you spell trouble. I bet money"—Shay grinned at her—"that you found the body."

"I did," Emma confessed, "and I jumped right to the conclusion that he'd been murdered."

"What," Shay asked, "made you think he had been murdered?"

"He was dead. And, as you just pointed out, in the polite circles in which I move, that means murder. Then I tried to call the police, and a lot of reasons why people might want to murder him began to pop up. Mr. Weatherbee's granddaughter and now Sauer."

Emma didn't mention Mary because, reasons or no reasons, Mary wouldn't have killed Horsack, and there was no point in prejudicing Shay against her.

"I don't believe," said Shay, "that I've heard you mention Mr. Weatherbee or his granddaughter. I could use a granddaughter."

Emma thought he probably could but hoped that Mr. Weatherbee's control would keep Susan in Denver. "Of course," she said, "I had her all picked for the murderer, but now I sort of favor her grandfather himself."

"I didn't think"—Shay took his elbows off the table so that the waitress could put down the steaks—"that this was a case of you know what."

"It isn't. But if it had been, you know, I've got it all figured out how he could have done it."

"You want coffee now?" the waitress asked.

Shay said yes, and Emma said no, and the waitress departed scowling because their disagreement meant an extra trip.

The steaks were small and rather too well done. Shay cut into his despondently. "Time was," he reflected, "when I'd have personally taken this back to the chef and told him what to do with it, but a protracted diet of rice has softened me."

Emma let it pass. It sounded inane to say, "Oh yes, what were you doing in China?" She knew that Shay had gone there to take pictures; the details, pleasant or unpleasant, were for him to divulge.

"I wish Hank were here," she said.

"Old Hank." Shay chewed gloomily. "Why don't you two get married?"

"He's stopped asking me"—Emma tried to speak lightly—"for the duration."

"Anyhow," Shay helped her out, "he's an awfully handy guy to have around in case of a—you know what," he finished, because the waitress was there with the coffee.

"I guess I'll have mine now too," said Emma, making an enemy for life.

"Merely to keep your mind off your food," Shay suggested, "begin at the beginning and tell me how you happened to be in on this—you know."

"Well," Emma began, "Hank got orders, and I got a letter from Mary. . ."

Shay did not interrupt her, except occasionally to put her back on the track of her narrative, until she came to the episode of Mr. Weatherbee; then he let out a whoop of laughter that turned the eyes of the now-full dining room upon them.

"Shush," said Emma. "You'll have a lot in common with the old devil." She spoke as though their meeting was inevitable, and continued, exaggerating her worries and fears to make the climax of the accidental death more pointed.

"And then Mr. Weatherbee and the sheriff went pussyfooting around to the side door like a couple of stock-company cops, and I went upstairs, and there was Mary—" She paused.

"Don't make it up," Shay warned her. "Tell me what happened. Was she washing her hands or burning the papers?"

"Don't be silly." Emma didn't sound convincing, even to herself, because of course it must have been Mary who had made the fire in the grate. "As a matter of fact, she was crying."

"Ah," Shay asked, "right out of the old crocodile's eyes?"

"Don't you think it. She was horribly upset . . . ." Again Emma paused, partly because something had just occurred to her and partly because she wondered if Shay would understand Mary's feeling about Horsack.

"Don't mind me," Shay assured her. "I like my women with homicidal tendencies; makes me feel right at home."

"Okay." Emma spoke bluntly because she wanted to get past this to the point she had in mind. "She used to be crazy about Horsack even though he beat her, more or less figuratively, and she said that she was glad that he was dead. Does that shock you?"

"No." Shay was equally blunt. "But the police aren't always so broadminded."

"She didn't get to the police, and that's funny, too, because she told me that Horsack had been on the trail of something—just that definite— that was dangerous, that she had thought he was bragging, but now it looked as though he wasn't."

"Yes, yes, go on."

"Well, they bring the police up to me and let me make a fool of myself telling why I thought it was murder, and then they tell me that Horsack had a heart attack, or fainted, and bashed his head on the doorknob, and that's all there is to it."

Shay put down his knife and fork and belched in what was undoubtedly the Chinese fashion.

"Well?" Emma urged.

"Well, indeed. And well enough. People have been fooled before."

Emma misunderstood him. "I know," she said. "It's my gaudy past that makes me suspicious. But all your talk about the Czechs and the Germans reminded me. Horsack claimed he was up to something dangerous; Mary said it looked as though he had been, but she believed it when the director told her it was an accident. You'd think she'd want to tell someone what she told me, but she hasn't mentioned it since."

Shay lit a cigarette and waved the match out airily. "Wishful suppression," he said. "She's so glad Horsack's dead, she doesn't want to think of anything else. Particularly now that I'm here."

"Oh, sure. Practically that, but you're the one who got spooky about Horsack's being a Czech and being dead, and then you acted to Sauer as though you thought he'd killed him. I try hard"—Emma was serious—"not to confuse the individual with the mass, but I could feel my hair rise when I saw Sauer. He looks so—so Prussian."

"I'm not civilized," said Shay. "I hate their guts, and don't forget that a lot of good fifth columnists have been yanked out of opera."

Emma's eyes brightened. "Wouldn't it be marvelous if we could find one—uncover a ring of spies, I mean? There are camps and plants in Denver, and it was probably sabotage and Horsack found out about it, and he was calling the FBI—"

"—and your landlady," Shay took up the tale, "or one of those tourists you mentioned, caught him at it and took him by the ears and whammed his head on the knob."

"You sound just like Hank—making fun of me. It was your idea."

"I didn't intend to start you on the underground movement. Horsack's death may have been accidental, and there may still be dirty work at the crossroads. Your friend, Mr. Fairbanks, would be the first to tell you to preserve an open mind. Which reminds me that this open mind could stand some preserving."

Shay stood up and led Emma toward the bar, an action which served the purpose of bringing the waitress running with his check.

"I can't drink again so soon after dinner," Emma protested when they were seated at a table.

"You can if you try. You can have a brandy or one of those nasty green things that women like. It settles your dinner, cools your stomach—"

"—or preserves my open mind."

"Atta girl. I always said I could love you."

"If you weren't busy loving someone else."

"That's you. Numbers has never stopped me."

A waiter finished reciting *The Face on the Barroom Floor* to a credulous group and came over to take their order.

"I presume," Shay inquired of him, "that there is historic proof that the historic incident commemorated in that poem took place in this historic spot?"

The waiter, who looked like a college boy, grinned. "You sound like that prof that stays up the street. He says it happened up in Nevadaville. All I know is they retouch the picture every spring. You in a hurry, or aren't you going to the opera?"

"I came to hear Horsack," said Shay, "but they tell me he met with an accident."

The boy's face hardened. "You ought to hear Sauer. Sauer is really very good." He took their order without further comment.

"Well," Emma inquired, "what does that tell your open mind? Didn't he like Horsack or doesn't he like Sauer?"

"Or is he in the pay of the Chamber of Commerce?"

"It's an awful habit," said Emma.

"I've tried all the cures," said Shay, "but they don't work."

"I don't mean drink, silly. I mean murder."

"Ah, yes," Shay murmured. "They say that gets you too."

"Dope! Oh, skip it—what I started to say was that my mind goes right on trying to figure out ways and reasons for Horsack's murder, even though I know it was an accident."

"Do you," Shay asked quietly, "know it was an accident?"

It was a few seconds before Emma answered him. "I suppose," she said, "that's what is bothering me. But on the other hand, I don't know it *wasn't.* And I've been brought up to respect the police, and they say it was."

"Now let me tell one." Shay grinned at her. "You may be civilized, but you're the most completely lawless person that I know. You'd break a leg trying to circumvent the law if you thought a friend of yours was involved, and I can prove it."

"You don't need to bother," Emma assured him hastily. "I'll be good. I promised Hank I would be. It's only that I keep thinking up ways he could have been killed while the opera was going on. At first I had it all planned out that it was Mr. Weatherbee, on account of his granddaughter, but Sauer was off stage too—I think. As I told you, I took a little nap, but I suppose we could find out."

"Not if it means sitting through a performance."

"No, of course," Emma agreed with him. "We couldn't make a sacrifice like that."

"An impasse."

"Remember the open door?"

"Waiter!"

"We'll get this thing yet." Shay frowned at his second drink.

"We could hire a spy," Emma suggested. "Someone might be willing to watch the show if they were paid for it."

Shay shook his head. "Sauer isn't Sauer any more. He's doing Horsack's part. Watching him now wouldn't tell where he was at when he was Sauer."

Emma giggled. "Come to think of it, Sauer is a horrible name for an opera singer."

Shay looked pained. "Don't distract me. I was having a thought. What we need," Shay went on, "is to find someone who has seen the show"— he lowered his voice to a grim whisper—"and make him talk."

"There's Mary. She'd do a lot for me."

"Ixnay. She's an interested party. She wouldn't tell the truth."

"She would so!" Emma flared out of the mood defensively.

"What we need"—Shay ignored her—"is the cold, unbiased opinion of the average man, the man in the street, a man like that little guy over there. . ."

Emma looked and snorted her derision. "That 'little guy' is anything but disinterested. He may look like Great-Uncle Hezekiah from the country, but that's Mr. Weatherbee."

The crowd in the bar had thinned out, some of the patrons being more receptive to the opera than Emma and Shay. Perhaps Mr. Weatherbee, standing in the door, heard his name; at any rate he glanced in their direction, caught Emma's eye, and bowed politely.

Emma beckoned with her finger. "You'll get an awful bust out of him," she explained.

Mr. Weatherbee nodded but paused at the bar before he joined them.

"At least he's a gentleman." Shay seemed to be of two minds about Mr. Weatherbee's company.

"How would you know?"

"Daddy spank. He's ordered his drink, so there won't be any of this oh-let-me-pay-for-it business."

Mr. Weatherbee approached, closely followed by a waiter bearing, on a tray, a bottle of whiskey, a jigger, a tumbler, and a pitcher of water.

"A drink, did you say?" Emma murmured.

"Looks like he's moving in for the duration."

Shay stood up. Emma went through the introductions. Mr. Weatherbee accepted Shay's presence with Emma as perfectly natural. So natural, in fact, that Emma felt bound to explain. After all, she had picked up Mr.

Weatherbee, and she didn't want him to get the impression that such procedure was a habit with her.

She explained Shay's presence in Central City and added firmly that he was an old friend.

Mr. Weatherbee dismissed the coincidence calmly. "A lot of folks get up here sooner or later," he said.

"My boss," said Shay, "seemed to think that this festival, the cultural standard which it represents, and these relics of America's past traditions justified my expense account."

"And Mr. Weatherbee," said Emma, "is just the person for you. He knows all about this place, background and local color and all that sort of thing, and, besides"—she smiled sweetly—"I hear that he's one of the backers of the opera."

Mr. Weatherbee looked reproachfully at Emma and poured himself a drink. As Emma and Shay were already supplied, he raised his glass in salute before he emptied it.

"Thought you was a reporter," he said to Shay. "We have 'em up here. Had a columnist last year. The local color got him all excited. He got himself some forty-dollar boots and a gun, and damn me if he didn't shoot a lady's toe off. You carry a gun?"

"Why, no," said Shay, and then added, "Do you think I should?"

Mr. Weatherbee's blue eyes opened wide in amazement at the suggestion. "We're a peaceable community," he said. "The Historical ladies just want us to look like the boom days—not act like 'em." He sighed regretfully, Emma thought, and went on. "Accidents"—he seemed to stress the word—"will happen, but the Historical ladies don't like it."

"Mr. Faber carries a gun," Emma said suddenly. "He carries it so much it's worn a hole in his pocket."

Mr. Weatherbee looked pained. "Sol got the habit," he explained, "years ago. Times have changed. Even the opera has changed. Why, there ain't a woman in the company that'd cast a shadow you could hide in. Boy, it used to be that when you put an arm around an opera singer you knew you had something." He broke off with a cackle and winked at Shay.

"Sir," said Shay, "you present an aspect of opera that never occurred to me, the cultural side being now somewhat overstressed."

"I never could understand why," Emma put in, "miners and prospectors and suchlike went in for opera anyway. I should have thought they'd have preferred vaudeville or burlesque."

Shay deferred with his glass to Mr. Weatherbee as the existing authority, and Mr. Weatherbee cleared his throat.

"Well," he said, "when you've struck it rich you want the best that money can buy. That's opera singers, or a house like Bert Estis built—or both." He cackled with laughter again and poured himself another drink.

"It's an amazing house"—Emma spoke to Shay—"what I've seen of it. You'll have to take pictures of that. Did you"—she turned to Mr. Weatherbee—"know Mr. Danforth?"

Mr. Weatherbee looked at her with only a trace of what might have been suspicion clouding his eye. "Yes," he said, "you might say I knew him, but I knew his father-in-law better. Old Bert!" He chuckled. "I knew him when the only other friend he had in the world was a walleyed mule by the name of Evangeline. Damned intelligent critter. Followed Bert around like a dog. Bert felt mighty bad when she died. Yes sir."

"How'd she die?" asked Emma, ever curious.

"Well, sir," Mr. Weatherbee took up the narrative, "it was in Blackhawk early one spring. We get a lot of landslides when you begin to get hot days and frosty nights. Bert left Evangeline outside the Silver Dollar Saloon and Billiard Parlor; didn't hitch her or drop her reins—just told her to stay there. Bert was a great billiard player, and he was playing with the Duke and Harry Mott-Smith, and there were a lot of side bets, because the Duke was pretty good—"

"Just a minute," Shay interrupted him. "Would the Duke you speak of have been Edward the Seventh?"

"Edward the Seventh," said Mr. Weatherbee firmly, "was never in these parts. This was the Grand Duke Alexis. He'd been on a hunting trip. Got three bears but no sheep. Disappointed he was, too. But as I was saying, it was three cushion billiards, and Bert had already run ten, when there was a great roar outside and somebody come in yelling for them to run; half the mountain was coming down. Now that slide took away the bar and half the billiard room, but Bert stayed right there and run her up to fifteen without a break. Only nobody believed it because nobody had stayed to see, and he never could collect the bets. Bert was pretty disgusted and went out to see where everybody'd gone to, but there warn't nothing to see. The saloon was gone, like I told you, and the First National Bank, but, by cripes, there stood Evangeline, right where the saloon entrance had been.

" 'Come here, you fifty-per-cent female,' says Bert, but Evangeline never moved. She was stone dead. A boulder must have hit her or something, but she'd stayed right where Bert told her."

Mr. Weatherbee paused and looked at Shay.

"Very interesting," said Shay. "Did you ever hear about the pet rattlesnake that went around the backs of the chairs in the poker game and rattled behind the high hand?"

"Cripes," said Mr. Weatherbee, "that was my rattlesnake."

"And that," said Shay, "calls for a drink."

"You're welcome to some of mine," Mr. Weatherbee offered, "but I know you won't like it. A man's taste in liquor is his own business, but dollar whiskey's good enough for me."

"You better haul in your leg, Shay," Emma advised, "or the waiter'll trip over it."

Shay grinned. "The one that was pulled or my wooden one?"

"You haven't got a wooden one."

"That's what you think," Shay cut her off and turned to Mr. Weatherbee. "The little beetle here says you did a nice job on her this afternoon."

Mr. Weatherbee smiled the deprecating smile of a man faced with his own masterpiece. "That was easy; she was scared anyway. I suppose she told you"—blandness again overspread his face—"about the accident?"

Shay nodded casually.

"I've got it!" Emma leaned forward. "Mr. Weatherbee is just the person we want. To tell us about the time Sauer was on the stage, I mean. You see," she explained, "we've been pretending, Shay and I, that Horsack was really murdered, and we're trying to figure out who could have done it. Now if you—"

As she went on Shay watched Mr. Weatherbee's face, but its expression of polite interest did not change. Then he watched Emma, rather hopelessly, because in the years that he had known her he had never been able to separate, for certain, her real from her pretended ingenuousness. She had said that she might have been suspicious of the old man. Was she trying to catch him up on whether he had himself seen all the opera that afternoon or not? Was she just sociably including Mr. Weatherbee in their game? Or was she seriously hunting for scraps of information, as she had seen Hank do?

Shay decided that people's faces probably registered everything but what they really thought and that Emma ought to have better sense than to try to get anything out of an old hand like Mr. Weatherbee.

"At first," Emma was saying, "I thought you did it—on account of your granddaughter, you know—but Shay thinks Sauer did it because Horsack was a Czech national. Now if you can tell us all that went on during the opera that sort of lets you out, and it may show whether Sauer had the opportunity."

"Nope." Mr. Weatherbee was equally blunt. "It doesn't let me out because I've seen that show seven times, as I said, thanks to my granddaughter, and I can tell you, almost to the second, where everyone was, but not because I saw it yesterday."

"Well," Emma went on cheerfully, "that leaves you in, and maybe I can find someone in the audience who saw you get up and go out, but what about Sauer?"

"Sauer was in the chorus," said Mr. Weatherbee, "and the chorus was on the stage in the tavern scene while Horsack was off. Only yesterday"—Mr. Weatherbee leaned forward conspiratorially—"Sauer didn't come on . . . ."

"That's my baby," Shay chimed in.

"Alvarado," Mr. Weatherbee persisted, "was hunting for Sauer because Horsack wasn't there and was having a fit because he couldn't find either of them."

"One of us will have to go backstage," said Emma, carried away by faked enthusiasm, "and check up."

"Look"—this time Mr. Weatherbee's expression was disturbed—"this is a nice game and a lot of fun and all that, but if it won't hinder your investigation too much, I wish you would stay away from Alvarado. You've no idea," he said sadly, "how excitable that man is. We've still got a three-day run, and I don't want the company to blow up in my face."

"That's not fair." Emma almost pouted.

"Don't worry." Shay nodded wisely. "My job is to take pictures of that bunch. I'll be upstage, backstage, and everywhere."

Mr. Weatherbee spoke to Emma, and his voice was soft as silk. "If you have any influence with that young man, you advise him to lay off the company, because"—his expression grew dreamy and far away—"*my* favorite suspect is Miss Dolan, who was also off stage at the same time as Horsack."

"You know"—Shay was watching Emma with some difficulty because part of the time she seemed to have two heads, but his voice was clear— "there are times when I keep forgetting that we are discussing an accident."

There was a pause, during which Shay got Emma's heads into focus and noticed, with some apprehension, that her mouth wore a mutinous expression. Emma would do a lot for a friend, but there were points beyond which she could not be pushed, either by threat or cajolery. Mr. Weatherbee was undoubtedly used to having his own way, but he didn't know Emma, who was herself not without guile. Shay decided it might be interesting to see a conflict between Mr. Weatherbee, the immovable body, and Emma, who gave in the middle but who attacked from both ends. He only hoped the little blackhaired beetle, bless her, didn't get caught in the crossfire.

Emma leaned forward and tapped Mr. Weatherbee on the sleeve.

"There's something I think you ought to know. Paul Horsack was engaged in some sort of dangerous work, probably for his government. He told Mary Dolan that much and said so much about the risk and the danger that Mary wrote me because"—Emma drew a long breath and decided to leave Hank and her past association with crime out of the picture—"I'm her closest friend, and she needed someone to talk to. Now if the police are satisfied that Horsack's death was accidental, so am I. But it looks mighty funny that he should die just as I get here and find an opera company full of Germans and—and"—Emma remembered the dark woman with the mole just in time—"Italians. You may be willing"—the fire of patriotism positively poured from her nostrils—"to harbor a nest of spies and saboteurs, but I'm not, and I personally intend to do something about it."

Shay started to cheer, but Mr. Weatherbee cut him off.

"Just what," he asked mildly, "do you intend to do?"

Emma, whose plan of campaign was as yet highly nebulous, fell back on the tried and true. "Keep my ears open," she said with dignity, "and—"

"Preserve an open mind," Shay finished for her. "Waiter!"

"When I was in the Civil War"—the light of reminiscence gleamed in Mr. Weatherbee's eyes—"I met a lady spy. She rode into camp on a big black horse, and she wore a long green riding skirt."

A crowd of people, the forerunners of those who had been at the opera, came noisily into the bar, breaking Mr. Weatherbee's thread of thought.

"From what I hear," he said, "spying's changed some since my day. I'll make you a proposition. If you'll let me take care of the opera folks I'll give you a couple of things I found."

Emma looked skeptical.

"One of 'em"—Mr. Weatherbee toyed with his tumbler—"was on the floor, sort of under Horsack's body."

Emma's open mind snapped to attention.

"The other came out of a grate. A grate where somebody'd had a fire."

"A pig in the parlor," said Shay profoundly, "is worth two in a poke."

"It's a deal." Emma ignored him and spoke quickly; more people were coming in. In a few moments Mary would be there . . . . Emma would trade the opera for whatever Mary had been burning in the grate any day. She'd not bother Sauer if the old man wouldn't bother Mary. It occurred to Emma that if Horsack's death were accidental both of them were being a little silly and that Mr. Weatherbee's promise to leave Mary alone was a promise purely of inference. That seemed to be the trouble with so many of Mr. Weatherbee's propositions. You had to take them at their face value or leave them alone. Still, she hadn't gone wrong yet. Emma held out her hand.

Mr. Weatherbee hiccuped and rose from his chair as though he had forgotten the matter they had been discussing. Then he paused, fished in the pocket of his coat, and emptied his closed fist into Emma's palm.

"Excuse me," he said, "for a few moments."

"Daddy, look." Shay craned his neck to scrutinize the two objects, though they were hardly that. One was a fragment of brown crayon, the waxy kind used by children in coloring; the other was a scrap of coarse paper, its edges burned but bearing certain marks. Shay peered close, and Emma pushed his head out of the way to examine the scrap herself. She thought she could make out a hat, a brown hat with a Tyrolean brush at the back. A hat like the one on the floor of the entry. Emma picked up the crayon and made a mark on the paper. The mark left by the brown crayon seemed to be the same color as that of the hat.

Well? Agatha Estis made childlike drawings—Emma explained about Aggie to Shay—and might lose a bit of crayon anywhere in her own house, but why should Mary be burning one of her pictures? The two scraps added up to Agatha Estis, but the sum didn't mean anything in connection with Mary. Or did it?

"Of course," said Shay, "we haven't looked at them under a microscope, but it strikes me that again our little girl has been had."

Emma, who hadn't mentioned the fire in the grate to Shay because she hadn't actually seen Mary making it, felt obliged to agree with him.

"He's such an old liar," she said, "that you can't possibly believe him. He couldn't have been in the Civil War."

"The heroic drummer boy—or maybe it was his mother was a camp follower. What was he muttering about the fire this had been burned in?"

Emma drew a long breath and told him, because of course she wasn't sure that Mary had burned it, but she wasn't going to compromise herself by withholding a trifling detail once it was asked for. To her surprise Shay burst out laughing.

"That blows it. I fell for the spy stuff and the eccentric old gent protecting the beautiful granddaughter, but the opera singer burning the papers lays it on too thick. I move we bring in a verdict of accidental death and dismiss the jury."

"Truth," said Emma stubbornly, "has been sounding strangely like E. Phillips Oppenheim of late. I wonder."

She wondered why Mr. Weatherbee had given her the scrap of paper and crayon. Was he turning over to her something that he couldn't or wouldn't investigate himself, or was he again guying her, playing up to the game she and Shay had been playing, just as he had tricked her in the afternoon? She wished mightily that there was some way she could get even with Mr. Weatherbee, but her head was buzzing with the turn and turnabout of events, and her weariness had returned. She wished Mary would come.

And then she saw Mary, whose progress through the crowd had been hidden because she was small. Mary was bowing and smiling to people and looked radiantly happy.

"Hello, darlings," she said when she got close. "You missed it. We were marvelous. I'm so glad for Rho. He doesn't belong in the chorus, and now they'll have to give him better parts. He's talking to Mr. Weatherbee and Alvarado now—about a raise, I suppose. How have you been getting along, you two? Did you miss me? I want something to drink. We had a marvelous house. Somebody said the Governor was here again. I met him the opening night. There are lots of people here I know from Denver. We ought to have fun."

Mary was her old self, Emma thought, happy and regretful at the same time, because Mary didn't act at all as though she wanted to go to bed. Emma did. And the evening began to take on a nightmare quality, unmitigated by sleep.

Mary drank. Mary ate. And Mary talked. Shay drank, and Shay talked. People came to their table and talked and went away and more people came. In the patio someone played the piano and sang topical songs. Feeling like a heel for not enjoying what was obviously a pleasant evening, Emma pinned a smile on her face and clenched her jaws to keep from yawning. Fortunately Shay and Mary were so busy talking, finding out about each other, that Emma did not have to join much in the conversation. She leaned her cheek on her hand and kept her eyes open by a determined effort.

Something sudden, a burst of noise, jerked her upright.

"How do you do?" she said, blinking.

Shay and Mary laughed again.

"You poor little thing," said Mary. "You were sound asleep, and your head went over—plop! I'm a dog to keep you up, and I'm going to take you home right now."

Some more people came up, and in the end it was Shay who took Emma home. He would return for Mary, who would come right away, she promised. Emma stumbled up the street, not caring, not noticing. She had not noticed that the other members of the company had not been among those who came to their table; she had not noticed that Mr. Weatherbee had not come back to them but to a corner table where he sat with the tenor, Sauer.

Only when Shay had unlocked Mrs. Danforth's front door and stood stock-still and silent did she notice again the hall's bristling array of heads and gleaming eyes.

"Well," said Shay finally, "thank God they're not pink." He raised and aimed an imaginary gun. "Beat it," he said. "Daddy'll shoot if they start coming down off the wall after you."

Emma fled silently down the rubber matting. Dimly, from the stairs, she heard the front door close; faintly, from a night light, she saw the row of doors, first Mary's and then hers. She groped for a light inside her room and, failing to find it, undressed quickly and crawled in below the cooing doves of her high black walnut bed without even thinking of them. That way, of course, she failed to notice the picture carefully placed on her bureau.

CHAPTER FIVE

WHEN Emma awoke the next morning the sun was pouring through the lace curtains at the windows, adding a confusion of pattern to the already overworked carpet. Through the window Emma could see a blue sky that outblued, she thought, the sky of the Southwest, certainly that of California. She stretched, decided that she felt very, very good, and wondered what time it was. She had been tired last night and for good reason. Yesterday had been, to underrate it, fatiguing, but today would be a different sort of day. She felt like doing a lot of things. First she would have breakfast; then she would get a guidebook and see all the things that one was supposed to see. She bet Mary hadn't seen anything. Mary had been raised in Cambridge and had never set eyes on the glass flowers until Emma had shown them to her. Mary's world was bounded on one side by her emotions and on the other side by her career. Emma wondered what time Mary had come in.

She got out of bed and, opening the double doors, found Mary's bed smooth and her room in order.

In the old days Mary would have no more straightened a room than she would have failed to do her morning trills.

Emma closed the doors, pondering on the ways of a just Providence that provided people to pick up after people like Mary. She had done it herself for four protesting years and had suffered serious misgivings about what would happen then. Well, it seemed that there was no problem. There was someone to pick up in Central City, and there had probably been someone to do it in South America.

Emma poured water into the Dresden washbowl, just so that she could say she had washed in one, and was surprised to find the water warm. That meant that Aggie-Agatha had tiptoed in while she slept, or Mrs. Danforth. Well, so what? She had enjoyed a good sleep, and the water was warm. Emma refused to consider the possibility that they could have murdered her in her bed. This was no morning for murder.

When she went to the bureau to brush her hair she saw the picture. Drawn on rough yellow paper, it presented three people eating at a table. Its color was vivid; the outlines were bold, but, like a child's picture, it had no depth or perspective. Two of the people were women, easily recognizable as Mrs. Danforth and Aggie. The third was a man, a rather plump man with glasses. That was all there was to it, except that jagged bolts of lightning were playing about the man's head.

Poor Aggie!

Emma found a skirt and a blouse not too wrinkled for wear and went back to the mirror to put on lipstick. She picked up a package of cigarettes to put in her bag and put in the picture too. It would amuse Shay or Mary when she saw them.

When she reached the foot of the stairs she saw Aggie arranging flowers on the broad dark dining-room table. Cornflowers and gaillardias; they were pretty, and Aggie was absorbed in them.

"Good morning." Emma spoke softly, gaily, but even so Agatha Estis turned with a start that knocked over the vase and sent a stream of water across the table.

At that moment Mrs. Danforth came in through the swinging door from the kitchen. She did not see Emma in the hall, but she saw the spilled water.

"You clumsy fool!"

Emma retreated two steps up the stairs and came down again, stamping to make herself heard on the rubber tread.

"Good morning," she said again, loudly. "Isn't this a perfectly marvelous morning?"

Mrs. Danforth came forward smoothly, and Aggie fled to the kitchen, but just before she reached the door she turned and asked plaintively, "Has anyone seen my brown crayon?"

Emma had half a notion to produce the scraps in her bag but thought better of it.

"What pretty flowers," she said.

Mrs. Danforth picked up a fallen stalk from the floor and smoothed a rumpled petal. "These are wild gaillardias," she said. "Aggie likes to pick them, and she arranges them well, but sometimes she is clumsy."

"Your house," said Emma, "is neat as a pin." The words popped into her mind because she knew from her experience with Mary what it was like, if you were an orderly person, to live with a careless one. The Danforth house was scrupulously clean; every hair, metaphorically, was in place, and Emma was willing to bet that it wasn't Aggie who kept it so. It wouldn't be any joke to live for goodness knew how many years with a person who was undoubtedly clumsy and who was pretty obviously foolish.

"Thank you." Mrs. Danforth smiled. "You haven't seen all of it yet. Would you care to?" Then because she realized that Emma had had no breakfast she added, "Later, of course."

Emma agreed that she would love to, later. Mrs. Danforth followed her down the hall and at the front door spoke softly. "If Aggie gives you any of her pictures will you burn them, or put them in a pile and I will? Don't, please, throw them in the wastebasket. It makes her unhappy."

Emma nodded and said, "Of course," as though such procedure were routine and idiot aunts were a matter of everyday occurrence to her, but she went down the steps filled with admiration for Mrs. Danforth. The old gal had lost her money; very well, she took roomers. She had a burden in the shape of Aggie, and she took care of her and protected her from possible slurs and taunts. There were pretty nice people in the world, Emma decided, and it was a day for nice people. White houses sparkled above her, clinging to the slopes, their yards gay and gaudy with flowers. The opera house, the street, even the dilapidated buildings, seemed freshly washed, as indeed they were, by a rain that had fallen in the night. Two small boys in jeans rushed past Emma, guiding a clanging iron wheel rim with sticks. A sedate woman puffed slowly up the hill with a bag of groceries. Emma drew deep breaths and hurried toward breakfast.

The patio of the hotel was bright with whitewashed walls and window boxes of geraniums; the surly waitress of the night before had been replaced by a younger smiling one, and in the midst of this brightness sat Shay.

Emma called, "Good morning," and went toward him.

Shay looked up with an effort, shielding his eyes with a hand. Shay did not look at all well, and when he spoke his voice was filled with gloom. "Must you," he asked, "be so noisy?"

Emma took in the glass of tomato juice, the cup of coffee, and the box of aspirin that seemed to comprise Shay's breakfast and smiled the smug smile of the virtuous. "Poor Daddy. Has he got a headache?"

Her chair scraped on the flagstone floor as she pulled it out, and Shay winced. "Daddy'll kick you right in the teeth if you don't keep quiet."

"And such a beautiful morning," Emma went on imperturbably. "I thought we'd take a nice long walk and see the sights, and you could get some pictures."

Shay looked at her as though her health and vigor were the crowning insult. "You'd make me sick," he said, "if it were possible to be any sicker. You look as though you'd even had some sleep."

"Whereas you"—Emma picked herself a hearty breakfast—"tossed and turned?"

"That old man"—Shay's voice was bitter—"is an insult to humanity. I resent being drunk under the table by an octo—nono—by an old man."

"Mr. Weatherbee, I take it, returned. Probably he was watering his drinks."

Shay snorted. "That water pitcher was just a buildup. He never touched it."

Emma knew that Shay was a quick drunk and a willing one, and at the rate he had been going when she left, Mr. Weatherbee's performance need not have been particularly spectacular. And with what she knew of Mr. Weatherbee, she wouldn't have put it past him to have had tea in his whiskey bottle, but she didn't say so. Instead she said, "How did Mary get along?"

Shay looked an impossible two degrees sourer. "Just the way I imagine she always does. Fine. Just dandy. She sat there and laughed at the old fool's stories just as though she believed them. She had no time for guys like I."

Emma suppressed her amusement. Most women lapped up Shay's exaggerated compliments, and if Mary were giving him the brush-off it might interest him even more.

"What," she inquired sweetly, "did Mr. W. add to the local legends?"

"I didn't listen to him. Just a lot of babble about the time the streets were paved with gold for General Washington. He's back in the Revolution now. Said he helped to do it."

"It was Grant," said Emma, "and silver."

"Gold. I heard that much."

"Silver. He told me about it yesterday."

"By tomorrow it'll be platinum, studded with diamonds. Anyhow, he's a pathological liar."

"They're aluminum now, if there's any aluminum in aluminum paint." Emma meant the bricks in front of the hotel, but she had to explain to Shay.

"Phony. Just like that face on the barroom floor."

"They have taken all the events that occurred around here and grafted them onto this hotel."

"Not a bad idea. Saves wear and tear on the tourists' shoes and increases the bar receipts."

"That reminds me." Emma got up and went into the lobby and returned presently with several pamphlets. "Now," she said, "we'll get it right out of the horse's mouth."

She opened a green folder; idly Shay took a blue one. " 'The Golden Kingdom,' " he read, " 'a record chiefly of Central City in the early days: Now what, pray tell, is a 'chiefly record'? A record can be good or inaccurate, but it can't be chiefly."

"What?" asked Emma looking up. "Oh, that. It's an adverb, silly; it modifies Central City."

"Silly yourself. An adverb can't modify a noun."

"All right, it modifies of or something. Don't bother me; it says here they've got graveyards."

"Boot Hill, probably, moved bodily from Dodge City. Say, that's pretty good for the state I'm in."

"What?" Emma asked again.

"Skip it. It exhausted me just to say it. But that's the way to use an adverb."

Emma paid no attention. "Listen to this: `Buried here are part of a troupe of opera singers brought directly from Germany, who died of scarlet fever during an epidemic. Headstones were raised by popular contribution.' "

"The poor devils."

Emma nodded. "But you'll have to get a picture of these headstones. Let's go now. I simply love graveyards."

"You would, you ghoul, but Daddy's legs are all bushed, and I've got to get another room. One of the bellboys is nuts on photography, and he won't let my cameras alone. He's probably up there now, breathing on lenses. Would that landlady of yours take me in?"

"Quick as a wink, if she's got room," said Emma, hoping that Aggie's art interest didn't extend to photography and that Shay wouldn't ask for a room next to Mary. "Come on"—she stood up—"and bring a camera. I've promised to look at the house, and if you say you want some pictures that'll get you in good. And that piece of crayon is Aggie's. She was asking for it this morning."

Shay got up wearily. "I bet Jeff is having a wonderful time," he said. "Why?"

"Because you aren't there cracking the whip. I bet old Hank is even enjoying the Navy. But what gets me is why, out of all the improbable places in the world, you had to show up here."

"I'm not," said Emma, nettled, "a slave driver. You came up here to take pictures, didn't you? It's your business, isn't it? You want to know about interesting places, don't you? Of course if you don't—"

"Maybe not now," said Shay. "Maybe I'm tired; maybe I need a nap, or—" His eyes roved in the direction of the bar and came back to Emma's stony gaze. "Oh, all right."

He went upstairs for his camera, and Emma went out into the sunshine to learn more historic lore to tell Shay.

"The Teller House, completed in 1872 . . . an inaugural ball and a series of parlor entertainments . . . elaborately furnished with the latest approved styles in walnut and damask and carpets of the finest Brussels. Adjustable windows . . . the register included the names of Chevalier Ernst de Hesse Worteg and Count Adam von Steinbeck of Prussia."

There was no mention of Mr. Weatherbee's friend, the Grand Duke, but perhaps he was earlier or, perhaps, as Shay had suggested, the old man had made him up.

". . . entertainments and dances by the Turnverein and the Fenian Brotherhood, less exclusive than the assemblies at the Teller House. . ." Emma would bet a nickel on that, but, all in all, she was rather disappointed in Central City's early history. There was mention of churches and evangelists and schools and the introduction of astrological instruments and the building of railroads, but there was no mention of the gaudier incidents at which Mr. Weatherbee hinted. Either the local historians were in a conspiracy to tone down the news, or Mr. Weatherbee's footnotes were decidedly extemporaneous. Emma knew what she thought and regretted it. As they walked up the street she discussed the matter with Shay, who about-faced and defended Mr. Weatherbee. There were many things, he said, that the long view of history omitted; it was conceivable that a history of the present war might be written without any mention of Bataan.

Emma asked if there was any news on the radio.

There wasn't, and the papers wouldn't be up till afternoon.

"It's funny how you go in cycles, isn't it?"

Shay waited for her to go on.

"When war was first declared I wanted to rush right out, and I read papers and was the best drugstore general you ever saw do something; then I sort of settled down to doing my job. Now that Hank's gone I'm all fidgety again."

"Yes," said Shay.

"Only I wasn't this morning. I was fine until you mentioned the news."

"I didn't. You did." Shay climbed upon the stone wall in front of the house and unlimbered his apparatus for a shot.

"You said something about Bataan. It seems incredible, doesn't it"— Emma looked up at the bright empty sky—"to think of war up here? You almost forget, the way I did this morning, and then that makes you afraid, because it's bad to forget."

Shay's hands were trembling as he put the cover back on his lens. "Will you shut up?" he said. "Do you think I like to be up here taking pictures?"

"Why, Shay," said Emma, "I hadn't thought—" They walked in silence to the house.

Mrs. Danforth emerged from the rear of the hall as they entered. Emma

made the introductions and explained why Shay wanted pictures and that
he might like a room.

Mrs. Danforth nodded cordially. "There have been many pictures taken
of the house," she said, "but none of them have ever been quite satisfac-
tory, to me at least."

Emma said that Shay's would be.

"Then we might as well begin with the gold room." Mrs. Danforth
bustled forward. "It will be easier for me if I follow the regular routine,
the one I give the tourists," she explained. "If I change the order I get
mixed up and find myself describing the wrong room."

As she spoke she threw open a pair of heavy dark doors carved with
swags of fruit and stepped inside, following another strip of rubber matting. "As I said," she began, "this is the gold room. . . ."

In the bright morning sun the effect was dazzling, and Emma, over-
whelmed in the doorway, was forced to admit that it was beautiful. If, of
course, you cared for the ornate. The walls were covered with yellow
brocade; from gilded cornices amber curtains flecked with threads of gold
cascaded over fine lace curtains to the tawny carpet, whose pattern of
brown and olive roses was dark enough to set off the gilded furniture. The
fireplace was faced with yellow marble; the great mirror over it was scrolled
in gold. Two enormous vases that Emma guessed to be Sèvres—she was
never sure about china—stood on the hearth.

"It pleased my father," Mrs. Danforth was saying, "because of his
mining connections. The curtains came from Lyons, France, and the carpet from Belgium."

"And the rocks," said Shay, "from Colorado?" He was looking at a
glass-doored cabinet, and Mrs. Danforth smiled.

"It may seem inappropriate, but it pleased my father. A collection of
ores from the mines in which he was interested."

It looked like a collection of rocks to Emma, but each specimen was
carefully labeled, some prosaically with numbers, and some with names.
There was the Nelly Bly, the Big Nugget, the Wilson, Spads Crossing,
and, on a bottom shelf, the Thunderbolt. That was the mine Mr. Weatherbee
had talked to Faber about, the one in which he and Mr. Estis had had a
stake. Emma was going to ask about it, but Shay was rearranging the
furniture, grouping the gilt chairs around a marble-topped console
with small regard for the chairs and no regard at all for Mrs. Danforth's
protestations.

Shay moved clumsily, but he seemed to know exactly the effect he
wanted and how to achieve it. It was all a mystery to Emma, whose pho-
tographic efforts had been made long ago with a Brownie Number 2.

When Shay had finished Mrs. Danforth replaced her chairs tenderly and gave a quick look around the room before she closed the door.

"One has to be so careful with the tourists," she said. "Once someone unscrewed a doorknob, and only yesterday I found a mustache on the bust of Apollo."

Emma smiled quietly to herself, remembering the man in the plaid coat, and stepped over Shay, who was on his back taking an angle shot of the head of a bighorn sheep.

"My father's trophies," Mrs. Danforth explained.

Shay took a flash of the stairway and a close-up of the illuminated bouquet on the newel post. Then he said, "Hello, what's this?"

He was in the corridor that led to the side entry, and Emma hesitated to follow him.

"A mummy and featherwork. Say! Is this stuff from Mesa Verde?"

"My late husband collected Indian relics." Mrs. Danforth spoke dryly, almost apologetically, and there was none of the enthusiasm that had been in her voice when she spoke of her father.

"These aren't just ordinary Indian relics." Shay went on babbling of knives and ceremonials and bridal chambers, glowering at the cases. "You can't photograph things in a case. I don't know that you could make anything out of this stuff away from its setting, aside from catalog illustrations, but I'd like to try—close-up of basketwork and that sort of thing— if you have a place where I could spread it out."

Mrs. Danforth turned to Emma, as though for help, and Emma understood what Shay's disruption would mean. "You can't do that here," she said. "This house has to be kept in order; it's on display, like a museum, and Mrs. Danforth doesn't want a mummy spread out on her dining-room table."

"Well, if I had a room here—"

Mrs. Danforth seemed relieved. "Perhaps," she said, "it could be arranged. Now would you like to see the meat hooks?"

Emma agreed hastily, not quite sure what was meant, and Shay got stiffly and reluctantly off his knees.

"Golly," he said, stopping again, "a ghost shirt. Sioux or Cheyenne?"

Mrs. Danforth didn't know.

"The origin"—Shay explained ghost shirts to Emma—"of the Superman legend."

He touched the leather gently. It was soft and supple in his fingers "I'll say this much," he concluded, "you keep things in good condition."

Emma and Mrs. Danforth exchanged the knowing glances of good housekeepers, and Emma said firmly, "Come on."

Down a corridor, to the left of the stairwell, they passed Mrs. Danforth's sitting room, rather more bright and ordinary than the rest of the house, and passed through the kitchen with its tremendous coal range, through another entry, and out into a brick-paved yard bounded by a wall, sheds, and coalbins. In the wall were embedded a row of huge iron hooks, high up, well out of reach.

"Lacking refrigeration," Mrs. Danforth explained, "meat was hung here in the open air. In my father's day there was plenty of bear and venison."

Without much enthusiasm Shay leaned two planks against the wall to make a shadow and took a picture.

Going back through the kitchen, Emma saw a table covered with a deep white cloth. It bore salt and pepper and a vinegar jug, and three chairs were arranged around it. Aggie's picture came back to Emma's mind, and she remembered the professor, who, it seemed, was privileged to eat here. Much handier, Emma thought, than having to trot over to the hotel, but not all boarders would care to eat in the kitchen; she didn't know that she would herself, with Aggie.

They went up the back stairs, and Shay took pictures of the doves on Emma's bed and of another bed, broad and long, with four posts as big as tree trunks.

"My father's bed . . . ."

Shay tripped over a rug and set a small table to rocking violently.

Emma wanted to show Shay the bathroom, a fantastic affair with an enormous tin-lined tub on a raised and carpeted dais, but she was pretty sure Mrs. Danforth would think it indelicate. If Shay were going to room there he'd find it for himself.

The end of the tour took them back to the dining room, dark with pictures of fruit and birds and bleeding rabbits that were repeated in the carving of a heavily laden sideboard. Emma's quick eyes appraised the silver as being mostly plate and badly Victorian, but she had to admit that the chandeliers, not one but two, that hung over the length of the table were superb. They were glitteringly clean, and Emma, who had cleaned many a chandelier for Jeff, knew what that meant.

Shoes removed, Shay lay on his back on the table for an upward shot, making Mrs. Danforth's recital of the list of notables who had dined in the leather-covered chairs rather breathless.

"P.T. Barnum, General and Mrs. Grant, Artemus Ward, Silver Dollar Tabor— Oh, do be careful," as Shay rolled over and the buttons of his coat came in contact with the polished finish. With a sigh of relief she steered him toward the register.

"If you don't mind . . ."

Shay picked up the pen and signed his name with a flourish.

"I didn't know you were left-handed," Emma remarked.

Shay grinned. "You should know me better. I brush my teeth left-handed too. Now"—he turned to Mrs. Danforth—"what about a room?"

"Oh, did you really want a room?" Mrs. Danforth fell back with a little sigh and surveyed Shay's aimless, clumsy bulk.

Emma could imagine her reviewing Shay's stumbling progress through the house, his open disregard for anything that did not have an unusual shape or cast a shadow, and was not at all surprised to hear her say, "I'm afraid I didn't understand. I don't have a room available. No, it would be impossible."

"Okay." Shay shouldered his camera and started out. "I'll give you some pictures." He went down the corridor without further argument, and Emma, following him, saw Aggie wandering in the hall, head down, as though hunting for something.

Outside the door Shay turned to Emma. "What did I do to get her back up?"

"Nothing." Emma didn't think she could explain about Mrs. Danforth's tidiness.

"You told her I wanted a room when we went in."

"Well, I guess she just didn't want you messing around with the Indian things."

"The hell with it. I won't use the pictures of her old house."

"Then let's go to the cemetery. There's one farther on up the hill, and you can crawl around on the graves with nobody to stop you. Come on."

With a lurch Shay sat down on the wall by the steps. His face was white, and he held the knee of his right leg in his hands.

"I can't go to any damn cemetery," he said. "Because why? Because I haven't got any goddamned leg. The rest of it's in China, and that's why I'm here. Now will you quit asking me to go places and climb mountains!"

"Shay"—Emma's sympathy was quick—"I'm sorry; you know I didn't know."

"For God's sake," Shay flared out, "don't be sorry for me."

Emma sat down beside him. "All right," she said. "All right. Show me how to work a camera, and I'll take some pictures for you. They might not be any good, but I might get a fresh angle." She hoped Shay would laugh at that, and he did.

"That's good," he said. "I'm supposed to be taking care of you, but I might have known it would end up with you taking care of me."

"You're supposed to be what?"

"Oops, sorry I mentioned it, but I happened to run into your chum Fairbanks in the Denver station, and he suggested that as long as I was there, Denver was a good place to light."

"So." Emma wasn't sure whether she was pleased or mad. "I'm not safe on my own."

"Well, the first thing you walk into is a murder."

"An accident."

"You tried to make a murder out of it."

"I'm still not absolutely sure . . . ."

"Forget it. Go take your walk. Daddy's going down to the hotel for some painkiller."

"But the pictures?"

"Mere crocheting. To make me look natural. But somebody'll buy them."

Shay went off down the street, trying not to limp. Emma remained seated on the curbing, feeling warm and cozy inside. Of course she was really annoyed, she thought, at Hank's lack of confidence in her, but it was nice to know that he hadn't forgotten her, that he had sent Shay to cheer her up. Or maybe Shay was the one that needed cheering. It wasn't exactly joyful to lose a leg. How? Emma's curiosity itched for details, but she suspected that they wouldn't come from Shay. Mary was exactly what Shay needed. Where was Mary? She might almost be said to be neglecting her guest.

Emma stood up. It was nearing twelve, but she would take her walk anyhow. She turned away from the opera house and continued on up the hill, past the ruins of the oldest machine shop in the Rocky Mountains, so the sign said. She pondered on the kind of people who had transported, with equal care, machines and Dresden china in the days when only mule or man could pick his way up the steep-walled canyon.

A man passed Emma, saying, "Howdy." Friendly people.

The world was bulging with nice people; Hank who would send Shay, Shay who would come, Mrs. Danforth who took care of Aggie. It was also the brightest, bluest day Emma had ever seen, just the day for visiting graveyards.

She halted and consulted the guidebook, which mentioned two "beyond the town, of interest to antiquarians."

At St. Paul's Episcopal Church, consecrated in 1876, the paving ended, and the board sidewalk became a path beside the road. Then the road branched, and Emma took the right-hand turn, pausing to admire before a small Victorian cottage, pink with chocolate trim.

A pleasant-faced woman weeding in the yard looked up and answered Emma's inquiry with minute and careful direction, though she admitted herself that she had never seen the graveyards. She also wanted to know Emma's name, where she came from, and where she was staying.

Because it was a nice day and she was momentarily at peace with the world, Emma did not feel her customary New England resentment against personal questions.

When Emma said, "The Estis Mansion," the woman came over and leaned on the fence.

"Didn't I hear something about that tenor Horsack's dying in Lizzie Danforth's side hall?"

"Entry," said Emma.

"What was he doing there?"

"Telephoning." It occurred to Emma to wonder to whom Horsack had been telephoning.

The woman sniffed as though that was a likely story.

"How much rent is Lizzie Danforth charging you?" she demanded.

Emma told her.

"Ten dollars a week!" the woman exclaimed. "She knows she ain't supposed to charge but a dollar a day during the season; the Chamber of Commerce sets the price, but that's just like Lizzie Danforth, thinking what she's got's better'n anybody else."

Emma, wondering what the Central City Chamber of Commerce did the other eleven months of the year, said that her room was exceptionally large and that she really must be going.

The first graveyard was comparatively modern; Emma prowled around among the monuments, noting the Mason jars of fresh flowers placed against their bases, and read the names. Many were of Germanic origin: Stass, Strauss, Beisendorfer. Some were English, but more were Irish; a few were Spanish or Mexican, and still fewer were French. The Irish were understandable; gangs of them had built the railroads through Kansas and Nebraska and had been on hand for the news of the gold strike, but why the preponderance of Germans? Emma decided that they had been the mechanics, machinists, and storekeepers. The Mexicans had oozed up from the south, but there was just no excuse for finding Frenchmen so far from home.

Emma found two monuments with faded photographs in glass-covered recesses, but otherwise nothing spectacular. No opera singers, no pet dogs. She climbed again, slowly, because she puffed in the thin air and because she stopped frequently to look at the mountains spreading out around her in darkening bands of green to other distant, barren peaks. She wondered if the men who had come there to grub in the ground for gold had ever looked at the hills? Some of them, surely. Perhaps those were the ones who had stayed on when the mines ran out. People like Mrs. Danforth, not like Mr. Weatherbee. He had gone away, but he was back, Emma was forced to admit, very much so. But only because of the opera.

Across a dry ravine Emma could see another graveyard with smaller, pseudo-Gothic headstones and sagging iron fences around the plots. That looked more like it. Emma puffed up the climb and sank on a fallen stone to get her breath. The view was different from here; through a gap in a nearby range she could see a distant snow-capped peak; two tiny puffs of cloud were white above it. Emma looked and looked again. The two clouds were joined by a feather of white that floated below them. The colors were ever shifting, ever changing.

Emma pulled her eyes back and found the grass at her feet thick with wild gaillardia. She got up and walked about, her steps making long furrows in the thick grass. Some of the stones were small and crudely chiseled; some were large and elaborate. Had there been a local stonecutter, or had the larger monuments, like the Dresden china, been brought laboriously up in pack trains?

Here was "Saml. Butler, gent., of County Tyrone, Ireland. Shot April 1, died April 10 1869. A mighty hunter."

Poor Sam, Emma thought, he must have taken an April fool seriously.

Here was a whole family—father, mother, and three children—who had died within a few days of each other in some epidemic.

That reminded Emma of the singers, and she found them: five headstones all in a row—Ettl Klotz of Baden, Herman Froemel of Neustadt, Gretel Geist of Mannheim. That was in Baden too, Emma thought; were they all from there? No, there was Marie Hynek from Posen. She was a Pole, or was she? Emma's history couldn't decide where Poland had been at that time, and she went on to Anna Eulalie, whose surname and origin were unrecorded. Five deaths might well have wiped out an opera troupe in those days, or nearly so, and the rest had fled, leaving no one who knew all the names. "Poor devils," Shay had said.

The sun was hot overhead, and Emma stretched out in the grass, leaning against the mound that had once been Anna Eulalie's feet, and meditated drowsily and not too unhappily on life and death. Death, in anticipation not too pleasant, once accomplished, was a fact that no longer concerned the anticipator. It made no difference to Ettl and Herman and Gretel where they were buried, but Shay was sentimental about it. That was odd for the tough guy, Shay. Or was it? Being Irish, he was probably sentimental about all his emotions; it was sentiment, not love, that made him pretend to be in love with every girl he met. She was the only one Shay wasn't in love with, but that was because he liked her. And liking wasn't love. But there was no love without liking. But Mary had said there was; Mary had been in love with Horsack, poor devil. Now she was being sentimental about him, and she was the only one, as far as Emma could tell, unless the Committee of Eleven or B4 or the FBI would miss him.

An exploring ant roused Emma; she sat up and looked at her view. It had changed again; the tiny clouds had swelled to big puffy ones that cast dark shadows on the mountains. It was an elegant view, Emma thought; she could stay there all day watching it. She got up and continued her ambling prowl.

She found Bingo, "a faithful friend," and Dash, and wished she really had taken Shay's camera. Coming upon a faint path, she followed it to a plot that was large and showed some evidence of care. The grass had been trimmed unevenly, as though with scissors or scythe, and there were flowers planted on the graves. Stone steps led up to a gate in the iron fence that surrounded the lot, and on the steps was cut the name "Estis." Emma unlooped an iron chain and went inside. Here, then, someday Mrs. Danforth and Agatha Estis would lie. The thought gave her a queer feeling, like the goose-walking-on-her-grave shiver.

Bertram Estis, born Dover, N.H., 1853; died Central City, 1909
Pioneer, citizen, father. "What hath God wrought?"

Emma didn't know and turned to the smaller, older headstone beside Bertram's.

Otille, dearly beloved of Bertram Estis
Born Frieburg, i.b., 18—; died Central City, 1897.

Emma blinked and read the inscription again. "Why, Bert Estis, you old son of a gun," she apostrophized in the manner of Mr. Weatherbee. "You married one of the opera singers."

Well, well, you never knew about the first families, did you? At least all of the troupe hadn't died. Here was a happy ending that she would have to tell Shay about. And Otille was Mrs. Danforth's mother; maybe she got her looks from her. Otille had probably been a lovely creature . . . .

Emma went off into a fantasy in which the beautiful Otille, the flower of the mining camp, had been nursed back to health by a devoted Bertram, who had then married her, or maybe he should have married her first— anyhow, ensconced in the Estis Mansion, she had queened it over Central City society, idolized by her husband and all who knew her.

Entranced by this charming picture, Emma paid scant heed to the marker on the grave of Alfred Danforth and no heed at all to the fact that the clouds of the northwest, over the mountains, were becoming tinged with black. She wandered on out of the graveyard and up the hill behind it, where a new view and more mountains opened out to the south. She kept on climbing because ridges interlaced and joined each other, and there was always a higher one that promised a better view. The sun was on her, in front of her, and not until she reached the big ravine did she look back and see that dark clouds now obliterated her snow-capped peak. The clouds whirled and tossed, settling lower and lower, blackening the valleys and diluting the sunlight to a greenish hue. It was fantastic and beautiful to watch, and Emma had no idea of the speed with which a storm could rise in the mountains. Suddenly the green light was all about her; she looked at the ravine just as the sun faded from it, the watery light making more vivid the orange and yellow tailings from pits and diggings, of which the ravine seemed to be full.

Emma looked back just as the wind struck, twisting, pushing her toward the ravine. Then the rain hit, icy-cold and driving fast. Emma fled before it, hoping, feeling, searching for some shelter. Most of the pits were just that, shallow excavations that went straight down and offered no protection; a few were larger and had their openings shored up with timbers, and for one of these Emma dashed, hoping that Mr. Weatherbee had exaggerated the danger of landslides.

A derrick of some sort rose over the opening that Emma picked, and the space below the flooring on which it rested was suddenly dry and comfortable. Emma drew breath, pushed the hair and water from her eyes, and saw a radio set.

It was a radio set to Emma, although its innards were not covered with a shiny wood case and the dials were multitudinous and complicated. There was a headset beside it on the seat of a dilapidated but well-padded chair.

Emma saw, but before she had time to think she thought she heard a thud, a thud of running feet; then there was a slithering thud, as though someone had fallen on shale or gravel, and a sharp exclamation.

It was the exclamation rather than the radio that sent Emma diving forward into a black opening. A lot of people she knew had radios, but none of her acquaintances were in the habit of saying "Zut!" She found herself in pitch-blackness, on rough dry rock, and huddled there, sure that her wet tracks would give her away and that in a moment she would be discovered by—

It was black in Emma's drift, but it was black outside, too, and whatever tracks Emma might have made on the dry dirt floor were obliterated by the feet of the man who came in.

Emma was sure it was a man. He moved heavily, like a man, and he smelled like one, sort of pipy. That was encouraging, in a way; if a bear or a rattlesnake came out of the darkness behind her she would take a chance on a man who smoked a pipe, even though he said "Zut." But it was so dark that she couldn't see the bear or the rattlesnake or the man, either, and she wasn't going to risk moving.

The man moved about; then a soft hum began, like the hum of a motor, and a dim light outlined the opening through which Emma had dived and shone above what Emma's exploring fingers discovered was a heavy plank partition. A very heavy partition. Stretching her neck as far as it would reach, Emma's eyes could not find a chink or a crack.

The chair creaked.

Aha, Mr. Heavy, Emma thought.

A match scratched and flared, and Emma nodded, as though the whiff of pipe smoke that came to her confirmed both her suspicions. All she had to do was to find a man who smoked a pipe, said "Zut," and was heavy, and she would know who had an outlaw radio station; she would be the one to track down the means by which ships were sunk and trains were wrecked and other aid and comfort given to the enemy. Emma was excited, because an outlaw station, of course, it was, and she was afraid, because it was equally obviously operated by the enemy, and Emma had not before come to grips with the enemy—figuratively speaking, of course—actual grips was what she hoped to avoid.

Suddenly and unexpectedly the shaft was filled with music. Emma had thought of messages—in code, certainly—but not music or music that was faintly familiar; then she remembered that music could be a code too. Not until a soaring tenor solo began did Emma recognize the music as that of the *Stolen Bride*, and she did so with the gooseflesh prickling her arms, because it was Paul Horsack's voice that came to her, correct in every intonation and detail, just as he had sung the count's solo, strutting on the stage the day before. Then the voice was cut off with an angry exclamation.

So, Mr. Heavy Pipesmoker didn't like Horsack's voice, which was odd, because his voice was the only thing to like about Horsack, but it was not odd if you considered that perhaps Mr. H.P. was thinking of the man and not the voice. Emma conceded that a dislike for Horsack wasn't going to help her identify her invisible enemy. It was, locally, a common trait.

There was a scrape and a rustle and the deep notes of a piano concerto. The man was playing records! Why not? He had some kind of power to run his lights and radio, and that power would also turn a turntable. That was the way he sent his messages. But the music broke off again; there was buzzing, crackling, whistling, and the sound of a typewriter being operated rapidly. He certainly was well equipped, was old Mr. Spy. Consternation broke over Emma. Suppose he lived there, with supplies of heat and food! Suppose he almost never went out, except for rare instances like the one that had enabled her to make her entrance; but suppose he was in now for the night, for the day, for the next week. For a moment Emma faced the possibility of dying there in her corner of slow starvation, or of revealing herself to face a fate worse than death but probably including it; then by her own peculiar brand of logic she saved herself temporarily. This man knew Horsack. Therefore, he had to have been in the village and have seen Horsack. Therefore, he was sometimes in the village and not always in his hole. Not necessarily. If this man was a spy he undoubtedly knew that Horsack was active among the Free Czechs, and his radio would bring him the news of Horsack's death. A spy could know all about Horsack without ever having been in Central City; spies were like that.

Emma gave herself up for lost and wondered how long it took one to die of starvation. She hadn't had any lunch, so she had a good start. Emma wished she hadn't thought about lunch; she was hungry right now, and the devil on the other side of the partition had stopped typing and was eating something. It sounded like an apple, a crisp, juicy apple. The saliva ran in her mouth, and she swallowed, audibly, it seemed. The apple was bad enough, but what if he cooked food? By tomorrow morning, say, how would she feel about the smell of crisp frying bacon and coffee? She could barely stand the thought now, and in the morning, when she was cold and stiff and Mr. Spy was just up from a nice warm bed . . .

Emma smiled and counted herself saved again. Mr. H. P. Spy didn't have a bed; Q.E.D., he didn't spend his nights there and she could get away. She checked her remembrance of the shelter carefully. Radio, chair, table, crates, and boxes, but no bed. She could have missed the typewriter, but she couldn't have missed a bed; the cave just wasn't big enough for one. And if Mr. Spy slept in the village she could find him somehow.

Time passed. Emma did not know whether it galloped or ambled withal, because, not having known when she came in, she did not know at what time her unknown moved about as though putting things away; the hum of the motor stopped and the lights went out.

"His nefarious activities finished for the day, the sinister creature locked his hideout and crept down the mountain. In the village to mingle, in another guise, freely, with his fellow men . . . ."

Emma was rather proud of the last sentence. It had a certain pseudo dignity about it. She wondered if it would be improved by putting the verb at the end. She tried it that way. She tried splitting the infinitive. She substituted "unsuspecting natives" for "fellow men," but discarded it as insufficiently high-toned.

It was very quiet in the shaft. Quickly, because she couldn't stand it another minute, Emma peered around the partition to see if her nefarious creature really had locked the door.

CHAPTER SIX

EMMA was amazed to find that it was still light when she left the mine shaft. After the darkness within she had expected darkness without, and she shrank back for a moment, as though the bright sky, now free from clouds, had tricked her. What if her late captor were watching from the long shadow of a scrub juniper? Emma took a couple of steps forward and bent as though to pick something, anything, from the scanty growths at her feet. There was no sudden movement; no shot rang out. Reassured, Emma straightened up and stared brazenly about her. He was a pretty silly Joe, this one, not to keep a better watch on his hideout. He must feel pretty secure—as though it didn't make any difference if he were found out, as though he had the backing of someone in authority. Emma knew who she would want on her side if she were running any nefarious project.

No; Emma, picking her way across the ravine, decided that it wasn't possible. Mr. Weatherbee might be a deceitful, double-dealing old wretch, but she could not imagine him in a traitorous role. Skirting the grave-yards, Emma conceded that Mr. Weatherbee was a vested interest, and there were those whose financial background had made them hostile to anything but a rugged, individualistic isolationism. Mr. Weatherbee was definitely an individualist, and the perverse streak in him might just exactly lead him to . . .

It fitted so beautifully: his sponsoring of a troupe in which the foreign-born would excite no suspicion; the equipping of an expensive station in a spot which, though relatively inaccessible, was well known to Mr. Weatherbee from days past; his benign, dignified supervision of the Festival, quite proper for a patron, that would excite no suspicion. His darkly planned murder of Horsack, the patriot, passed off as an accident. Which, of course, it wasn't.

Emma sat down on the curbing of St. Paul's Episcopal Church, remembering the doorknob. That was what had been in her mind all the time, nagging at her. That was how she knew Horsack's death hadn't been an accident. Because when she had been in the side entry the door-knob had been bright and shiny. Mr. Weatherbee had said that there was blood on the doorknob, chancing that she wouldn't remember. He had done better than that. He had suggested that they check details at the scene of the crime; then Nitti had mentioned the knob. If she had said that there was no blood on it Mr. Weatherbee would have thought of something else, but as long as she hadn't he figured he was safe. It was a good thing, Emma reflected, that she was so dumb. Now she was one up on him, and he didn't know it. And the way he had tried to throw her off the track with that crayon and scrap of paper.

Horsack had got wind of something, and Horsack had been killed, but Horsack had talked too much. She, Emma, would not make that mistake. Not she! She'd go sniffing around with that piece of paper in her hand, pretending she didn't know a red herring when she saw one. That reminded Emma that she was hungry.

There were people still in front of the opera house but none coming out; that meant the matinee was over and that Mary would be coming out soon. Emma wondered if Horsack had really told Mary anything; she hoped not. Emma felt that Mr. Weatherbee would have no more compunction in wiping Mary out than he had Horsack. She decided not to tell Mary of her afternoon's discoveries. Mr. Weatherbee was already pointing the finger of suspicion, if not death, at Mary, and what she didn't know couldn't hurt her.

It was later than Emma had thought. Mary, in her room removing makeup, hailed Emma as she came down the hall.

"Where, in the land of saints, have you been?"

"I took a walk"—Emma hung her head—"and got lost."

"Why, you poor little thing, you must be dead. You really shouldn't go wandering off by yourself. There might be bears or rattlesnakes."

"Phooey," said Emma grandly. "I was perfectly safe; only I got caught in the storm and had to wait in a cave."

"How exciting. The storm put the lights out—it always does—and we sang for two minutes in dark daylight. It was just before Rho's entrance and it made him late, and I give you my word, when the lights went up and he wasn't there I had the oddest feeling. But he took his cue off stage perfectly."

"Tell me"—Emma fingered the dinner dress laid out on the bed—"have you noticed how much Sauer says 'Zut'?"

"Why, no"—Mary took the towel from around her neck—"I hadn't. Sometimes, I guess."

Could it possibly have been Sauer? Emma wondered. He had been late on his cue, and the opera didn't begin until three, but she was completely confused as to the time of the storm and the time she had been in the mine.

"Darling," Mary was going on, "do you mind dreadfully? I have to go to this dinner. They're having it early because it's really for me. Some man who used to have a lot of rubber is giving it, and Alvarado thinks it's important. I wonder it Aggie remembered to turn off the hot-water heater; she'll blow us all up someday."

Mary hurried across the hall to the bathroom, leaving Emma feeling half neglected, half relieved that she would have time to think things over by herself. Now that she was sure Horsack had been murdered, things

were different. She had to go back and put the pieces of the picture, as
Hank would say, in place again. She wished Hank were there. Hank would
know what to do. Shay? Emma wasn't sure about Shay. If she told him
she had spotted an enemy radio station he would very likely laugh or
demand to be shown. Emma didn't like to be laughed at, and she didn't
want to risk another trip to the shaft. There was no knowing how far or
how deep it went. . . .

Emma went into her own room to wash and to change her shoes. As
she reached for a towel she saw, with a feeling of annoyance, that Aggie
had been there again. Another fantastic drawing lay atop the towels. Emma
put it on the bureau, half looking at it as she dried her face. This time
Aggie was going in for clocks, along with the other surrealists, only this
clock didn't drip; it stood primly on a scarf draped shelf, pointing to seven.
Emma scowled at the clock; instead of numbers it had letters, and there
weren't twelve of them. "March 7," Emma read.

"Here's where I get off," she quoted to herself and laughed at the
improbability of Aggie's knowing the old joke. More likely March 7 was
Aggie's birthday. Poor Aggie, the comedy relief.

Mary was still in the bathroom, so Emma wandered around aim-
lessly because she had been in the room so little that it was still strange
to her; there was as yet no place to which she instinctively went to sit
down. There was a bouquet of wild gaillardia on the bureau—Aggie's
touch again—and a pile of magazines on the stand by the bed: *Look*
and *Time.* Emma rearranged the magazines because *Time,* being the
smallest, ought to be on top. Horsack's death ought to make *Time,* but
not this week's. And when the news of his murder came out it would
make it again.

Hello, this wasn't even this week's *Time.* The cover was familiar.
Emma looked again; it was the issue of March seventh. March 7.

Emma glanced quickly behind her, as though someone were in the
room. That was what the clock said: March 7. The clock was time. Look
at *Time,* the magazines said.

Hearing Mary's voice in the next room, Emma took the drawing from
the bureau and put it in her bag. Mary wouldn't get it. Mary was too
absorbed in Mary right then to do anything more than laugh at Aggie's
foolishness, but it was just as well not to take any chances.

"Darling," Mary was saying, "you come over to the hotel and find
Shay and have dinner with him; I feel like a dog leaving you like this, but
I have to stay in good with Alvarado, the greasy pig."

"Look at *Time.* " The words were insistent in Emma's mind; she picked
up the magazine, her bag, and joined Mary.

"That Shay," Mary was saying, "I never heard anyone like him. He was telling the most amazing stories of his experiences in China this noon, in a most amazing fashion."

Emma could tell an amazing thing or two, she thought to herself, but aloud she said only, "Amazing," and wondered why Shay would open up to Mary and not to her.

"I think"—Mary was quite serious—"that he could be had, if, of course, I weren't absolutely off men."

"Absolutely," said Emma, smiling to herself. The wind was blowing all right in that direction. Mary would be surprised at how easily Shay could be had.

"Forevermore." Mary came out of her trance of self-absorption. "Say something. Don't just stand there repeating words."

"That's a knockout dress," said Emma. "Turn around and let me zip it up."

"It's just a little old thing." Happily Mary ran a comb through her short hair, poked at a curl or two, and put on lipstick. She picked up a short fur coat, opened the door, and made a gesture of caution to Emma.

Down the hall, Aggie, tray in hand, was standing in front of a closed door.

"She told me to bring it," they heard her say, and Mary nudged Emma's ribs.

They heard no answer from within the room, and after a minute of wavering indecision Aggie put the tray, which contained a glass with a drinking rod and a plate bearing a sandwich, on the floor.

"She told me to bring it, and I'll leave it here while I fix Miss Dolan's room."

She turned to Mary, taking in the details of face and dress fondly, lovingly. "Have a good time."

Emma jumped as though she had been stuck with a pin, but Mary, with a friendly smile, hurried her on, then stopped with a muttered exclamation. Telling Emma to wait, she ran back upstairs.

Emma waited, then she went on downstairs and stood looking at the Indian curios in which Shay had taken so much interest. Shay was amazing all right. She looked at the door ahead of her, the door to the side entry. It stood ajar, its frosted- and cut-glass panels reflecting colors from the stained-glass window beyond it. So they were using the side entrance again, were they? Everything was all over, all hushed up. Oh, it was, was it? Little old butter-wouldn't-melt-in-his-mouth and his stooges were in for a good stiff jolt. Emma was wondering whether she had decided that Mr. Weatherbee or one of his gang had killed Horsack, when she heard Mary coming, and then Mrs. Danforth appeared from the dining room, saying "Good evening" and gently, firmly, herding them out the side door.

Mary left Emma in the lobby of the hotel, ascending grandly, for one who was so small, the broad, sweeping staircase to the mezzanine where the party was to be held. For no very strong reason Emma felt alone and abandoned, until Mary, at the top of the stairs, turned and waved. That made things better again, made her feel that Mary, at least, knew she was there. That was like Mary; she might seem self-centered and selfish and then all of a sudden she did something that made you know she had been thinking of you all along. You had to be self-centered to get along. Emma decided that it would be a fine idea for her to be a little self-centered in the next few days or she would find herself dead in a telephone booth, having hit her head on the doorknob! That was such a silly story! She shouldn't have fallen for it in the first place, but in a way it was lucky she had. Old Mr. W. thought everything was clear. It was, to her.

Her bag and magazine under her arm, Emma entered the bar because that was the most likely place to find Shay. She hadn't decided how much to tell Shay, but under the guise of their game of suppositions she might get her thoughts straightened out. Shay was in the bar all right; his huge bulk was leaned across a table, and he was talking fast and earnestly to a creature in a greenish-blue dress, a blond creature that Emma did not need a double-take to recognize as Susan Weatherbee. From the looks of things Shay had not only forgotten Mary but had gone completely over to the enemy.

Emma jockeyed around, moved her bag from one arm to the other. Did everything, in fact, but cough and beckon to get Shay's attention Finally Shay looked up and saw her, or, more accurately, became slightly aware of her, as of a pinpoint on the horizon.

"Hi, kid," he said and turned back to Susan Weatherbee.

Well, it came eventually to every woman, Emma thought, the realization that she was not first with all her male acquaintants, but it griped particularly to be given the brush-off for Susan, who made matters worse by looking at Emma casually, blankly, as though Emma could not possibly be of the slightest interest or importance.

Of all the confident, conceited little—

Emma stalked haughtily through the bar, into the patio, and ordered her dinner.

They'd find out—Susan Weatherbee wouldn't be so smug when her grandfather was revealed as the brains of a spy ring. Susan was probably in it, too, avid for new excitements, after a jaded life . . . .

Emma opened the copy of *Time*. Book reviews, movies, religion. With some dismay Emma realized that she hadn't the faintest notion what she was looking for; there was nothing to do but to read every word with the hope that somewhere a bell would ring or a light would break. In the middle of "Business and Finance" and halfway through her soup, Emma decided that whatever the message was, she probably wouldn't get it. "Metals and Mining" caught her eye, with a reference to molybdenum and Climax. Climax was somewhere near; she'd seen it on a map. But the article was full of figures of increased production and had no reference to sabotage or Mr. Weatherbee. With her fried chicken Emma scanned "Radio," but the Reds were fighting the Blues and paying no attention to outlaw stations.

With her pie and ice cream Emma decided that she had thought the whole thing up herself. She was a silly to think that a silly like Aggie could devise such a complicated device for conveying a message, much less have a message to convey. The thing was a coincidence. Half convinced, and feeling much more normal for having eaten, Emma started to read "People" purely for entertainment. Some of the store's customers occasionally popped up there doing strange things: leaving their money to a pet poodle, or giving a yacht to the Navy—a yacht like Mr. Whoosit's, where the beds zipped from stateroom to stateroom at the press of a button. Jeff had told her about that. But this time there were no familiar names. A movie actress, four times wed, was having another go at matrimony with a band leader, a mere lad of three tries. Adolph Burkhardt, who had been decorated by Hitler for a scholarly analysis of the economy of the Third Reich (see a previous issue of *Time),* had resigned from the chair of history at Tupelo University. Professor Burkhardt gave a throat ailment rather than academic pressure as his reason and would devote himself to his hobby of geology. One Timothy Smith, a plumber by trade—

A professor of geology . . .

Emma took a spoonful of coffee instead of ice cream. He wasn't that, of course, but Mr. Faber had said that Burkhardt was his name.

Emma hastily opened her bag and took out the picture, not of the clock, but the earlier one of the three people eating, the one of the two women and the short heavy man with the flashes of lightning around his head. Radio! Sound waves, not lightning! That was what Aggie had been trying to convey, and her warped mind could not do it by words, only by pictures. But how had Aggie found out about the secret station? Emma remembered the wild gaillardias and the crudely clipped lot in the cemetery. Aggie, in her quest for flowers, had stumbled onto the professor's hideout. She also knew the professor's name and had connected him with the article. How had she learned about that? From the professor himself? That seemed hardly likely, until you stopped to consider why the professor was the favored roomer, the only one who was also boarded, and remembered that Otille, the dearly beloved of Bertram Estis, had been born in Frieburg and that Mrs. Danforth was half German. That didn't have to mean anything, or it might mean a lot; at least it gave the professor and Mrs. Danforth something in common, something to talk about, and the professor might have talked too much. Emma balked at the idea of making Mrs. Danforth an accomplice, but the professor could have shown her the article in *Time*, could have enlisted her sympathy with a tale of academic persecution without divulging why he had chosen that out-of-the-way spot for his retirement. Aggie had overheard his story and had added her own discovery to it.

The waitress coughed, and Emma realized that her place was needed for more practical purposes than that of speculation. She paid her bill and went straight to the lobby. Shay, for his pains, was going to be scooped of a nice fat story. She was going straight to the police.

No, she wasn't.

The police, probably including the honest but obvious Dominic, were straws in Mr. Weatherbee's incalculable wind. She had to go over the police, to someone. The FBI? Of course! Only she wasn't exactly sure how you got hold of an FBI-er. Hank knew some, but Hank knew some of every kind of cop and, besides, Hank wasn't there. Emma went to the telephone booth, vaguely remembering that there was something on the front of phone books, a number or something. But the Central City, Nevadaville, and Blackhawk exchange was only interested in what to do in case of fires, forest and otherwise. Emma took the Denver directory: fire, long distance, special operator—ah, there it was . . . .

"Hello," said Mr. Weatherbee. "When you get through I'll buy you a drink."

Emma let the phone book fall the length of its chain. "I can't," she said. "I've got to go to Denver." She blurted it out because she suddenly realized that that was what she had to do. She couldn't make her call with Mr. Weatherbee standing there, and even if she got rid of him he doubtless had spies in the local exchange.

"The train"—Mr. Weatherbee seemed to think her desire perfectly reasonable—"doesn't go until twelve. You've got plenty of time."

Emma didn't want to wait until twelve; at least she didn't want to spend the intervening time in the company of Mr. Weatherbee and his uncanny habit of reading her mind. Also, she didn't, judging from his past performance, think it was possible to get rid of Mr. Weatherbee, who was probably supposed to be at the party but who would leave it flat if the fancy struck him. Emma wished, for the umpteenth time, that she had her car, any car. . . .

"On the other hand," Mr. Weatherbee was saying, "there's my car if you're in a hurry. What you got?" He grinned affably. "What my granddaughter would call a hot date?"

Emma's smile was a triumph of coyness and deceit. "Don't tell Shay—Mr. Horrigan—I don't want him to know. But I couldn't think of troubling you. Won't you want it? I might wreck it."

This was wonderful, Emma thought; this was colossal. Taking Mr. Weatherbee's own car.

"Anything to oblige a lady. I was young once myself." Mr. Weatherbee leered. "And Chew'll drive you. He can make better time; he knows these roads like I know the mountains." He chuckled.

Ha, ha, yourself, Emma thought. She knew something about the mountains too. "I see your granddaughter came back," she said too sweetly.

Mr. Weatherbee looked at her searchingly. "She's just a little girl," he said. "And I kinda thought—" For the first time he seemed at a loss for words. "I got the idea that your— Damn it," said Mr. Weatherbee, " 'intended' is a silly word, but 'boyfriend' is no improvement."

"You mean"—Emma had to help him out—"my guy's in California and," she added in not quite such an amiable tone, "what Mr. Horrigan does is not of the slightest importance to me."

"Uh-huh," said Mr. Weatherbee. "Well, let's get off to this hot date in Denver."

"Oh, it's not really that. . ." Emma's voice trailed off as she realized that Mr. Weatherbee had her range, from not one point but two. What Shay did was nothing to her because her true love was far away, so she had said. She had also said that she was going to Denver for a hot date.

"Or it could be"—Mr. Weatherbee, not unaware of his advantage, chose to be kind—"that it's none of my business."

With all her defenses shot away, Emma trailed him to the door while he whistled up Chew and the black car.

"I better tell Miss Dolan where you've gone." The old man was solicitude itself. "And there's no hurry about getting back. I can go down the mountain with m'daughter, but if I've got any sense I'll bed down here for the night. You better go to the Brown; it's a good hotel.

"And it might interest you to know that the telephone operator says that Horsack had asked her to call the Denver FBI. But he—er—died before she put the call through."

Mr. Weatherbee watched the taillight of his car until he saw which turn it took; then he chuckled as he went back into the bar. Chew liked to drive the canyon road.

For once Mr. Weatherbee did not pause in the bar; he went straight through to the telephone booth in the lobby and put in a Denver call.

There were times when he seemed like such a kindly old man. Emma, looking at the sparse, bristly hairs on the back of Chew's neck, almost felt ashamed to be using his car and his chauffeur for what she was going to do. Maybe he didn't know anything about the radio station in the mine; maybe he had just killed Horsack to protect his granddaughter, who was obviously in the habit of throwing herself at any man in sight. Looking at it that way, Emma felt almost sympathetic toward Mr. Weatherbee, though murder, as a habit, was something that she deplored. On the other hand, Emma had a feeling that Mr. Weatherbee knew about the radio station, partly, she conceded, because she didn't think that there was much that went on in Central City that he didn't know about. With a regretful but virtuous sigh Emma decided that she would have to tell her story as she knew it; if investigation showed that Mr. Weatherbee was involved— well, it was just too bad.

The car swooped around a curve; Emma braced her feet and looked out. It should have been dark by now, but a bright moon was shining high among the clouds, illuminating, as though by daylight, green meadows that stretched away.

Emma looked again. Those weren't meadows; those were the tops of trees—big trees—far, far below! The car swooped again with a screech that must have taken a good two hundred miles off Mr. Weatherbee's tires, and Emma climbed, panicky, to the other side of the car. The view from there was not pleasant either. Jagged rocks that cast black shadows in the moonlight towered high above her—over her, for in some places they seemed to be driving in a half tunnel excavated from the cliff. She didn't blame Chew for hugging the inside track. . . .

She climbed back to the other side of the car and snatched a quick look, then shut her eyes. There was no inside track. They were hurtling down the mountainside at breakneck speed on a single-track road. Even if they made all the turns, which seemed impossible, a single car—just one little old Ford—was all that was necessary to send them off—off over the tops of those gigantic trees, crashing, smashing on a hidden ledge, to broken bits of nothingness.

Emma pounded on the glass in front of her. She yelled, but the head in the stiff black cap did not turn; the pace did not let up. This was Mr. Weatherbee's doing—Emma saw it now—this was a diabolical plan to send her off to be killed, mangled, maimed, there on the lonely mountainside. That Chew would perish, too, meant nothing to Mr. Weatherbee; he probably had dozens of chauffeurs all fanatically devoted to their master, all willing to die for his whim.

Emma's eyes fixed themselves on the road ahead; she was driving now, feeling every jolt, anticipating every turn, braking much more frequently than the Flying Tiger in front seemed to think necessary. Suddenly a ridge of earth loomed up in the lights, a long winding ridge left by the scraper, too high to straddle, too close to the edge to avoid. If they skidded in that, all was over right then—all but the sickening, dizzy fall.

Emma was forced to a grudging admiration. Chew could certainly drive a car. He pulled out to the right, out to the edge—here Emma shut her eyes—and turned his wheels sharply. There was a lurch as the right wheels hit the ridge almost squarely and a rattle of gravel like shot against the mudguard; then they were over, speeding on down the mountain.

The rest of the trip was an anticlimax. On the almost level streets of Idaho Springs, Chew turned to Emma with a broad grin of elation, and Emma forced herself to grin back. No chauffeur was going to have the satisfaction of knowing he had scared the pants off her. Sheepishly she felt for her shoes, which she had removed at some unknown point of the descent, her monkey instincts telling her, no doubt, that she could cling better with her toes. Somewhere on the broad stretches of Route 40 a motorcycle cop pulled up behind them, noted the license number, and sped past with a wave. Emma was chalking up another instance of authority for Mr. Weatherbee when she looked at the speedometer and was amazed to find that they were only doing a little better than forty. She wondered dizzily if they had been doing no more than that down the mountain; it had seemed like a hundred. They approached Denver, long sprawled out along the road, and Emma's feeling of light-headedness increased. What had Mr. Weatherbee said about a hotel? She tapped on the glass, but Chew, with another grin, kept on going, over a viaduct, through a nondescript section of filling stations and warehouses, to a brightly lighted corner.

Then a man in a blue uniform was opening the door, and Emma found herself in front of an ornate old brownstone hotel. She tried to say something to Chew, to tell him not to wait, that she'd go back on the train, on her hands and knees, any way but in that car, but Chew only nodded and turned the car into a garage across the street, leaving Emma to wobble up the steps into a lobby from which tier after tier of gilded iron railings rose around a huge central well. Emma looked and felt dizzier and groped her way toward a slipcovered davenport, reviewing, because her stomach was often her undoing, what she could have eaten to upset her. Fried chicken never hurt anybody, and the soup had been good, though unnameable from any obvious ingredient. It was probably just the excitement of finding herself alive after flirting with that old wolf, death.

Emma looked about for a telephone booth and saw the woman at the newsstand closing up for the night. It seemed reasonable that she would know the location of the telephone booths, and Emma went to ask her, went unsteadily in a wavering line. The woman at the stand watched her suspiciously.

"Please," said Emma politely, "where is the nearest phone?"

"Around the corner. Right in front of the entrance."

Emma felt like saying that she hadn't come in the entrance—she had come down from the top floor on a rope—but she only walked away with as much firmness as she could assume.

Around the corner she saw a model of a frigate over an oak door that was lettered "Ship's Tavern." That was what she needed, she thought, a glass of grog; that would clear her head and steady her feet; then she saw the telephone booths and decided to put business before medicine. It was close in the booth, so Emma left the door open; that prevented the light from going on, and Emma had to hold the directory outside in order to see.

". . . Cherry 9000, and you will be connected at once with the Washington office."

Emma didn't want the Washington office; she wanted immediate action, so she dialed information.

"The FBI, please." That didn't sound explicit enough. "I want the office of the Federal Bureau of Investigation."

"I am ringing your number."

So soon? And so casually? Emma was a little taken aback.

"Yes?" said a pleasant voice.

"Look," said Emma, "I never did this before."

"Yes?" said the voice. "Where are you calling from?"

"That doesn't matter." Having so suddenly obtained her objective left Emma completely flabbergasted, and she rushed on: "This may sound awfully silly, but I want to talk to someone about something I found in the mountains up by Central City, beyond a graveyard—well, beyond the *second* graveyard really. I can't tell you over the phone. I'm wearing a plaid gingham with a clip on it that looks like a donkey . . . ."

"Just a moment. If you'll tell me where you are I'll meet you."

"Oh, thank you so much. I'll be in the bar because I sort of need a drink."

And with those explicit directions Emma hung up, not realizing until she had ordered the hot grog that she had neglected to say what bar. She was unutterably stupid and would have to go through the whole thing again, but first she would have her drink. But the drink was long in coming, possibly because the bartender had to look up the recipe or wait for the teakettle to boil, and before the waiter had brought it a tall man walked into the bar.

Emma noticed him because he would have stood out in any crowd. He was thin but broad-shouldered and so tall that he looked down from under habitually drooping eyelids. He walked past Emma's table, and Emma watched him admiringly. He turned and walked back, watching Emma. His eyes were haughty, piercing; the look of eagles, Emma thought.

More likely a wolf, she corrected herself sternly, and she wasn't the kind of girl to be picked up in a bar—not tonight, anyway. Then she realized that the tall man had stopped and was gazing pointedly at the pin in the collar of her dress, the donkey pin that she had given as identification.

"How on earth," asked Emma, "did you know which bar I meant?"

"To a great many people," said the tall man, "this is the only bar in Denver; it's the place I'd look first."

Just routine, Emma thought, old stuff to him. He really was handsome, and he looked more FBI-ish than the pictures of J. Edgar Hoover.

"Won't you," she said, "sit down?"

"If you have something to tell me," said the tall man, "I think we better go somewhere else."

Of course. Emma felt abashed. A bar was no place to conduct government business. She rose quickly, wavered, and reached for the back of a chair, but the man had his hand under her arm, steadying her, leading her toward a side door. Outside she felt better and pulled away from his arm. It would be horrible if he thought she was drunk and wouldn't believe her story. He had to; he'd have to investigate at least, and if he investigated he'd find out that what she said was true.

They crossed a street and continued down it.

"Denver is quite a large city, isn't it?" said Emma.

"What? Oh yes. Is this your first visit? Hey, look out!" for Emma had narrowly escaped collision with a lamppost.

After that the conversation languished. Emma concentrated on putting one foot in front of the other; she didn't know what ailed her; she only hoped that she didn't pass out or do something foolish. They crossed a second street, went around a corner, and, somewhat to Emma's surprise, into another bar.

"Hello, Mr. Strike," said a waiter.

That was it, Emma thought; here he was well known and safe from interruption. "That's an odd name," she said, because it seemed time for someone to say something.

"Yes," said the man, "my father—"

"Was a Strike," Emma finished for him, thinking herself rather cute and not noting that Mr. Strike seemed startled rather than pleased at her remark.

"Er, quite so," said Mr. Strike, excusing himself and going into conference with the bartender.

Emma wished he would light and pay attention before the whirling in her head got the better of her; she also felt as though she had a mouse in her throat, a mouse that scurried up and choked her and then retired to brood somewhere down in her chest.

Mr. Strike came back and asked abruptly if she would like something to drink. Emma, who didn't feel that her mouse would care for alcoholic stimulant, said she'd like a glass of milk.

Mr. Strike said, "Quite so; make it two," and the waiter looked at him with solicitude.

"Of course," said Emma, "I just happened to think. You traced the phone call."

Mr. Strike looked blank.

"I mean that's how you found me. It was silly of me not to think of it. You traced the call to the hotel, and I'd said I would be in the bar. Hank says it's surprisingly easy to trace people, especially if they're trying not to be traced. They do all sorts of strange things that you can catch onto, whereas if they'd just be normal it would be much harder."

Mr. Strike looked toward the door and then at Emma curiously.

"But," Emma was going on, "I don't need to tell you that."

The milk came; the waiter watched Strike take a long drink and walked away, shuddering.

"Now," said Mr. Strike, "what was it you wanted to tell me?"

But before Emma could swallow her mouthful of milk the waiter came up and said, "Phone call."

"Come with me," said Strike. "This may take a little time."

His voice had a note of authority that had Emma out of her chair and halfway down a back corridor before she realized that the door in front of them led into an alley rather than to a telephone booth. Emma hung back, but Strike, behind her, pushed her through, into darkness and a sharp spatter of rain.

"I don't think I like this," said Emma suddenly.

Mr. Strike laughed. "Quite normal," he said. "That was a code message which meant for me to go to a certain place at once."

"Spies?" asked Emma, mollified. "Or dope?"

"Violation . . ."

Emma thought he said, "of the milk ordinance," but she stumbled over a half-filled carton of empty bottles and couldn't be sure.

It was raining harder now, and they ran around the corner into a brightly tiled cafe of the open-all-night variety. Strike got a cup of coffee and a bottle of milk and led Emma to a table well to the rear.

Emma filled her glass and took a sip.

"Tastes all right to me," she said. She examined the cap. "It's pasteurized."

Strike shook his head. "Somebody must have tipped him off; sometimes we catch him selling raw milk."

Emma laughed. "It sounds just like a raid during prohibition."

"Quite so." There were crow's-feet of laughter around his eyes, Emma noticed, and she imagined that he had a lighter side when, of course, he wasn't on business. He really was very attractive.

"Now," he was saying, "out with it."

"I hardly," Emma said, "know where to begin. . . ."

But she began at the beginning, which was her finding of Horsack's body, and told, for her, a reasonably connected story, omitting impressions and sticking to facts. She did, however, rather elaborate on the character of Mr. Weatherbee because she felt that he was important.

Mr. Strike's crow's-feet deepened when Emma told of what had happened to her in Mr. Faber's office, and he murmured, "The old devil."

"Oh, he is," Emma assured him. "Wait till you hear the rest."

She told of the finding of the hidden radio apparatus and of the identification of its operator through Aggie's pictures.

"I've got the article right here." She handed over the magazine for Strike to read.

He seemed impressed. "Although," he said, "you realize that he will have to be caught in the act."

Emma nodded. "That's where you come in."

Mr. Strike nodded, and Emma went on. When she told him that there was no blood on the doorknob when she had first found Horsack—she had already explained why Horsack's death had been called accidental—Strike interrupted her sharply.

"You're absolutely sure about this?"

"Absolutely. I don't always remember things all at once, but if I do remember them, they were so."

Strike did not seem entirely convinced, but . . .

"Have you told anyone else about the doorknob?"

"Not, a soul." Emma smiled happily. "Particularly not Mr. Weatherbee, because his not knowing I know makes me one up on him. You must have heard of the Weatherbees," she went on; "they seem to be terribly important around here, and that granddaughter, Susan—"

"Yes," said Mr. Strike, "they are well known in Denver."

"And likely to become notorious." Emma's tone sounded so vengeful, even to herself, that she promptly relented. "Of course it's a shame in a way. A family that has stood for so much . . ." Emma wasn't exactly sure what the Weatherbees stood for except money and power, so she skipped on, "But that's exactly the kind that get delusions of grandeur and think they're stronger than the government, just because they can bribe the local cops, and think that the only way to rule is by individual authority, just because they've always done so."

"Let me get this straight," Strike interrupted her. "You think that the old man, Mr. Weatherbee, is at the bottom of the whole thing, (a) that he instigated or connives at the secret listening post for the purposes of sabotage, and (b) that he murdered, or had murdered, Horsack, because Horsack was onto him? Is that it?"

It sounded bald and ugly, the way he put it, but that was what it boiled down to. Emma nodded. "He just admitted to me that Horsack was trying to call the FBI." She half expected Strike to argue, to try to bring Sauer into the picture—Emma had touched rather lightly on the relationship between Mary and Horsack, not to be dishonest but because the case against Mr. Weatherbee was so much stronger-but Strike seemed to agree with her.

"It certainly looks," he said, "as though the old man had overreached himself this time. Criminently," he broke off, "look at it rain."

The windows of the cafe were streaming, and when the door opened the wind and rain rushed in halfway across the room. "If it's raining like this in the mountains you can't get back tonight. How did you get down? You were too early for the train."

"I borrowed a car," said Emma, and then, because she thought Mr. Strike would appreciate the joke, "Mr. Weatherbee loaned me his."

"That's a good one, but you can't drive it back tonight. The road is probably washed out in half a dozen places by now."

"There was a chauffeur," Emma admitted, "that went with the deal. A demon like his master. As a matter of fact, I thought he was going to kill me coming down that canyon."

Mr. Strike seemed to find it amusing. "Quite so," he said. "The canyon road is a little steep the first time. I better phone for a taxi."

Someone turned on a radio. "Warning to all motorists. Stay off Route 90. Route 40 closed beyond Idaho Springs. Warning to all motorists. Stay off Route 90. This is the Highway Patrol warning all motorists.

"Folks, this is Byron Kelley, your announcer, telling you that it sure is coming down in the hills. Of course it's only breast-high on my duck, but it's too deep for cars. Folks, we may have some bad news in the morning about some of you that didn't heed the patrol warnings, but right now Mrs. Sadie Hoffspringer has got word to us that she's all right. Mrs. Sadie Hoffspringer of Longmont says to tell her folks that she got out of her car and to a cabin O.K. And good old engine Number 6 got the folks down from Central City before the storm broke. Folks, if any of your friends or family were at the opera tonight you don't need to worry; good old Number 6 got 'em down safely. Of course I can't promise that they went straight home. . . ."

Life in Denver, Emma thought, would have little privacy with that man at the mike. Strike came back with word that the taxi was there, and together they made a dash that only half wet them.

"Did you hear the radio?" Strike asked. "Route 90 is part of the less sensational way to Central City, and the canyon road joins Route 40 the other side of Idaho Springs, so you couldn't go that way if you wanted to, which," he added, "I guess you don't."

"It's all right," Emma assured him. "I left word that I might stay all night. I gather that yellow peril of Mr. Weatherbee's took me down the canyon road just for the ride. But if there had been a car coming up he'd have been just as dead as me."

"He didn't tell you"—Mr. Strike's voice sounded very much amused— "but that road is one way up before the opera and one way down after it. There's not much traffic these days, but the rule is still enforced."

"Oh," said Emma.

"And by the way"—Strike's tone became serious again—"I hope I don't need to tell you that whatever opinion I may have given you about what you have told me is not for publication. The matter"—he spoke gravely—"is out of your hands now."

Emma sighed her relief. The load was off her mind, and the mouse in her throat seemed to have also vanished.

"And for Pete's sake," he added, "don't tell anyone about that door-knob. Don't tell anyone anything until we get hold of the guy that killed Horsack."

"You mean because it would be dangerous," Emma agreed, "but you think they're the same, don't you—whoever killed Horsack and the one who is running the radio?"

"I think," said Mr. Strike emphatically, "that you better not know what I think."

The taxi sprayed to a stop in front of a marquee, and a doorman in a maroon uniform held the door for them. Emma didn't notice the door-man, but she did notice the low, broad lobby.

"Hey," she said, "what are you doing? This is the wrong hotel."

Strike looked perplexed; then he looked at Emma as though he expected her to start screaming. "Don't misunderstand me," he said; "this is a very good hotel."

Emma blushed to the back of her neck. "I'm sure it is," she said with dignity, "but I said I'd be at the Brown Palace. Mr. Weatherbee recommended it."

Strike turned toward the door. "Suit yourself." His dignity outstripped Emma's. "Mr. Weatherbee happens to own part of the Brown; I have no interest in this one."

"Oh, don't be absurd," Emma flung at him. "Of course I'll stay here. It was just that—I was just surprised that it wasn't the Brown. Good night."

"Good night."

Emma marched haughtily to the desk and haughtily asked for a room; she grew even haughtier when the bellboy inquired innocently for her bags and was only slightly mollified when the clerk suggested that she had been caught by the storm. Anyone could see that, because her dress was wet and her shoes were muddy; anyone could see that she wasn't the kind of a girl . .

Oh well, she supposed that long association with the most desperate criminals had warped Mr. Strike's opinion of the human race.

Emma watched the bellboy through the ritual of opening windows and turning on bathroom lights and tipped him carefully. That would show the kind of girl she was. Then she closed the windows and took a hot bath, because it had turned cold with the rain, and her teeth were chattering. The warm water relaxed her, and she lay in it comfortably, thinking over the evening. She had done the right thing in telling her story to Strike; she was sure of that. He hadn't laughed or been suspicious of her motives; that was gratifying. But she was a little surprised that he had seemed more concerned about the doorknob and its bearing on Horsack's murder than he had been about the listening post. She would have thought that the murder was the affair of the local authorities. Of course she had gone to him because the local authorities were purblind and he needed proof of the murder, whereas he could catch the professor red-handed. Anyhow, as Strike had said, the matter was out of her hands now.

Emma sat up slowly, tensely, in the bathtub, because a voice was talking in the next room. A voice that she knew.

"Darling," the voice was saying, "you know I love you, and there isn't the slightest danger of our being found out."

Emma couldn't hear the next remark.

And then the voice said, "You don't have to worry about her. She's at the Brown."

The voice was Mary's.

Emma got out of the tub quickly, shut the shower-bath door, and, climbing into bed, pulled the covers over her ears because she didn't want to hear any more.

And the man? Shay, of course. Who else could it be?

CHAPTER SEVEN

WHEN Emma got back to Central City, Aggie had just found the professor. It was midmorning because Emma slept late and had breakfast in her room, not wishing to run the chance of meeting Mary. She had pondered the problem of her return but on leaving the hotel found her answer in the person of Chew in casual conversation with the doorman of the Brown. The Brown was right across the street. She could have, Emma realized, stayed there just as easily as not, but it was too late to cry over spilled milk. Chew was there, waiting for her, and to return with him was the obvious thing.

Chew was full of stories of the storm. Cabins set too close to the creek had been washed away, straying stock and motorists who had failed to abandon their cars had been drowned. The town of Danvers, below the confluence of Bear and Rabbit creeks, had all but been destroyed by an eight-foot wall of water. And yet a crate of chickens from an overturned truck had been deposited miraculously safe on the roof of a garage.

She had been well advised, Chew thought, to stay in town.

Emma didn't argue with him. She tried to listen and looked dutifully at the gullies and washes that Chew pointed out. The road they were taking was broad and ascended the mountains by easy stages, following the grade of the railroad. Chew drove slowly, circumspectly; he had had his fun the night before, Emma thought. Men were piling rock at the base of a trestle, and Emma took off her hat to the men who had first constructed that line. It had probably seen many storms like last night's, but it still skirted the edge of the creek or clung to the side of the mountain, swooping, sagging, climbing, but still there. It ought to be endowed or made a national monument.

"Who owns that railroad?" Emma asked.

"The boss," said Chew.

She might have known it, Emma thought.

A patrol car came up behind them, its siren screaming, and shot past. Chew picked up speed and stopped talking, but when he pulled up in front of Mrs. Danforth's the patrol car was already there, with a small, black, dejected figure sitting on the running board.

"Some people," said Mr. Weatherbee as Emma got out, "have all the luck."

Chew went quickly and stood beside his boss.

"What?" asked Emma. "Why?"

"You were in Denver," said Mr. Weatherbee, paying no attention to Chew. "I stayed up here. I did worse; I paid a social call on your landlady, and now I'm a suspect."

"I suppose," Emma said politely, "that you strangled her?"

"No," said Mr. Weatherbee. "I always sort of admired her guts, but somebody poisoned the professor."

"Oh no!" Emma spoke sharply.

Mr. Weatherbee nodded. "Deader'n a doornail when Aggie found him."

Emma looked at Mr. Weatherbee with something like admiration. With the professor dead, all proof of Mr. Weatherbee's connection with the listening post was probably gone. And the professor had conveniently died just as she had gone to the FBI with her story. And Mr. Weatherbee was attempting to disarm suspicion by claiming to be suspect. But Mr. Weatherbee didn't know that she knew about the doorknob. A gratifying elation swept over Emma, to ebb just as quickly. It was her word against Mr. Weatherbee's—the word of an unknown against that of a pillar of society—and Emma wouldn't have given a last year's hat for her chances of being believed. And the police, under able direction, would probably find that the professor had taken his own life.

"Of course," said Mr. Weatherbee sadly, "he could've poisoned himself."

Emma sat down on the curbing with the feeling that Mr. Weatherbee undoubtedly knew all about her trip to Denver, and wondered why he hadn't instructed Chew to push her over a cliff. It would have seemed much more practical to have done away with her rather than with the professor.

"Tell me about it," she said. His story was bound to be interesting.

"All there is to it. What I told you. When he didn't come down to breakfast Aggie went up and started screaming. I happened to be walking by, sort of looking for you and Chew," Mr. Weatherbee put in brazenly, "and I went in and sized things up and called the police."

Yeah, Emma thought, and incidentally destroyed any evidence that might be around. A thought flashed through her mind. Was Mrs. Danforth his accomplice? He had said that he visited her the night before, and they were friends from the boom days. Why not? He could make it worth Mrs. Danforth's while, now that the tourist business was on the verge of being ruined by the war.

"How do you know he was poisoned?" As soon as the words were out Emma could have bitten her tongue off. She had tipped Mr. Weatherbee off to his first mistake, and he was well aware of it because he was staring at her fixedly.

"That's right," he said softly, "I shouldn't have known that, should I? Except," he went on, "that he wasn't stabbed or shot or choked to death, and a fellow that's seen 'em die most any way you can think of can't be blamed for making some deductions, can he?"

"Perhaps," Emma suggested helpfully, "his body was frightfully contorted or there was the smell of bitter almonds?"

She had him now, she thought; she could check whatever he said with Aggie, with the police findings. He was bound to give himself away somehow.

"The body was relaxed. It would be after twelve to fourteen hours."

Emma tried not to raise her eyebrows at this display of knowledge, but Mr. Weatherbee seemed to know what she was thinking.

"Look here," he said hastily, "he was alive at six o'clock. Aggie says she took his supper up then and talked to him."

"That's right," Emma conceded, "I heard her. I saw her. But I didn't hear him. You don't suppose"—Emma's eyes grew wide and she forgot for a moment her desire to trap Mr. Weatherbee—"you don't suppose he was dead then? Because she spoke to him twice, and he didn't come to the door. Then she said, 'I'll leave it here. She spoke sort of loudly, as though she thought he might be in the bathroom."

Mr. Weatherbee straightened up and looked more cheerful.

"By gum," he said, "maybe you've got something. Something that'll help."

Help him, Emma thought, and wished she hadn't spoken.

"The only trouble is we can't find the tray."

"No tray?" Emma asked sweetly, because of course Mr. Weatherbee had done away with the tray.

"No tray."

"There was a sandwich on it," Emma persisted, "and a glass of milk with one of those glass straws in it."

"Pack rats!" Mr. Weatherbee exclaimed. "Mrs. Danforth was telling me last night there was a nest of them in the attic. Do the damnedest things. Feller had some canned goods in a cupboard and some potatoes in a bin. One day when he came home the potatoes was in the cupboard and the canned beans was in the bin. Pack rats did it." He peeked at Emma from under the brim of his hat.

"Well," Emma asked him, "what do you think this pack rat left in place of the tray?"

"Nothing," said Mr. Weatherbee cheerfully. "Humans ain't got the sense of dumb animals." He looked up and seemed to see Chew for the first time. "Hey," he said, "skedaddle down to the hotel and get us a couple bottles of beer." He waited until Chew was out of earshot before he spoke again.

"You still got that crayon and paper I give you?"

Emma nodded.

"Done anything with 'em?"

Emma thought a moment, knowing that Mr. Weatherbee would not have kept them if he had not examined them. "The crayon," she said, "was Aggie's, and it could have been the one used to draw the hat."

"And the hat was like the one Horsack wore?"

Again Emma nodded.

"And you haven't figured out yet what it was doing in your grate?"

The blow caught Emma off guard, and her "No" was stammered.

Mr. Weatherbee looked his disapproval. "My," he said, "you're slow. Half a dozen people know Miss Dolan went to Horsack's room after she found the body. Well," he amended, "at least two."

"And why shouldn't she?" Emma flashed. "Nobody wants to have her letters read in court."

"No," the old man agreed, "particularly if she said half the things he deserved to have said to him."

This time Emma saw the bait and said nothing.

"What puzzles me," Mr. Weatherbee went on after a pause, "is why she burned up Aggie's picture."

"Maybe she didn't. Maybe it was crumpled up in the grate and got burned with the—the rest—"

"Well, now I never thought of that." Mr. Weatherbee seemed satisfied; at least he changed the subject partially. "Your friend Miss Dolan isn't here," he added.

"Oh, isn't she?" Emma, tried to sound surprised.

"I thought maybe you might have run across her in Denver. I told her where you were staying."

"I didn't stay at the Brown. It was raining, and I got out of a taxi on the other side of the street and stayed there." Emma tried not to sound triumphant. So he thought he had known where she was, had he? At least she had crossed him up to that extent. But Mr. Weatherbee's next remark made her wish she hadn't been so previous.

"You don't think she's run out on us?"

"Good heavens, no. She—she'll be back for the performance. Why, singing this lead is more to her than life . . . ." That didn't sound good to Emma, and she started again: "She'll be back; she wouldn't do anything to jeopardize her career."

"No," said Mr. Weatherbee. "She'd try to protect that."

His inversion of her words annoyed Emma, and she flashed out at him: "You make me tired: You're always trying to drag Mary into this. She was in Denver last night. You said so yourself," she put in quickly. "She hasn't anything to do with this. Why, I don't know that she ever saw this professor."

"Did you?"

"No."

"She was with you? Yesterday afternoon?"

"She was with me in the hall when Aggie brought up the tray." Emma stopped short. It had no connection, absolutely none, but she had just remembered that Mary had gone back upstairs alone.

"Ah yes," Mr. Weatherbee countered, "but just a minute ago you were saying that he might have been dead then. Were you with her before that?"

"You're being perfectly ridiculous." Emma was angry and upset. Upset because she was remembering Mary's words: "Quite all right . . . . There isn't the slightest danger . . . ." and angry with herself for defending Mary, the Mary who had thought Emma safe at the Brown. But there it was; you couldn't let your friends down, no matter what they did to you.

"Your granddaughter was up here last night," said Emma. "And you admitted you were right in the house."

"Here we go again," said Mr. Weatherbee affably. "Maybe we'd see more if we stopped trying to cover up for our relatives and friends. Sort of declare a truce, eh?"

"You brought it up," said Emma shortly. He needn't think he could pull the wool over her eyes. He'd find out when the FBI men got there. Emma sighed, remembering that the professor was dead and that Mr. Weatherbee would disclaim all knowledge of the radio station.

"I'd hoped"—Mr. Weatherbee's voice was bland—"that you could alibi each other."

He said it as Dominic and the sheriff came down the walk, and all Emma could do was glare at him.

Dominic said hello to Emma and asked her what she knew about this. Emma answered his questions. She had seen and heard Aggie in the hall, but she had not heard the professor. Dominic asked her about the tray, and Emma described it, but he did not ask her if Mary had gone back upstairs.

" 'S a funny thing. None of 'em in there know anything about that tray after it was left in the hall. If it wasn't for that tray I'd think he died from an overdose of one of these here." He pointed to a pasteboard box full of medicine bottles, large and small, that the sheriff carried.

"He took this," said Mr. Faber, "before meals, for his stomick. And this after meals, also for his stomick. There's something for his throat, and headache powders and eyedrops, and even Mrs. Danforth don't know what the rest of them are for. He was a sick man if he took half of it."

Emma looked at the bottles; there'd be one there, she was sure, with the same stuff that they'd find in the professor's stomach, if they bothered to look.

"If it wasn't for that danged tray," Dominic repeated, "I'd say he got mixed up and drank the eyedrops and let it go at that."

Yes, Emma wondered, if the professor had been poisoned from his own medicine shelf, why had Mr. Weatherbee done away with the tray? Why the tray and the plate and the glass? He should have at least left the glass with the professor's fingerprints. Taking everything made even Dominic suspicious, though Emma supposed Mr. Weatherbee could handle him. He didn't ordinarily make mistakes. She supposed he was getting caught in his own coils, being forced to work faster because of her trip to Denver and the danger of being discovered.

But Mr. Weatherbee didn't know why she had gone to Denver. Or did he? He had caught her hunting through the front of the phone book, and she obviously wasn't reporting a fire. She had said she wasn't calling long distance, but he had sent her to Denver and had set Chew to watch her. Chew, the soft-footed Oriental. Emma purposely ignored the fact that Chew wore sturdy black shoes and clumped when he walked and would have been very conspicuous in any of the places to which Strike had taken her. Chew had warned his master of what Emma was doing, and Mr. Weatherbee had hastened to call on Mrs. Danforth. Whoa! The professor was already dead before Emma had made up her mind to go to Denver; that wouldn't wash. But they didn't really know when the professor had died. Of course Mr. Weatherbee had jumped at her suspicion that the professor was dead when Aggie brought the tray! He wasn't, and he hadn't died from eating anything on the tray. The removal of the tray was merely to throw suspicion on Aggie or Mrs. Danforth. If the professor and Mr. Weatherbee had been in the radio deal together they had probably talked together before, casually, not to arouse Mrs. Danforth's suspicions. And last night Mr. Weatherbee had called, not to see Mrs. Danforth, but the professor. Though Mrs. Danforth, for a consideration, would say that he had called on her.

Emma felt sorry for Mrs. Danforth, who would certainly be an unwilling party to any such transaction, but while she was being sorry she was wondering if she could get a connected story out of Aggie. Aggie might have heard or seen something that her addled mind would think unimportant.

"Just how crazy is that other one?" Dominic was asking.

Mr. Weatherbee shrugged. "She's been like that for years."

Mr. Faber nodded.

"I was getting at"—Dominic was doggedly pursuing an idea—"old maids get funny notions; you don't suppose she poisoned him?"

Mr. Weatherbee moved restlessly, got to his feet, and peered down the street. "I sent that heathen for some beer. Who, Aggie?" He turned back to Dominic. "You'll know better after the autopsy and the report on that assorted painkiller, and you better get going." As Dominic and Mr. Faber acted on the suggestion Mr. Weatherbee followed them to the car, saying something that Emma could not catch. As Dominic listened his hand moved upward to his throat and then downward from the ear.

He'd attend to it. He'd attend to everything. The body would be out of the way before the matinee. Everything would be all right.

And how! Emma thought, but she had to admit that Mr. Weatherbee was sporting. It would have been so easy to throw the blame on poor Aggie. Mr. Weatherbee played a game that was definitely not cricket, but he played himself and took his chances. She could not recall that she had ever heard him cast so much as a thread of suspicion on anyone. Except Mary. And Emma half thought that he did that just to keep her riled up when she got her nose too far into his business.

Chew came panting up the hill with the story of having dropped a bottle and been forced to make another trip.

"You lie," said Mr. Weatherbee. "You didn't want me drinking in front of the cops."

Chew grinned and retired to the car.

"To your health," said Mr. Weatherbee.

"To yours," said Emma, because one had to be polite and because there was something about the old rogue that made her want to like him, if only he wasn't mixed up in this business of sabotage. Emma told herself that murder was bad enough, and sabotage was much worse, but she drank the beer anyway.

"You going to move," Mr. Weatherbee asked, "or you going to stay put?"

It took Emma a couple of winks to realize that he was referring to Mrs. Danforth's and not to her seat on the curbing. It hadn't occurred to Emma to move. Mrs. Danforth's house was where things were happening, and right in the middle of that was where Emma wanted to be; however:

"I shall stay," she said primly, "as long as Mary does."

"Um," said Mr. Weatherbee. Then: "You know shorthand and typing?"

"Mercy, no!" Emma spoke rather more forcefully than was necessary because the question was unexpected.

Mr. Weatherbee was apologetic. "I hope you don't mind my asking. I got the idea you was secretary to some feller."

"I am," said Emma. "But I don't." She was saved the need of explaining that being secretary to Jeff Graham involved many complicated duties, but not necessarily a knowledge of shorthand, by the approach of Mrs. Danforth. She moved toward them smoothly, elegantly, but her face was distressed.

Emma stood up, and Mrs. Danforth put her hand on Emma's arm.

"I'm very glad that you weren't here last night," she said. Then she turned to Mr. Weatherbee. "About the house," she asked, "what shall I do if anyone wants to see it?"

"Dominic close his room?"

Mrs. Danforth nodded.

"Oh, show 'em the downstairs; that's enough. You might get them," he added, "to hunt for the tray."

Mrs. Danforth's distress deepened.

"I can't understand it. I know Aggie took that tray up because I saw her go myself."

Mr. Weatherbee explained that Miss Marsh and Miss Dolan had also seen the tray. Mrs. Danforth looked at Emma, her speculation the more apparent because she said it at once:

"And I saw you go out." Then after a moment's pause. "I know Aggie is peculiar sometimes, but you don't think—that policeman doesn't think—that she did it?"

"No." Mr. Weatherbee spoke honestly. "I don't think Aggie did it."

A quick expression of relief crossed Mrs. Danforth's face, and then it was somber again. "So many things happen," she said wearily. "I don't suppose"—she did not look at Emma—"anyone will want to stay here now."

"I'm staying," said Emma, "and so is Miss Dolan." She'd see to it that Mary did. It was too late in the season for Mrs. Danforth to get any more roomers, but perhaps by next year the whole thing would be forgotten. Perhaps by next year the war would be over and tourists would come in their former numbers. Emma knew quite a lot of people that she thought ought to be interested in the Festival; she started compiling a list of those to whom she would recommend Mrs. Danforth's.

Alvarado came puffing up the street. "The train is in," he shouted between puffs, "and Sauer—is—not here—and Miss Pinzi. Where is she?"

"Keep your shirt on," Mr. Weatherbee advised him. "I don't know about Sauer, but I saw Miss Dolan—Pinzi—go in the house a spell ago."

Sneaking, Emma thought, up the back steps to avoid them.

Alvarado shook his fist at the house and departed in search of Sauer. Where had *he* been? Emma wondered.

"Oh, dear," Mrs. Danforth sighed, "I better go tell her, unless—"

"I'm hungry." Emma ignored the suggestion. "I'm simply famished. I'll be at the hotel if anyone wants me."

With that she walked away. But not so fast that she failed to hear Mrs. Danforth's remark: "I wonder what it was that he wanted to see you about last night."

Tourists were spilling out over the town now, jolly and bright, quiet and staring. The old-time fiddlers that played for the square dancing were tuning up in front of the livery-stable door. The air was heady and sparkling, as it always was after a rain. Emma wished that she were a tourist with nothing to do but to enjoy the Festival.

Emma wondered if, by exposing Mr. Weatherbee, she would put an end to the festivals. She had heard that there would have been none this year if he had not agreed to underwrite any deficit. That would be characteristic of him: to go high-handedly ahead in the face of war and the shortage of transportation. Of course there was another side. There were the townpeople like Mrs. Danforth—utterly dependent on the tourist trade. The profits, if any, would go to Army and Navy Relief. And, Mr. Weatherbee's railroad made the use of gas and tires unnecessary. Oh, he'd done it very well—there was no doubt about that—in order to keep an eye on his radio station.

Reminding herself that Mr. Weatherbee wasn't exposed yet, Emma turned into the hotel and saw Shay talking to Susan Weatherbee.

"Hi, babe," Shay yelled. "Have a chair, have a drink."

"Thanks," said Emma coldly and walked on, followed by Shay's whistle of surprise.

Over a cold plate she considered her attitude toward Shay and Mary. She had hoped they would like one another and—well, obviously they did. She had wanted it, had thought it would be good for Mary, so what was she fussing about? Was she motivated by distaste for the assignation at the hotel, or was she more hurt by their attempt to keep the knowledge of it from her?

Wearily she decided that she had other things to worry about and dragged her mind back to Mr. Weatherbee. What had Mrs. Danforth meant by her remark: "I wonder what he wanted to see you about?" Who was "he"? Obviously the professor. Mr. Weatherbee had implied that a call on Mrs. Danforth was the object of his visit to her house. But her remark sounded as though the professor had sent for him and that Mrs. Danforth knew it. If Mr. Weatherbee and the professor were working together it would be perfectly natural for them to have a conference. Had Mr. Weatherbee gone upstairs and found him dead, or had Mr. Weatherbee killed him to keep him from revealing Mr. Weatherbee's connection with the station? But that presupposed that Mr. Weatherbee knew the purpose of Emma's trip to Denver.

Well, if it wasn't Mr. Weatherbee, who was it?

Mary? Mary might, by some, be said to have had a motive for murdering Horsack, but she had none for murdering the professor. Unless he knew that she had murdered Horsack. If Mary had found out about the radio station she would have gone to the police.

Susan Weatherbee? That was hardly likely. She had had a kid's yen for Horsack and was always underfoot, but having Mr. Weatherbee for a grandfather seemed to be the worst there was against her.

Robert Sauer? Here Emma paused. Sauer had kept pretty much in the background, but Emma wasn't sure he should be skipped over lightly. He was a German. An Austrian, Mary said. Horsack had been trying to reach the FBI. She had assumed it was to denounce Mr. Weatherbee and the professor, but might he not have intended to include Sauer? Sauer obviously hated Horsack, and it might have been for more reasons than the one of professional jealousy. And Mr. Weatherbee had said that Sauer was off stage at the probable time of Horsack's death. She had seen Mr. Weatherbee talking with Sauer.

Mrs. Danforth? Two men had died in her house, but she had no apparent motive for killing either of them and she had been convoying a party of tourists when Horsack was killed. She had refused Horsack a room, but that seemed to have been in anticipation of moral turpitude. She was of Bavarian descent, and so was the professor. That was a flimsy connection but pointed to friendliness rather than murder. In fact, the blackest mark against Mrs. Danforth came from her knowledge that Mr. Weatherbee had intended to call on the professor. Had she gone up and rapped on his door? Called, as Aggie had done earlier, and assumed that he was asleep because he did not answer? Or had Mr. Weatherbee gone up, done his wicked deed, and finished off the evening by having a polite chat with Mrs. Danforth?

Always, whichever person Emma thought about, they all seemed to have some connection with Mr. Weatherbee.

All but Aggie.

Emma had left Aggie for the last because it didn't seem sporting to bring in the mentally deficient. Emma realized that the reason she was not sitting quietly back, minding her own business and waiting for the FBI, was that she enjoyed pitting her wits against Mr. Weatherbee's. Emma had always played a modest second fiddle to Hank's virtuoso conducting, but right at this point, as her spoon sank into her chocolate sundae, she knew that she had always thought that she could do as well herself. Hank and Jeff had always tried to protect her, to keep her in a safe woman's place, but that wasn't where she wanted to be. She loved the smoke of mental battle, and if the best battlefields seemed to be littered with a few corpses—well, that was deplorable, but that was where the fun was.

Emma reproved herself for unladylike tastes but went right on to decide that if she could outguess and outmaneuver Mr. Weatherbee she would have done something of which even Hank would be proud. And into her feud with Mr. Weatherbee which was waged in a rarefied atmosphere, not unlike the realms of higher mathematics, Emma hated to inject Aggie's unreasoning mentality. Playing against Mr. Weatherbee was sport; Aggie was a subject for doctors and psychiatrists.

But, Emma sadly admitted, her attitude was wrong. Murder was not a game; it was an antisocial act, and the perpetrator should be brought to justice as soon as possible. She proceeded with the case against Aggie.

Old maids, as Dominic, in the fullness of his wisdom, had stated, sometimes got funny notions. Mary had jokingly said Aggie had a crush on Horsack. If she found out that Horsack had been making fun of her, might she not kill him? Might she not kill him anyway on the old no-one-else-shall-have-him theme? Aggie was supposed to have been picking flowers while Mrs. Danforth was showing the house, but Mr. Weatherbee had found a piece of her crayon under Horsack's body.

And the professor? He lived in the house; he was ailing; her thwarted maternal instincts would lead her to love the professor, and Aggie, most of all, had had access to the professor's tray. Except for the lack of connection with the radio station, Emma had to admit that Aggie was the best suspect, next to Mr. Weatherbee, of course. But Emma remembered the drawing with the flashes playing about the professor's head. If Aggie had found out about the professor's nefarious occupation, her faint, distorted brain might have told her that it was her patriotic duty to kill him. It might have; who could say? That was the trouble with the mentally unbalanced: one couldn't tell how far they confused real and unreal motives.

The only good thing about Aggie, viewed as a suspect, was that Mr. Weatherbee was being a little cozy about her. He had said nothing to Dominic about the piece of brown crayon, and he had assured Mrs. Danforth that he didn't think Aggie was guilty. Did those two things add up to the same? Or did they cancel each other?

If Mr. Weatherbee had thought the crayon of no importance, why had he given it to her? There was an easy answer to that: throw the seal a fish; give her some beads to string; keep her idle hands harmlessly busy. That was O.K. if Mr. Weatherbee really knew Aggie was innocent, but Mr. Weatherbee was just as smart as she was—perhaps, Emma conceded magnanimously, more so—and he could not fail to see the case against Aggie, even though he might not want to turn her in.

That was it! Mr. Weatherbee, being bound to the Estises by the ties of long acquaintance and financial relations, did not wish to be the one to point the finger at Aggie. He didn't think she had done it, oh no! But he was perfectly willing for Emma to be the finger man. He would give Emma the crayon, point out that Aggie had carried the tray, and let Emma bear the local unpopularity of having convicted a poor, half-witted creature. Such a trick would be exactly like Mr. Weatherbee, the more so if he himself were guilty! The enormity of Mr. Weatherbee's perfidy made Emma's eyes open wide, wide enough to see Shay standing in the doorway, beckoning her.

Emma got up because she had paid her check and there was no excuse to linger; she tried to pass Shay in the doorway, but he blocked her way.

"I want to talk to you."

"Well?" Emma was polite but haughty.

"Not here." Shay took her by the arm and led her out into the garden. "What's eating you? Are you stuffy just because I made a pass at one of your friends? For God's sake, you know I always do that; you know it doesn't mean anything."

So, Emma thought, he admitted it. Why did people do things that didn't mean anything? How did Shay know that it hadn't meant anything to Mary? Her voice hadn't sounded that way.

"I am quite aware," said Emma, "that my friend's morals are none of my concern." Her tone implied the opposite.

"Morals!" Shay's voice was faintly startled but amused. "What's that got to do with it?"

"We won't discuss it. What did you want to talk to me about?"

"I think you ought to move." Shay spoke bluntly. "I'll go even farther. I think you ought to get out of town."

"And why, pray?"

Shay rumpled his hair. "None of my business, eh? You forget that it's my business to look after you. Not that I want to, God I knows, if you're going to act like an old-maid aunt, but because I said I would. Rumor hath it that the professor died in his bed, and it seems to me that that house ain't healthy."

"So that's the story he's spreading." Emma was thinking out loud. "Where did you hear that?"

"I hear a lot of things in my little eyrie among the bottles, things that would surprise you, or maybe they wouldn't."

Shay had guessed right; Emma's curiosity was stronger than her scruples. "What things?" she asked.

"Oh, so you want to make friends. Well, come down off your high horse and say please. Pretty please?"

Emma wavered and gave in. "Oh, Shay," she said, "I don't care what you and Mary do; it was your sneaking off without telling me."

Shay did not change his expression. "Well?"

"Well, it's none of my business. Skip it. What do you know?"

The character of what Shay had been going to say had changed profoundly in the last few seconds. He had been going to tell Emma to warn Mary to lie low, that her public attitude of indifference to Horsack's death did not look well coupled with the ugly rumors that were coming from backstage. The story that she had been in Horsack's room immediately after his death had wider circulation than Mr. Weatherbee thought. It was repeated that she had thrown Horsack over for a bigger fish; it was whispered, not too quietly, that she had killed him because he stood in her way. Mary was on the way up professionally, and such stories might have no surer foundation than jealousy; that her name had been coupled with Mr. Weatherbee's, Sauer's, Alvarado's, and his own showed the uncertainty as well as the scope of the stories. Shay was flattered that he was included in the list, but if Emma thought that he had been sneaking off with Mary, to use her own words, that story might well have come from Mary, and he felt the need of a conference with that lady herself. Shay was willing to be the fall guy but only if he could share in the profits. Mary wasn't a bad little piece, but whatever she and he were supposed to have done had upset Emma. Mary needed Emma's loyalty and defense, whether she thought so or not. Shay would tell her about that. And, he ventured to guess, would get kicked for his pains. She-stock, in Shay's mind, were notoriously inconsistent and unreliable.

But he had to tell Emma something.

"The professor," he began, "is something of an enigma, or puzzle, to the local boys."

Emma managed to conceal her smile of superiority.

"There are those as claim he was dumb, meaning dumb, but a certain member of the Weatherbee tribe says she caught him talking Chinese to Chew."

"She"—Emma couldn't resist the dig—"being thoroughly conversant with Chinese?"

"She majored in it at Ann Arbor," Shay lied profoundly to save the point. "Anyhow, he could talk, but apparently he didn't choose to."

"I'm thinking of giving it up myself," Emma declared. "It only leads to misunderstanding."

"May I live to see the day," Shay said piously. "Look here, do you want the dirt or not?"

"So far it ain't been pay dirt," Emma snapped back in the local idiom.

"Little grains of sand," Shay compiled, "make the mountains as well as the molehills. Don't you want the pieces? I'm Old Dog Tray, bringing you the parts to put together. Or"—Shay threw out another piece of bait—"can I tell Hank that you've ceased to play the lady sleuth?"

"Phooey," said Emma. "Go on, though it's only habit that makes me interested."

"Well"—Shay settled himself comfortably on a bench, leaving a corner for Emma—"the professor has died, but nobody seems to know what of." He was having a hard time making copy out of the professor, when what he had come to talk about was Mary. "What could a guy have, besides laryngitis, that would keep him from talking?"

"A foreign accent." Emma spoke without thinking, or rather because she was thinking about the professor and reminding herself that Strike had warned her not to tell what she knew.

Shay hitched himself around to look at her. "Now why, I wonder, did you say that?"

"Cancer"—Emma recovered quickly—"of the throat."

"Possible."

"Mm. If he did have cancer, that might account for his taking poison."

"Poison? Who said anything about poison? Maybe you better tell me what you know."

"Nothing." Emma was enjoying herself. "That's one way to die, isn't it?"

"Do you want Daddy to shake you until your little teeth rattle?"

Emma giggled because it was fun to be friends with Shay again. Surely, she thought, it could do no harm to tell him the gist of her speculation with Mr. Weatherbee. She had also thought up a job of legwork for Shay. She was beginning to realize the necessity for legwork. Hank seemed to be able to solve his murders from a recumbent position, but that was only because he had Donovan and a highly trained city police force checking details of times and alibis. Emma could have used several men right at that moment: one to tail Mr. Weatherbee, one to watch the mine shaft, one to do spadework among the opera company, as well as one for the job she had in mind for Shay. She reminded herself that she was only an amateur and very likely to make mistakes.

"Give," Shay demanded.

"Last night," Emma began, "Mr. Weatherbee said he called on Mrs. Danforth. But I heard Mrs. Danforth ask him what he supposed the professor wanted to see him about. No." Emma tried to be accurate. "What she said was, 'I wonder what he wanted to see you about.'

"Which might mean that Mr. Weatherbee didn't see him, or"—Emma wriggled her brows as another thought came to her—"if he did, that Mrs. Danforth was fishing to find out what about."

"Or," Shay put in, " 'he' may refer to two other people."

"And this morning"—Emma ignored him—"Mr. Weatherbee just happened to be standing in front of the house and he heard Aggie's scream. . . ."
She went on to narrate Mr. Weatherbee's timely, if suspicious, doings.

"Now note carefully," she pointed out. "On the face of it, the only curious thing about the professor's death was the absence of the tray . . . . But Mr. Weatherbee jumped at once to the conclusion that he had been poisoned. I caught him up on that, and he gave me a lot of hocus-pocus about the body being relaxed when it ought to have been stiff, and how would he know that, when nobody knows when he was poisoned, if he was?"

"I follow you," said Shay, "with difficulty. At least I get the idea that you think the old gent has his foot in it well above the knee. Have you whipped up any reason why he had so suddenly to give the professor the permanent hot foot?"

"There"—Emma avoided a direct answer—"is where you come in. You take the pictures you took and see if you can find out whether or not Mr. Weatherbee actually saw the professor. Aggie will be your best bet for information, but I better warn you that she will probably fall in love with you and may try to finish you off. Because if it wasn't for Mr. Weatherbee, I'd think she killed Horsack and the professor."

Here Emma gave in detail the case against Aggie. "You may find out," she wound up, "that she did it, but I hope you don't."

Shay looked profound. "I think I get it. I go to Mrs. Danforth and say, 'Madam, here is a picture of the front parlor.' If she says, 'Get out of my house,' we assume that the professor was slain by Mr. Weatherbee before he could blow up the opera house. If she says, 'I'll take a dozen and one of the crayon enlargements,' why, it's apparent to the simplest mind that Aggie killed him. The only flaw in the flue is that the negatives haven't been developed."

"Send them in to Denver; send them to the newspaper; you ought to have some kind of a drag there. And don't be an idiot. Talk to Mrs. Danforth the way you do to Mary or Susan Weatherbee—and you are sure to find out something."

"And suppose I refuse"—Shay was serious—"suppose I refuse to print the pictures or to do your snooping; will you drop this business and go home or at least drop it?'"

Emma shook her head.

Shay grinned at her. "I didn't think you would.

"But consider carefully"—he was serious again—"it could be that you'd get your fingers burnt, that you'll find out something you'll wish you didn't know. Will that cure you of trying to run Hank's business as well as Jeff's?"

He couldn't be talking about Mary, Emma thought; she hadn't told him about Mary's trip back upstairs, and he must think he could alibi Mary from the opera on. And when Mary had said: "There isn't any danger," she had referred to a possible discovery of her rendezvous with Shay. Mary's trip back upstairs the night of the professor's murder had been for a handkerchief, lipstick, or some forgotten object. That was the way it was. The way it had to be.

"I'll take a chance," she said.

Shay didn't have any problem; he wanted to get to Mary as quickly as possible.

After Shay had departed, presumably to attend to his pictures, Emma's conscience gave her a faint poke. She was reasonably certain that she was sending him on a wild-goose chase, because when the FBI men came it would be all over but the shouting. They wouldn't need the professor to prove that Mr. Weatherbee was involved; they were smarter than she was. That was one way to look at it. That was the way Emma looked at it for possibly ten minutes; then she considered how silly she'd look pitting her word against Mr. Weatherbee's; then she got to thinking about Aggie. Her mind went uneasily from corner to corner of the triangle.

Mr. Weatherbee's motives were rational; Aggie's were irrational—but not to Aggie. Which was more important: motive or evidence? One could conceal a motive; she thought guiltily of the piece of crayon and the paper in her bag and conceded that one could conceal evidence also. That was nothing; Mr. Weatherbee probably bulged with concealed evidence. She wondered what the autopsy would show; she wondered when Mr. Strike would appear.

She continued to wonder.

CHAPTER EIGHT

SHE WAS WONDERING if she should go back and see Mary, when Mr. Weatherbee's black car shot past, with Chew grinning on the front seat and Susan and Shay laughing merrily in the rear. Emma didn't laugh; she didn't turn back toward Mrs. Danforth's; she kept on going down the street, wishing she had never spoken to Shay. The man obviously had no sense of decency. He was a wolf in tweed clothing; he was pretending to run with the hare, but actually he was hunting with the Weatherbees. It wasn't necessary personally to escort his films to Denver; he could have sent them by Chew. Emma positively stomped past Mr. Faber's office, past the Mercantile Supply and Dry Goods Company, past three boarded-up buildings, and turned the corner onto the street that approached the railroad station. She could see Engine Number 6 standing there, being oiled, greased, and put together with baling wire for the return trip. It was a wonder it didn't jump the track and land its trusting passengers in the creek. But no. Mr. Weatherbee's luck was too good for that. The Midas touch. Gold is where you find it. Gold in them thar hills—or was it bears? Golden-voiced: that had been Caruso. Another tenor.

A dingy sign in front of her read "Antiques," and Emma went in because she was sick of gold and tenors and faithless men in general and Shay in particular. Emma might not have been born with a Paul Revere spoon in her mouth, but she had worked for Jeff Graham for so long that an antique shop was practically home to her. And, Jeff being the man that he was, his name was, from coast to coast, an open sesame to recognition, welcome, and reminiscence.

The interior of this shop was as dingy as its sign, and there was little enough in its collection of ironstone china, early Woolworth, and bentwood chairs to justify the name antiques. Either the Denver dealers had taken the cream or there were few establishments in Central City that had boasted even the Dresden and black-walnut elegance of Mrs. Danforth's.

Two drab-looking women broke off their conversation as Emma came in, but not before Emma had heard: ". . . always was too big for her boots."

The women looked Emma over with open curiosity; then the smaller one picked up her bundle and went out. The other woman, as broad as she was drab, leaned dejectedly on the battered glass showcase.

"I ain't got no barbed wire or branding irons," she announced wearily.

"Well," said Emma bluntly, "if that's what people want, why don't you get some?"

The woman stared at Emma and then came out from behind her barricade to point to row upon row of assay cups that lined one wall. "Looka there," she said. "Two summers ago they come up here a-wanting them things, and I didn't have any. During the winter I bought up all I could find, and now nobody wants them. Ain't nobody up here got branding irons anyway. This ain't cow country."

"It's mining country," said Emma, racking her brain to think of something miners used besides picks. "Have a lot of things the miners used."

The woman sniffed and picked a battered tin mining lamp from a basket of junk. "They say they're too small."

The lamp was small, too small to use alone, but Emma could imagine Jeff recommending a row of them behind a bar or over a sofa in a game room. The woman had no imagination, no ingenuity; she would never be anything but a lap or two behind the fickle taste of the buying public. She said, only with the hope of keeping the conversation going: "The houses around here—some of the families had nice things."

The woman looked at Emma pityingly. "Them as got 'em hangs onto 'em, mostly." She looked Emma over carefully, as though trying to estimate the cost of the gingham dress, the square-toed shoes. "You interested in silver?" she asked diffidently.

"Mm," said Emma casually, fingering a plush album for all she was worth. "Solid silver?"

"It ain't marked," said the woman; "they didn't mark things sterling in them days." She made no move.

"That's right," Emma flattered encouragingly. "What is it? A bowl? A pitcher?"

"A tea set," the woman conceded grudgingly. "A child's tea set."

It could be anything, Emma thought, or again it could be something special, something that would take the taste of this trip out of her mouth and make Jeff forgive her prolonged absence. If she could ever get Old Lady Inertia to show it to her.

"She wants—I'm supposed to get a hundred dollars' for it."

The old stock price. Anything that was antique was worth a hundred dollars. "Cash?" Emma asked. That ought to fetch her.

"You'll have to come back here."

The woman led the way behind a golden-oak china closet, opened a drawer of a roll-top desk, and produced a faded leather case. "It's kinda queer," she said, pressing the catch.

Emma choked down an "Ah" of delight and stretched out her hand to touch, for there on dim green velvet rested three silver donkeys, the tallest no more than five inches in height; the smallest, two. The workmanship was good, robust rather than delicate, but the detail was there, from feathered hocks to bits of rope. The teapot donkey, the biggest one, arched his neck and swung his tail. His packsaddle was hinged and tilted back; the one on the sugar bowl lifted off, but Emma laughed out loud at the cream pitcher. That donkey was stubbornly reared back, ears flattened, mouth open, functionally to yield cream, but realistically in the manner of donkeys resistant to whatever use was being made of them. She looked for marks. There were none, but the silver was smooth and soft and solid. Jeff would love it; anyone would. A child would utter squeals of delight, though it would be a fortunate child on whom such a gift would be lavished.

"I can use it," said Emma.

The woman stared at her incredulously. "You mean you're going to buy it?"

"Sure." Emma felt inclined to be jovial now. "Why not?"

The woman shut the case quickly. "I never thought anyone would."

She hesitated, and Emma opened her bag, knowing that the sight of money sometimes ended argument. Still the woman seemed to hesitate.

"You got to promise," she said finally, "not to say you bought this. Particularly not up where you're staying."

It was the first hint Emma had had that the woman knew her, but it wasn't surprising, because Central City was a very small town. And it wasn't surprising that Mrs. Danforth should be selling her things or that she shouldn't want anyone to know of it.

Emma got out her money. "Wrap it up in a newspaper," she said. "I won't tell a soul."

She left the shop feeling very pleased with herself, glad that she had found something in an unlikely place and happy that she had lightened Mrs. Danforth's load temporarily. It was her general feeling of good fellowship, as well as the satisfied one of having done something smart, that made her pause in the door of Mr. Faber's office. She smiled tolerantly at the row of little bags on the counter. She knew what they contained now.

Mr. Faber was tilted back in his dusty chair.

"Come in," he called jovially. "Got something there you want disposed of?"

"Just a couple of odd bones," said Emma. "Nothing I can't handle myself."

Mr. Faber slapped his thigh. "That 'Loss, he's a card. Have a chair. Have a drink?"

"No, thank you." Emma remembered the nature of Mr. Faber's spirits, but she sat down, resting her bundle on her knees. "Have you heard anything more about the professor?"

Mr. Faber shook his head. "Waiting for a call now."

Mr. Faber seemed open and frank, at least by comparison with Mr. Weatherbee, and Emma struck out boldly. "How did he happen to come up here in the first place?"

Mr. Faber scratched his head. "I don't rightly know. He was always going around with his little hammer, chipping rocks, and we got plenty of that here to chip. He looked kinda sickly; maybe he come for his health. Looks like we run out of that for him."

The telephone rang, and Mr. Faber got up to answer it.

"Yup," he said.

"Yup."

There was a pause.

"So?" said Mr. Faber, prefacing another pause.

"Yup."

He hung up and came back to his chair.

"Cancer," he said. "Cancer of the throat. Too bad."

"You mean—" Emma was incredulous. "Was that the call about the professor? You mean he died of cancer of the throat?"

"That's what he had."

"What about the poison?"

"Poison?" asked Mr. Faber, as though the word were new to him. "Poison?"

"Yes," spelled Emma, "p-o-i-s-o-n. What you were all so sure he died of this morning. Remember? Remember the box of medicine and Aggie and the tray? You were sure enough he was poisoned then. Mr. Weatherbee said so."

Mr. Faber hung his thumbs in the armholes of his vest and tilted back his chair.

"It just goes to show," he pronounced, "that it don't do to be too hasty."

Emma made a derisive sound, but Mr. Faber continued, unabashed

"Why, if he'd of been poisoned, we'd have to be looking around for whoever give it to him."

"Doesn't anybody," Emma burst in, "care when murder's done up here? Doesn't anyone respect the law at all? Don't you? You're the sheriff."

"Shucks—-Mr. Faber looked modest—"I ain't running for reelection this year."

Emma could find no words to express her outraged civic virtue.

"Or take it this way," Mr. Faber went on; "if he knew he had that there cancer, he might have taken poison himself, but he'd of died of the cancer anyway, and what's the use of mucking around in his insides to find out if he hurried up the job? I had a great-aunt die of cancer once; it ain't a way I'd want to go."

The argument was irrefutable, though it wasn't the same one they had started. Mr. Faber, Emma conceded, needed no lessons in sidestepping from Mr. Weatherbee.

"And so," she heard him say, "he dies of cancer, leastways until day after tomorrow."

"What?"

"Tomorrow night's the last night of the opery. Season's over, and God knows when we'll ever have another one."

Emma got it. After tomorrow night Mr. Weatherbee, his opera, and his station would be safe. Interfering tourists like herself would come no more. The cast would be disbanded, taking whatever they knew of Horsack's death to San Francisco, Chicago, New York. After tomorrow Central City would sink back to contemplation of its ghosts, not caring if a few new ones were added. Emma set her jaw. She had only a little better than twenty-four hours, but she'd do something. If only the FBI man would come! Perhaps he was there now, looking for her. Emma stood up. Maybe there was a call for her at Mrs. Danforth's.

Mr. Faber stood up too. "See you tomorrow night at the shindig."

"What?" Emma's thoughts were up the street.

"Party. Over in the livery stable." Mr. Faber did a nifty buck and wing. "Always have one to sort of celebrate the strike. Old folks, young folks, everybody comes."

A party! Emma thought that was the last straw. A party to celebrate two murders. She wasn't being exactly fair, Emma knew. Horsack's supposedly accidental death would mean little to the townspeople, and precious little more, she was willing to admit, to the cast of the opera company. The professor meant nothing to the cast and very little more to the town. Death had often been sudden in Central City, and in these days one lived with death. Emma's heart contracted. Death's dice did not need to be loaded; they were being rolled steadily. Let people dance while they could.

Emma nodded and hurried away.

CHAPTER NINE

EMMA entered the Estis Mansion by the front door. Mrs. Danforth or no Mrs. Danforth, she avoided the side entry whenever possible. This time only Aggie caught her. Aggie, in her artist's costume, was down on hands and knees peering into the dark recesses behind the hall tree. She started up as Emma came in, and one of her strings of beads caught on a protruding knob, a string of round red beads that hit the floor pop-pop-pop as they fell from the broken cord. Aggie began to cry.

"It's only me," said Emma. "Never mind, I'll help you pick them up."

Aggie cupped her hand, hoping to check the popping cascade, and sat whimpering as Emma felt along the edge of the rubber matting. The beads were easily found; they were red and smooth and shiny, just like Mary's. Emma pretended to hunt in a corner. They were so exactly like Mary's as to make it practically certain that they were Mary's. Probably that was why Aggie was crying; she had taken—well, say borrowed—Mary's beads and broken them.

"Here you are," she said. "You better string them and put them back."

Aggie nodded and leaned closer to Emma. "I'm making you a picture," she confided in a whisper, "but I can't find my brown crayon."

She ought to quit talking about that brown crayon. Emma's eyes went guiltily to her bag that she had put on the floor beside the newspaper-wrapped bundle. Aggie's eyes followed hers and bored into the parcel. Emma got quickly to her feet and picked up her belongings. This would never do; in a minute Aggie would be asking what it was. The parcel would have to be hidden somewhere, well hidden from Aggie's snooping eyes. She would be one of the ones Mrs. Danforth wouldn't want to know.

"You do me a picture"—Emma hastened down the hall—"without the brown crayon. I like your pictures."

She was part way up the stairs when the phone rang. It would be for her, of course, but she waited for Aggie, who had followed her to the bend of the hall, to answer it. Aggie, however, hung back. The phone rang again.

"Answer it." Emma spoke sharply.

But Aggie cringed away. "You," she said. "I don't like to go in there."

Emma rushed to the phone. Where was Mrs. Danforth? The crowd had been leaving the opera house as Emma passed; if they came here Mrs. Danforth ought to be on hand to show them around. Emma also wished Mrs. Danforth were there because it was giving her a creepy feeling to be alone with Aggie. Aggie, who had no more sense than to keep asking for her brown crayon and who wouldn't go into the entry where Horsack had been killed.

"Hello." Emma spoke rather breathlessly.

In a moment she was back. "Some woman from the Ladies' Aid"— she spoke carefully—"wants to know if Mrs. Danforth can make two dozen cookies for the party tomorrow night."

Aggie's eyes brightened. "The party!" she exclaimed.

"You won't forget to tell her?"

They both looked up because someone was coming downstairs. The dark woman with the mole, the one who had been snippy to Emma. She was still in costume.

"Miss Pinzi," she asked, "iss not in yet?"

She ought to know, Emma thought; she had just come from up-stairs. No wonder there were murders in this house, the way people went in and out.

"No," said Emma.

The woman flashed a white smile that was completely devoid of mirth. Secret Agent 97.

Emma told herself that she had been seeing too many movies. The woman looked exceedingly sinister, but she had probably come to bor-row a spool of thread. In this day and age spies didn't look like spies.

Mrs. Danforth came in the front door; the dark woman went out; Aggie went toward the kitchen, and Emma fled upstairs, her bundle hidden un-der her coat.

Past the professor's door, tight-closed; past Mary's, partly open; to her own, which was locked. Fumbling with her key, she wondered why she bothered to use it. She could go in the way anyone else could, through Mary's room. A happy thought.

The room was bright when she got inside it. Bright and tidy, with a bowl of purple flowers on the dresser. Aggie's touch. Aggie had been there. Had she noticed that the copy of *Time* was gone? Emma looked at her pocketbook; she looked at her bundle. The copy of *Time* was gone all right! What had she done with it? She tried to remember what she had done with it when she had had it last. In order, she visualized herself in the car, talking to Mr. Weatherbee, eating lunch. She must have left it at the hotel; anyhow, it was gone, like the professor. She didn't have time to think about it now; she had to find a hiding place for the tea set before Mary came, or Aggie, bringing unneeded towels. The bureau drawers were no good; Aggie probably went through those. Not the commode, and not under the bed. Emma went to the tall wardrobe and pulled out a suitcase in which she packed the soiled clothes as they collected on the trip. It was a new bag with a set of keys still unused in the inside pocket. Luggage keys, Emma had found, never got lost if they weren't used, but she'd use these and take a chance.

She had the bag out and the lid raised, but she did not put the tea set in; she sat staring, gaping open-mouthed in astonishment, because there on her best slip lay the lost tray, the plate, and the glass straw. Only the tumbler was missing. No. It was tucked down in a corner. All the evidence was there, all complete and all washed clean.

Emma didn't need to ask herself who had put the articles there; it was Aggie, of course. Aggie had washed them but had been afraid that wasn't enough. Aggie hadn't meant them for a plant; she was just trying to hide them, and but for the purchase of the tea set the bag might have gone on to Boston unopened. That was one of the breaks that one hoped and prayed for. Only, in their washed condition, the tray and the plate and the glass were something in the nature of white elephants. They were no good unless they were tested for traces of poison and fingerprints, and Aggie might be crazy, but Emma didn't think that she had left either. Furthermore and besides, Emma could not remove the bag without giving away the fact that she had discovered its contents. Aggie had her neatly by the heels unless she was ready for a showdown, and Emma wasn't—not quite yet. What would a clean tray prove? Not even that Aggie had hidden it.

Emma peered at the tray. It was spotless; so was the plate. But the glass sipper was another matter. Aggie had slipped up there; there were particles of moisture still on its hollow interior, and even though it had been rinsed, there might be particles of something else. Of course the professor might have drunk directly from the glass, but the fact that the straw was there at all seemed to indicate that he habitually used it. Some people took medicine that way. Emma got up, took a clean handkerchief from a drawer, and carefully lifted the straw. Then she held it in her hand, wondering what to do with it. She had to get it to Denver somehow. She put it in her bag, protecting it as much as she could with the handkerchief, and heard steps outside in the hall.

Quickly, but not too quickly, not daring to waste time by a false movement, she took the key from inside the bag, added the tea set to the other contraband, and shut and locked it. She considered swallowing the keys but added them instead to the contents of her pocketbook. Even as she did so Mary called:

"Hello, stranger!"

"Hello," said Emma feebly.

Mary looked at the bag. "Going somewhere?" she asked with a hint of stiffness.

"Clothes," Emma explained, "dirty clothes that I was packing." She felt like the liar that she was, but she couldn't tell Mary what she knew about the professor, and she didn't want to give Aggie away just yet. There was plenty that Mary didn't tell her. The thought of that made her a little abrupt.

"Why didn't you tell me that the show closes tomorrow night?"

One of Mary's eyebrows shot up. "My dear girl," she said, "whether you realize it or not, I have hardly seen you for the last two days."

"I wasn't invited to the dinner, if you remember."

"You went tearing off to Denver—"

So did you, Emma thought, all her innate dislike of the implications of Mary's trip rising again within her.

"—not that it matters. I know you don't like opera, and I can understand your staying away from that, but I thought you came up here to see me."

"Fat chance I've had. Not being included—" Emma didn't mean the dinner to which she had not been invited; she meant Mary's trip to Denver, but Mary misunderstood.

"Why do you keep harping on that?"

They were glaring at each other now, and the silly part of it was, Emma knew, that they weren't really angry at what they were talking about. They had jumped each other because they both were guiltily aware that they had been holding out. The dinner was the least important of their troubles. Emma thought of all the horrible things they might say, the accusations they might make, and realized the quarrel had better stop right there.

Mary must have been thinking somewhat the same things, for the sparks faded from her eyes, and she sank down on the bed. "I've been a beast," she said, "to you and everybody—"

"No, you haven't." Emma was all contrition now. "I've been the one—"

"I had no excuse—"

"You did so . . . ."

Now they were as equally determined to take the blame as they had been previously to give it and, seeing their absurdity, they both laughed, closing the gap between them. Almost.

"It's a good thing"—Mary stretched her arms and fell back on the bed—"that tomorrow night is the end. If I had to keep on much longer I'd explode. Singers are a bunch of cats, male and female, and I'm no exception. Alvarado is so fidgety he's got us all on edge, and it may be my imagination, but the whole cast is acting as though I'd poisoned someone."

The words startled Emma. "Did Mrs. D. tell you about the professor?"

"Yes. Poor old thing. God rest his soul."

The regret was routine, impersonal. Mrs. Danforth must have been sparing of detail.

"He had cancer of the throat," Emma added.

"The saints preserve us!" Mary's hands went to her throat.

The idea would be horrifying to her, but what struck Emma particularly was that Mary's gesture was the same one Dominic had used that morning in the car.

"Mr. Weatherbee knew that," she said aloud. "He told them what to look for." And if they found cancer they wouldn't look for anything else. One could die of that. And Mr. Weatherbee's knowledge was another twist, binding him to the professor.

"What are you talking about?"

But if she had guessed right, the tube in her bag would show something else, something that would be in the professor's stomach. Then Mr. Weatherbee's tricks would be of no avail. Emma scowled. Was she proving a case against Mr. Weatherbee or Aggie?

Mary sat up and snapped her fingers under Emma's nose. "Come out of it."

"I have to go to Denver."

"You were just there. Darling, what are you up to? Please tell me."

It was no good to tell her, to upset her more, but she ought to warn Mary about Aggie. Aggie surely knew about Mary and Horsack, and she might transfer her pattern of hate to Mary.

"You ought to lock your door," she said. That would serve the double purpose of protecting the suitcase as well as Mary. "Aggie seems to be a touch light-fingered. She was wearing your beads this afternoon."

"Oh, that's all right." Mary looked down at the spread and picked at it. "Actually, I gave them to her."

It didn't sound like the truth. Why should Mary give anything to

Aggie? She barely noticed her existence. If she knew that Aggie had taken the beads, why was she protecting her? A bribe?

Emma crossed to the mirror and began to comb her hair. She had promised herself not to think things like that of Mary. She had plenty else to think of and so much to do.

Mary came over to the bureau and fiddled with the catch of the purse, sending cold chills up Emma's spine.

"I'll lock my door," she said, "if it'll make you happier, though it won't be necessary."

She seemed about to say something else, but Emma took the purse from her, pretended to hunt for something in it, and then put it safely on the commode while she washed her face.

Mary looked at her watch. "Good heavens, it's late. Let's go grab a bite."

As they entered the hotel Emma looked for Shay, but he was not in his accustomed place in the bar. Probably dining off the vine of the land in Denver, with Susan Weatherbee. But Susan was in the dining room, eating demurely with her grandparent. They all nodded politely. Shay might be up on the train, if he hadn't found a friend.

"He's a cute old character, isn't he?" Mary said.

Emma almost swallowed the menu. It wasn't the way she'd describe Mr. Weatherbee.

"And actually, my dear, the granddaughter is right nice. I was a fool to think what I did about her and Paul. And will you look at the front on that woman!"

Emma looked and said it was another case of nature imitating art.

Mary eyed the two remaining French fries on her plate and then deliberately ate them. "Paul liked skinny women," she said.

Mary must be well over her feeling for him, Emma thought; she talked about him casually now, not avoiding his name. Now was the time to ask questions. "You've never told me," she said casually, "what you meant in your letter about needing Hank professionally. Was it about that business of Horsack's? Whatever it was that he thought was dangerous?"

Mary glanced about quickly, at the Weatherbees, at the dark ugly woman at the bar.

"I was joking about Hank." She spoke lightly, but her eyes did not meet Emma's. "And I think he made it up, I mean, to sound important."

It had been important to Mary, too, Emma remembered, when Mary had thought Horsack had been murdered. Again she contemplated the idea of taking Mary into her confidence and then decided against it. If Mary wasn't giving, she'd be darned if she would either.

"Rho is an alien," Mary was saying. "He only has his first papers and he wants to enlist."

Rho? It took Emma a few seconds to make the connection, and then she thought it was remote. Who cared about Sauer, except as a suspect?

"I wish you'd come tonight." Mary sounded as though she meant it. "Rho is infinitely better than Paul ever was, and you've never heard him. And honestly I'm not so bad myself."

"Kid," said Emma, "you'll never be any better to me than you were when the glee club did *The Pirates of Penzance,* but I'll come."

They left the hotel together, seemingly at peace with the world and each other. Mary took her to the box office, got her a seat, and then hurried backstage.

Emma watched the orchestra seats fill gradually with people. Some of the audience, she noted, looked up at the blazing chandelier, stared at the murals and the names on the backs of the seats, chattering and pointing. Those were newcomers, strictly tourists. Others came in quietly, took their seats, studied their programs. Those had been there before; perhaps, conceivably, they liked opera. Finally, escorted by two ushers, Mr. Weatherbee and Susan entered. Emma scrunched down in her seat, glad when the Weatherbees were placed well up in front. The orchestra swung into the beer-drinking song; the house lights went out; the curtains rose, revealing the courtyard of the count's castle.

Emma woke with the old familiar start, jerked her head from the shoulder of the man in the next seat, and blushed furiously in the dark. It was positively disgusting that she couldn't stay awake at an opera. It showed a lack of intelligence, certainly a lack of character. She sat bolt upright, gritted her teeth, and gazed at the stage. Mary was not on. The chorus was doing some kind of dance. The Maypole scene. Round and round the dancers went, round and round and in and out, until their bright costumes blended together, mingled with the lights . . . . Round and round . . . .

Good heavens, she was dropping off again! Suppose she slept on and on, after the opera was over? Suppose she was locked in and missed the train for Denver? Emma clutched her bag—suppose she had dropped it?— and crept quietly from her seat.

The comparatively warm night made it simple for her to slip out the open doors onto the balcony. There she hesitated a few moments, deciding what to do until traintime. If she went to the hotel she might become involved in a group from which her departure would be noticed. Mr. Weatherbee would be sure to return to the hotel after the opera, and on this trip she wanted no help from Mr. Weatherbee or his Flying Tiger. The best thing to do was to go back to her room.

There was a light in the hall of the Estis Mansion and a light in the

dining room. As Emma passed the doorway she saw Mrs. Danforth bending over the register of her paying visitors and paused. Shay was in Denver, but she might pick up some information for herself.

"By the way," she said, "some woman telephoned and wanted two
dozen cookies for the party. Did Aggie tell you?"

Mrs. Danforth looked up from the register with a frown of annoyance. "No, she didn't tell me."

"I thought maybe she hadn't."

They exchanged commiserating glances.

"Two dozen cookies," Mrs. Danforth sighed. "Sugar."

"Well," Emma was sympathetic, "at least they don't have to be made
of rubber. Do you burn wood here in winter?"

"No, coal. It has to be trucked up and it's very expensive, but the
trees were all cut down long ago, for the mines. I have to close most of the
house and live in the kitchen."

The expression on her face was so revealingly distasteful that Emma
averted her own gaze, looked down at the register open before her, and
saw that there had been only two paying tourists that day. She wondered
if Mrs. Danforth knew that the tea set had been sold. She wanted to tell
her, to assure her that she would have that money, but knew that in so
doing she would hurt Mrs. Danforth's pride.

The register was a thick old ledger, encompassing several years. Mrs.
Danforth was turning back the pages, turning back to where more than a
page was necessary for a day's names.

"Oh, may I look?" asked Emma. "You must have some interesting
names, and I might find someone I know." It was vaguely in her mind that
some of the signatures might be valuable, though she doubted if she would
find Button Gwinett's.

"Why, certainly," said Mrs. Danforth. "I have the late President
Coolidge—no, he's in another book, but I think Spencer Tracy is in this
one. I'll go get it."

She left the room, and Emma stole a quick look at her watch. The
opera would be out at eleven; she had to get away before then, but there
was still plenty of time.

She turned back to the dear, dead days of 1940, when a majority of
citizens had exercised their inalienable right to go streaking across the
country at sixty m.p.h. You could argue the homely virtues of staying at
home, but it was for these wanderers that good roads had been built, paid
for, and, in many instances, by the tax on the gasoline that they used. It
was a fine thing to picnic in the back yard and get acquainted with the
neighbors, but it had also been good for the shop worker from Haverhill
to see the immensity of Boulder Dam and the equal immensity of the

Kansas wheat fields. The low-priced car had been the magic carpet of the little people, and it was wonderful and heartening to Emma that they had given up their ticket to adventure without a whimper.

Only people like Mr. Weatherbee still drove cars . . . .

People were not alike. Look at the slanting, upright, backhand signatures that persisted after years of struggle with the Palmer method.

People were just the same. There was one in every crowd that signed himself "Edgar A. Poe" or "Flash Gordon."

Mrs. Danforth had done pretty well in 1941 too. Thirty, forty sightseers at twenty-five cents a head, but this year ten had been a big day. Emma's eye was caught by a sprawling signature. Here was where Horsack had registered below Mary and had been denied a room. Moved by a sudden thought, she turned to the day of her arrival. It was a far cry, but it was just possible that among the names of that day might be a clue to Horsack's murder, might be the name of the murderer himself, if she was smart enough to recognize it. There was her own name, primly set down, and then a group, all from Denver. That would be the giggly bunch that had been leaving as she had come in.

"Mr. and Mrs. Hubert Fox, Margaret Lund," she read on down the list. They looked innocuous enough. Here was another scrawl: "David Albert, WBZM"; she recognized the call letters of a Denver station. David Albert was one to get his plug in.

There seemed to be nothing there. She turned another page as Mrs. Danforth returned, and then turned back to look again.

"Here they are," Mrs. Danforth was saying. "Mrs. Coolidge was a lovely woman."

"Yes indeed," said Emma, restraining a smile, because the late President's prim signature was very like her own. Which didn't mean a thing, any more than did the fact that Shay Horrigan and David Albert of WBZM had a similar angular scrawl. Horsack wrote that way too, though she would not embarrass Mrs. Danforth by going back to prove it. Shay and Horsack were left-handed; she could stop in tomorrow and check up on David Albert. If she wanted to be taken for crazy.

Mrs. Danforth was running her fingers lovingly down the long column of names. Emma realized that, aside from the money, they had represented the outside world to this woman who lived with the ghosts of a better past. Actually, for Aggie was no better than a ghost. Where was Aggie?

Where was Aggie? It was a refrain that kept coming back. Aggie or Mr. Weatherbee?

It was time for Emma to go.

"Things will be good again sometime," she said, because she had to say something.

"I am an old woman."

Time, for Mrs. Danforth, might not be long enough.

Emma picked up her bag. "See you tomorrow," she said hastily.

She stopped at the hotel for a magazine, but it was not until she had taken a seat in the waiting train that she realized that she had not asked Mrs. Danforth a word about Mr. Weatherbee's visit; she had been too busy being sorry for her. Glumly she began to read. She was reading when the train began its slide down the mountain, so she failed to notice that Mary and Sauer had slipped into the rear car.

CHAPTER TEN

EMMA left the sipper at the Mile-High Chemical Laboratories shortly after nine o'clock and was promised a report before noon. She felt that she should do something constructive with the intervening time, but what? The report would determine her future actions, but until she got it she was held in abeyance. She thought of trying to reach Mr. Strike, but there again the situation was the same. She had handed over the knowledge she possessed for him to use; she was waiting for him to act. And she wished he'd hurry up about it; it must be only in the movies that the FBI moved with lightning flash.

On the purely personal side, she didn't have time to get a wave; she didn't need a manicure, but she could, by golly, buy a hat.

She had walked half a block from the laboratory now, but the section seemed entirely given over to supplies for farming, mining, and ranching. In a window beside her a pretty girl was arranging a collection of serious-looking spurs on a Navajo saddle blanket. The girl was pretty. Emma walked in and asked her where she could buy a hat. The girl turned to a showcase filled with tremendous felt shapes: black, tan, brown, and white. They were, Emma realized, hats.

"Oh no," she exclaimed. "I meant a hat that you could wear."

The girl turned, half insulted; then she saw Emma's hands making gestures of smallness and laughed.

"Oh," she said, "you mean a hat."

Then they both laughed.

The girl gave a name and address that meant nothing to Emma, then took her to the door, pointed out a high tower, and counted the blocks and turns. The blocks were long, and there was no taxi in sight. Emma plodded along in the sun, wishing that her suit was not so heavy. Maybe she didn't need a hat; maybe the one she had was all right; it had always been a good hat.

Finally the store was reached and Emma read the directory in the elevator. Millinery was on the third floor, and Station WBZM was in the tower. Interesting, how radio stations always seemed to perch on the top of things.

Emma got off at the third floor, delivered herself over to a salesperson, and lit a cigarette.

It certainly was a coincidence, WBZM being right in the same building.

No, she didn't want anything dressy, and she didn't like light blue.

Mr. Albert probably wasn't in.

Amusing? Yes, Emma thought the concoction of violet bows being placed over her right eye certainly was.

It was only the middle of the morning; maybe he was.

"Look," said Emma, "I just want a hat to wear with a suit sort of like this one." She indicated her brown felt nestling dingily among the discards.

The salesperson said, "Oh," haughtily, and went away. She was gone a long time. Emma decided that she was making a hat or that she had gone down to the bargain basement. Emma felt that her old hat had been insulted; she put it on quickly and marched herself to the "Up" elevator.

Station WBZM did itself rather well. It was long and low and, modern. A woman in a blue dress rose from behind a chartreuse leather desk and said, "May I help you?"

"Mr. Albert?" Emma asked. "Will you tell him that Miss Marsh is here? Tell him WXOR." Emma had picked the biggest station she could think of and hoped that she gave the impression of being connected with it without having said so.

"Just a moment." The woman pressed a buzzer. "I will see if Mr. Albert is disengaged."

Emma refrained from asking if Mr. Albert did rope tricks or was only tangled up in red tape and swept into the granted interview as though she bore a contract from General Foods.

When the door, also leather-padded but this time in dark brown, closed behind her Emma was relieved to find that Mr. Albert was the man who, frolicking in the plaid jacket, had taken a picture of her on Mrs. Danforth's lawn only a few seconds before she had gone in the side entrance. He was a youngish man with hair receding only a little from his temples and a nice smile. He was smiling as he came forward.

"Didn't I take a picture of you?"

Emma nodded. "And I'm not from WXOR; I don't even listen to it." She had to get that misrepresentation off her mind.

"O.K. What are you selling? I'll buy it. Want to see the picture?"

He got a bunch of prints out of his desk, found the right one, and held it out, talking a rapid run of jargon of light and lenses and exposure that would have endeared him to Shay but which was lost on Emma. It was a good picture, though. Emma searched it carefully.

Beside her figure there were the corner of the piazza, the top of the steps that led up from the opera house, and the background of mountains. That was all.

"Keep it," said Mr. Albert, "if you want to."

"Thank you." Emma put it away in her bag. "Are you left-handed?"

"Yes. And I wear pajamas and like pancakes for breakfast. And if you're interviewing me you better sit down, because I like to talk about myself."

Emma sat down on a long leather couch that was so deep it put her at the disadvantage of having to look up and worry about her skirt at the same time.

"That," she began, "about your being left-handed really isn't important; it just slipped out. What I really wanted to know was, when you were going through that house, the Estis Mansion, did you see anything of another woman? A woman in a smock with a lot of beads? Sort of crazy-looking?"

Mr. Albert sat down on the corner of his desk. "No," he said gently. "Have you lost her?"

"I'm not," said Emma with some spirit, "crazy."

"No indeed," said Mr. Albert, reaching behind him toward a row of buttons. "No," he said conversationally. "I'll tell you just what we did in that house. We had some guests and we took them up to see the sights— the opera, you know, and so on. Only we didn't go to the opera; we'd stayed too long in the bar. I'm afraid we were a little noisy going through the house. Some of us were in the parlor when the good lady wanted to show us the dining room, but we didn't see anyone in beads or touch anything that we shouldn't."

Mr. Albert broke off at the sound of a knock on the door.

The woman in the blue dress said that Mr. Higgins was waiting.

"Thank you so much for coming." Mr. Albert spoke graciously to Emma. "I'm sorry that I'm so busy."

There was nothing for her to do but get up. The interruption was phony; she suspected that he had rung for help, thinking her at least a crank. But if he hadn't seen Aggie there was no point in staying longer, and he hadn't seen Aggie or he wouldn't think she was imaginary. As it was, Emma couldn't resist living up to her role. She picked up her bag, cradled it in her arms, arranging imaginary covers.

"Come on, honey," she crooned to a hypothetical infant. "Daddy's too busy to talk to us."

Let him try to explain that!

Aside from the fun of her little joke, all Emma had gained from Mr. Albert was the knowledge that Aggie had not been roving the premises at the time of Horsack's death. Or that he hadn't seen her.

Walking back to the laboratory, Emma decided that that was pretty small potatoes. But Aggie had been very much in evidence when the professor had died, and Emma was definitely cheered to learn that there was strychnine in the glass sipper, although in view of her recent experience, she was a little sensitive about the way the clerk looked at her when she asked:

"Enough to kill a pack rat?"

The clerk assured her that the concentration was strong enough to kill a horse.

Then Emma had a smart thought. She instructed the clerk to put the sipper and the report in a safe place and to keep them for her. From now on she had to tread carefully, and she didn't want to be hampered by the literal burden of proof. And she still had to show that there was strychnine in the professor.

How did one go about that? One didn't, she was sure, hop around to the police station and say: "Take another look at that there corpse." At least not in Mr. Weatherbee's own bailiwick, one didn't. It certainly made things difficult, this having the police against one. Now in Boston . . .

Still and all, it hadn't been a bad morning. Emma caught a bus back to the train and, walking through to find a seat, was only momentarily taken aback to find Mary and Robert Sauer sitting together and positively beaming. At least they were until Sauer caught sight of Emma, and then Sauer's face fell.

Mary certainly got around a lot, Emma thought, but she said: "Hello, folks, what's new?"

Mary glanced at Sauer, but Sauer shook his head. He offered Emma his seat, but she waved him aside and found one for herself farther forward.

The train was crowded, and Emma remembered that it was the gala day, the day of the shindig, as Mr. Faber put it. The last day. She would have to work fast, and, if it wasn't presumptuous of her to think it, Mr. Strike ought to be stirring himself too.

Mary and Sauer joined her as they got off the train. There were children on the platform selling war stamps which, they were told, would be legal tender for that day. Teenage girls in long dresses and bonnets were offering corsages of stamps.

Sauer bought a handful and made a bouquet for Mary. He was very gallant about it, and when he smiled, Emma had to admit, he

wasn't bad-looking. Then she reminded herself that she hadn't fully decided that he wasn't the murderer.

Cowgirls in soft, fringed leather outfits that had never seen a cow
rubbed elbows with them as they walked up the street. A group of men in
jeans and bandannas were draping the front of the livery stable with
bunting. If the personal decor smacked more of the rodeo than of mining
it made no difference to the spirit. It was as though the town, faced with
the last of the opera, perhaps for a long time, had determined to go down
with flags flying. Mr. Faber, his badge of office prominent on an unbut-
toned vest, patrolled the street on a pinto pony, his coat discarded, but his
gun peeping from an equally well-worn holster.

The spirit was contagious.

"Whoopee," said Mary. "I hope that pistol is covered with rust."

"Not pistol," Emma corrected her. "Gun, six-gun, or shooting iron.
At least that's what they're called in *True Westerns*."

Mr. Faber had ridden up to them, setting his pony neatly back on its
heels and drawing his gun. "Git into that store," he shouted, "and git a
costume. Everybody's supposed to be in costume. Not you"—he recognized Mary and Sauer "you can wear your show ones, but this here ten-
derfoot—"

His gun went off at Emma's feet, and she leaped into the air in a
manner that she had always imagined was another *True Western* exaggeration. The surrounding crowd roared with laughter; the pinto danced
and rolled a white eye. Mr. Faber was thoroughly enjoying himself, and
there seemed to be no rust on his gun.

The Great Mercantile Dry Goods and Supply Company was doing a
landoffice business in jeans, frontier pants, neckerchiefs, and bright-col-
ored shirts, all paid for in stamps. Mary took time to help Emma select her
regalia—reasonably well-fitting levis and an orange shirt that had to be
tried on in a crowded, curtained-off alcove—and Sauer shyly presented
her with a green scarf which said in red: "Ride 'em Cowboy!"

Mary and Sauer went to the opera house, and Emma, going to Mrs.
Danforth's to leave her city clothes, found her landlady wringing her hands.
There were tourists mobbing the parlor and a smell of burned cookies
coming from the kitchen.

"That Aggie—" Mrs. Danforth greeted her distractedly.

Where was Aggie?

Emma couldn't cook, but she took over the tourists, trying to give
them their money's worth. She showed them everything; what she couldn't
remember of Mrs. Danforth's spiel she made up, adding McKinley to
Grant as an overnight guest and seating famous names drawn at random
around banquets of local game and imported delicacies.

"Solid silver doorknobs," she assured them, "of ore from the Estis mines. And the treasures of Europe brought here by covered wagon."

It was a hectic afternoon. The sightseers became increasingly full of frolic and banter. They refused to proceed orderly; they met each other coming and going and insisted on taking each other back to view the elegancies of the gold room or to laugh at the pictures of dying fowl in the dining room. They wrote jokes in the register and pried into everything. They raided the kitchen and ate up the cookies, keeping Mrs. Danforth tied to the mixing bowl, but they left their twenty-five-cent stamps. One wag, to be sure, insisted on sticking his to the back of Emma's shirt. He seemed to have taken a fancy to Emma, for he made the tour over and over, prompting her if she missed a detail. Once she found him entertaining a new group with a solemn war dance, attired in the chief's bonnet from the side entry and brandishing the tomahawk. Horrified, Emma rescued the relics and put them back, the bonnet on its nail and the tomahawk by the entry door, quickly, before Mrs. Danforth should know. Emma couldn't keep track of them all; she had not seen the dark singer with the mole come in, but she saw her go out just before the five o'clock lull that marked the concentration at the hotel bar.

Emma helped Mrs. Danforth pack the cookies, ate some, and went upstairs to rest her feet.

From the hall, before she reached Mary's door, she heard the sound of sobbing. She had not seen Mary come in, but that was understandable; what was less so was the sight of Mary now, flung across her bed, crying with deep, heaving sobs.

"Angel . . ."

Mary had not heard Emma, and she sprang up at the sound of her voice, only to sink back again, her tears increasing. This time there was no hint, as there had been once before, of the theatrical in Mary's tears. Her tears were real.

"Pet"—Emma went around the bed and stroked Mary's head—"whatever is the matter?"

"Go away! Oh, I wish I were dead."

Emma sat down on the bed and continued to stroke the black curls. Mary continued to cry; she cried until she was exhausted and had to gasp for breath. For a while she lay still and then she rolled over, looked at Emma from swollen eyes, and spoke through swollen lips.

"I've committed bigamy."

Emma, thinking of Shay and Sauer, wondered if that was the word she meant.

"Rho and I were married this morning."

"Whatever for?" Emma, in her complete surprise, couldn't help saying.

"Because we're in love. You were right; Rho was my tenor, but you didn't like him; Shay didn't like him. And he's so sensitive about his looks—people always think he is German—and he knew you didn't like him and he was afraid you would try to stop it. Oh, I wanted to tell you; I didn't want to leave you out—"

"I thought it was Horsack."

"That was all over, but Paul wouldn't leave me alone after he found out about Rho. He made me go places with him—to the Weatherbees' parties—we were the two leads, and he said I had to. And he made love to me in front of Rho, and Rho threatened him, and we were having the most horrible time—about getting married—because he is practically an alien, and that's why I said I was glad when Paul died, and now I wish—oh, I wish I had never married him. You aren't angry with me? Please don't be; it was just that I was afraid you'd try to stop us, and now I wish you had!"

"It's all right." Emma swallowed the hurt of being left out. "Honest it is."

Her mind was racing.

It had probably been Mary and Sauer, not Shay, in the hotel. . . .

The way Sauer looked at Mary. . . .

She was a fool not to have guessed.

But what a beautiful, believable motive it gave Sauer for murdering Horsack!

"And you're absolutely right," she said. "I would have tried to stop you."

"Dear God," said Mary. "If you only had!"

Had Mary found out something? Something about Sauer and Horsack?

"Why?" Emma asked. They had been happy on the train. What had happened to spoil it?

"Because I've been married before. I'm still married, and that's bigamy." She lay back limply on the bed and went on in a lifeless voice: "Before the war. When I was in Rome. Count Gabriel Galeazzo." Her lips twisted in a grimace. "Everyone called him 'Sonny.' He was a mess. But I was young and romantic and I suppose the fact that he was a count had something to do with it."

All this was news to Emma.

"But then," said Emma, "you shouldn't have married Rho."

Mary sat up straight.

"But of course I thought he was dead! I heard that he had been killed in Africa. He was a Fascist. But Nella says not; she knows he is alive."

"Nella who? And how does she know?"

"Nella Randano, the soprano. She is a cousin and says she has heard from the family."

The dark woman with the mole. That explained, Emma thought, why she had been trying to see Mary. She was exactly the type to enjoy such a situation.

"Maybe she's wrong," Emma tried to console.

"Maybe. But I have to find out. And what will I tell Rho?"

"Tell him the truth; he'll understand."

He would if he wasn't a heel like the rest of Mary's men, including the count.

Life came back to Mary's voice. "Oh, but I couldn't! He doesn't know anything about it and he's fantastically jealous. He threatened to kill Paul. He's queer and chivalrous and sweet and I love him, but he'd fly into a rage if he knew I had been married before!"

There it was; it was hopeless to hope that Mary would pick a man who was normal.

And Sauer had threatened to kill Horsack . . . .

But a wife couldn't testify against her husband . . . .

But if he wasn't her husband . . . .

Sauer hadn't killed the professor; Aggie had done that job with strychnine.

Or Mr. Weatherbee?

Well, whoever had done what, first things came first. Mary, Emma suddenly bethought herself, had a job to do at eight o'clock and she couldn't fall down on it on the last night. The last night.

Emma sighed. Some might think that solving the murders came first, but no. In the afternoon it had been Mrs. Danforth's cookies. Now it was Mary.

Emma got up, wet a washcloth in the water pitcher, and put it over Mary's eyes.

"Don't worry, sweet," she said. "If the count isn't dead yet he soon will be. Or maybe old pickle-puss just made it up to make you unhappy. How did she find out you were married—over again, I mean?"

Mary lifted the washcloth from her face. "I don't think she knows about this morning. She said she was telling me because she thought I'd be glad to know. The old hypocrite. She knew what he was like before I married him."

" 'Latins are lousy lovers,' " Emma quoted.

Mary almost laughed. "I bet I'm a sight," she said with returning normalcy. "But what will I do about Rho?"

"Tell him nothing," said Emma cheerfully. "Act as if everything was all right. After tonight old P.P. won't be around to know what you do."

Mary looked shocked. "Oh, I couldn't do that, and tonight is—well, tonight is—"

"Your wedding night," said Emma, blunt, because half the time Mary talked like a trollop and the rest like a prude. "But if you're fussy you can get so pie-eyed that I'll have to put you to bed."

Mary giggled. "Would you care to go on our honeymoon?"

Emma stuffed a wet towel in her mouth. "Shut up," she said. "Think of your voice."

Professional concern swept back over Mary. She got out gargles and sprays and went to work on herself while Emma went to the hotel for hot soup and ice. It took Emma a long time. The town was a roving, seething mass that was fast coming to a boil, and a great part of it seethed and roved around the hotel. Trying to get to the dining room, Emma ran into her friend of the war bonnet, who picked her up bodily and carried her to the crowded bar. He was a nice man, and Emma didn't want to offend him.

"What's your name?" she asked.

"Ohio."

"I don't believe it."

"It is too. My family came from there. And don't call me Beautiful. Spent my life hitting people for calling me Beautiful."

Emma said she wouldn't think of it and instinctively looked around for Shay. The setting was a natural for Shay. Shay ought to be up on a table leading the singing.

A man in a broad-brimmed hat came up and slapped Mr. Ohio on the back. "Hello, Beautiful," he shouted.

Beautiful hit him, and in the ensuing tussle Emma sped away, found a harried waitress, and eventually achieved her wants. She got most of the soup back to Mary, having passed Sauer on the way and persuaded him that Mary was resting. She held an ice bag to Mary's head while Mary ate; she brushed Mary's hair; she pressed the costume that Mary had wrinkled; she answered telephone calls and received a box of flowers from one of Mary's Denver admirers. She passed Mrs. Danforth in the hall, visited with her in the kitchen, but of Aggie she had never a glimpse.

She was so busy being nurse, valet, and spiritual adviser that she hardly went into her own room. She got Mary to the opera house on the dot, and this time she stayed for the performance. Her clothes were all right; most of the audience were in costume of one kind or another. All but Mr. Weatherbee, and yet his dingy black suit seemed quite in keeping. The Weatherbees made an impressive entrance. Besides the old man there was Susan, her blond hair set off by powder-blue buckskin, a tall handsome woman in full black silk—she might be Susan's mother—several men in slick tight pants and smooth-fitting stockmen's shirts, and finally, at last, Mr. Strike.

It was about time for him to show up! He brought up the end of the Weatherbee procession like one shepherding a bunch of convicts to a prison movie; he kept his eyes on his charges, looking neither right nor left.

The Weatherbees seemed to make light of his presence; they bowed and smiled. Mr. Weatherbee spotted Emma, caught her eye, and winked. If the rest of the Weatherbees were unaware of Mr. Strike's identity, Emma felt the old man wasn't. Was he signaling her that the jig was up? Or was he betting that he could get out of the fix even yet?

Somewhat to her surprise, Emma enjoyed the opera. She tried to think about Aggie and Mr. Weatherbee, to sort out their parts in the two murders, but instead she found herself listening to the music, watching the gay, bright colors on the stage. The audience was in a good mood; the cast felt it and were in top form. The chorus sang with spunk and precision; the dances were lively. The mole-checked Nella, as the village hag, had a soprano voice of surprising brightness. But it was Mary and Sauer who were delighting the audience. Sauer, his Teutonic brightness darkened by his makeup, was a handsome and compelling hero; his voice, deep in range for a tenor, was sweet and compelling. Mary was outdoing herself. Rich, liquid, pure, her tones were sincerely gay or tender. She could act as well as sing. There was a catch in her voice as she sang the renunciation scene that brought down the house, though Emma wondered, herself, whether it was caused by emotion or a still-swollen larynx.

The curtain finally went down, to go up again, and down and up. There were applause and flowers and more applause and a speech by Alvarado, who looked as though he had been put through a wringer while still damp.

"If it were the last it had been the best . . . ."

"Highly successful . . ."

"Cooperation of leading citizens . . ."

There was a clatter of hoofs outside and a volley of shots.

Mr. Weatherbee's head went up like a fire horse's at the bell. "Come on, folks," he shouted. "Celebration's just begun!"

And from the vantage point of his front seat he ducked out the rear door with Strike in hot pursuit.

The old man was making a break! Emma wondered if he could get away with it. She had visions of Chew piloting a wild dash down the mountain and then decided almost regretfully that Mr. Strike would have foreseen that chance and would have taken steps to prevent it.

Emma had to worm her way through the slowly moving crowd to get backstage.

"Stick with me," Mary had begged, "so I won't be alone with Rho."

She needn't have worried. Behind the set and in the dressing rooms was amiable pandemonium. Singers who had not spoken during the season were kissing and crying. Chorus men were complimenting each other and telling their draft classifications. No one was working; the stagehands had already started the migration to the hotel. Only a few lackluster spirits were packing to catch the down train; the rest stepped on them and over them.

Mary, wide-eyed and glowing, was thoroughly enjoying the adulation of those crowded around her, was sharing it with Rho, with Nella, with anyone who passed near her. She seized on Emma.

"Come to the hotel with us. Alvarado is breaking the habits of a lifetime and buying a bottle of champagne. I feel that this is going to be a night."

Emma thought so too. If Mr. Weatherbee hadn't made good his escape, at what peak of celebration would Mr. Strike snap on the handcuffs?

Sauer touched her arm. "Mary has told me that you know about us. Please, you are not angry?"

He sounded eager, beseeching, and sincere, and because his matrimonial troubles were greater than he knew, Emma couldn't be cross with him.

"It's all right with me," she said. She no longer had to worry about Sauer's guilt; Strike was going to arrest Mr. Weatherbee.

"But you better be good to her," she added darkly.

They went out through the garden, though that was only slightly less crowded than the street. People milled about, calling, laughing, shouting. A man in the cutaway and loud vest of a gambler had taken over the supplies of a stamp girl and was loudly crying his wares. An old stagecoach, drawn by four horses and flanked by cowboy outriders, careened down the street and pulled up in front of the opera house. In a moment Susan Weatherbee climbed up beside the driver, and the equipage moved forward into the crowd to the accompaniment of a fusillade of shots.

"Somebody could get hurt, no?" Alvarado worried.

Emma didn't bother to answer him; she was feeling sorry for Susan Weatherbee.

"It is like my father's stories of Colonel Buffalo Bill," Sauer was saying. "He saw him in Vienna. He shot glass balls from under his horse's neck, and my father broke his leg trying to do it. After that he stuck to dressage."

No one tried to separate Sauer's father from Buffalo Bill. In front of the hotel the stagecoach was held up by a group of masked men who unloaded bag upon clinking bag from the interior. It probably wasn't the actual cash receipts, but it made a good act. Someone in the crowd yelled:

"String 'em up!"

And the effigy of a man with a black mustache and a dangling lock of black hair was hoisted to the top of a lamppost amid boos and hisses. One of the masked men brought Susan a drink, and she toasted the dangling figure.

Someone yelled: "Remember Pearl Harbor!" Then a miraculous shot parted the rope; the effigy fell, was caught by many hands, and struck, torn, and stamped upon.

"String 'em up again!"

Another figure slid into the air. Alvarado drew back. "It is not pretty." They followed him into the hotel.

"No, but it's such fun."

Mary was wonderful, Emma thought; she was either up or down. Tonight she was up, and nothing would bother her, not even the hint that the celebrating throng could turn to a vicious mob. She hoped Mr. Strike knew his business. It seemed to her that leaving Mr. Weatherbee loose on such a night was foolishly courting disaster.

The bar was jammed, but there was a table for them and a cold bottle. A waiter had to open it, Alvarado's hands shook so. Sauer ordered another bottle.

"To your success . . ."

"To all our successes . . ."

"To your happiness," Emma whispered to Mary.

People pressed around them, members of the company, strangers, saying good-by, congratulating. Alvarado pulled himself together and made another speech, during which Sauer pulled Emma away to the bar. He ordered a double scotch, but Emma shook her head.

"Say, is it all right with you, really?"

Emma nodded.

"She is so beautiful." Sauer drank his scotch at a gulp. "It is good not to have to sing tomorrow."

Emma thought he better look out if he wasn't used to it, but she said nothing to spoil his fun.

"My father would have liked her. Have I told you about my father?" Sauer ordered another drink, and, to save time, the bar boy handed him a bottle. "He was a major in the Austrian Army. The Imperial Austrian Army. He was with a cavalry regiment on the eastern front. A beautiful Hungarian princess gave them her stable of race horses—oh, fine horses that could run like the wind—have I told you about Hungarian horses?"

He paused for another nip, and Emma reminded him that their acquaintance had practically just begun. With Mr. Weatherbee as good as in jail, she found herself liking Sauer.

"Look at her talking to that fat swine, so beautiful! As I was saying, beautiful horses that run like the wind. And one morning they are out on a scout, and my father says, 'Come on, let's see how fast these horses can run: So they race, and the horses like it; they are trained to race and they race and they race, and there is no stopping them, right into the Russian lines. But the Russians are good sports. They have seen the finish of the race, and they know how anxious are the rest of my father's regiment, who only saw the start. So the next day they send over a plane and drop a note which reads: 'The major's gelding won by a nose.' "

Emma did not know that Shay had come up behind her until he said: "So that was your father? I never heard the guy's name before. Say, that's nothing; a while ago the sheriff repeated history by riding his horse right up to the bar."

"And I suppose," Emma helped him out, "the horse said, 'Hey, Wilb, how about a bottle of beer?' "

"No," said Shay, "that was the Englishman in the bathtub."

Emma laughed at the blank look on Sauer's face and decided that Mary had made a mistake. Only people who laughed at the same jokes should get married, but by that token she ought to marry Shay, heaven forbid.

Shay reached for Sauer's bottle. "Nice party. Let's ask the same people next year."

"I can come." There was no use in being stuffy, Emma thought. Shay knew as well as she did that there wouldn't be any next year. Of course he didn't know about the trap that was about to spring on Mr. Weatherbee.

The old man was squarely in front of her.

"They've taken m'granddaughter home," he announced. "Yippee!"

"Sir," asked Sauer, "did I ever tell you about my father? He was a doctor—"

"My father," Mr. Weatherbee interrupted him, "was a Mormon."

"Fascinating occupation," said Shay. "Mine was two Marines."

Mr. Weatherbee surveyed him skeptically. "What you all need," he told them, "is exercise. Come on, let's go dancing."

Joined by Mary and Alvarado, they threaded their way across to the livery stable. Shay pulled out handfuls of stamps to pay for their admissions.

"Mercy me," said Mary, "so 'twas you held up the stagecoach."

"I didn't have to." Shay waved them inside. "There's a roulette wheel and somebody dealing faro at the hotel and a bingo game in the basement of St. Francis' Church."

The livery stable, built to accommodate express wagons and freighters, was broad and roomy; seats had been built in the stalls and a platform raised at one end. Here the slightly less rambunctious natives and outsiders were gathered, mothers, children, babies, watching from the seats, waiting to take their turn in the intricate figures for which the fiddle, the banjo, and the clarinet played.

"Choose your partners," shouted the caller.

His arm around her waist, Mr. Weatherbee swept Emma into a set that was forming.

"But I don't know—" Emma protested.

"Do what the others do and hang on."

> *"Greet your lady and lead her out,*
> *Next time round and in and out . . ."*

The sets began to move, bowing, retreating, weaving. The fiddle squealed. Faster, faster . . .

> *"Ladies step in, and the gents step back . . ."*

The words were a blur to Emma, but she found herself in the center of a ring.

> *"Change your partners and dos-y-do.*
> *First couple forward and the rest stay back.*
> *Swing your partner . . ."*

A stout man whirled Emma until her feet left the ground and tossed her on to another. Finally she began to see the pattern, to get her breath, and to enjoy herself. It was fun; it was sociable. She said hello to the drab woman from the antique shop, who didn't look so drab with her hair curled and a pink dress on.

"Fun . . ." said the drab woman before she was snatched away.

Everyone talked, though Emma didn't see how they had the breath to do it or could hear each other above the music, the calls, and the swish of feet. She began to listen for words and phrases.

". . . trouble with his wife . . ."

"Two pleats in the back . . ."

". . . shut down the gold mines . . ."

"Have you seen her?"

". . . bought strychnine . . ."

Emma heard the last from behind her and whirled around, losing step, but could not tell from whom the words had come. Who had bought strychnine? Where?

"Promenade!"

The dance had brought Mr. Weatherbee, fresh as a daisy, back to her.

"How you doing?"

"Swell, but I'm dry as a bone."

Mr. Weatherbee reached toward his hip pocket, but Emma made for a table laden with punch and cookies.

"There ain't nothing nourishing in that," Mr. Weatherbee objected.

"These cookies are good," said Emma. "I practically helped make them."

Mr. Weatherbee gingerly helped himself; others were doing the same.

"Hm," a woman beside Emma sniffed. "That's Lizzie Danforth's recipe. I am surprised. Last year she got out of sending any by saying Aggie forgot to tell her."

"Have you seen her?"

The woman looked around and then leaned forward to whisper to her companion. Emma leaned forward, too, but Mary and Shay pushed in, panting and laughing.

"More fun," said Mary.

"Cookies!" said Shay, taking a handful.

"The true folk spirit," said Alvarado, also helping himself liberally. Sauer was nowhere to be seen.

"Choose your partners for the Virginia reel!"

Shay took Emma, and Mary had to suffer Alvarado, because Mr. Weatherbee had vanished. As they joined the long lines on the floor Shay said casually:

"My spies tell me there's an FBI man in our midst."

Emma tried not to look superior; she also looked around for the tall figure of Mr. Strike and, failing to see him, said, "Not here."

Shay laughed at her. "They don't carry a sign."

A gasp that quickly turned to a titter swept the assembly and, looking up, they saw an amazing sight. Mr. Weatherbee was leading out Miss Agatha Estis, leading her serenely to the head of the line. Emma held her breath; it would be horrible if everyone laughed.

"The Statue of Liberty," said Shay, "as I hope to kiss a pig."

"She's been making it," said Emma. "That's where she's been."

Aggie was draped from shoulders to toe in red, white, and blue cheese-cloth. She carried a torch fashioned of cardboard, and under her rayed headdress her pink face was absurd and utterly happy.

"If they laugh at her," said Emma, "I shall cry."

Shay began to applaud; the crowd, easily influenced, followed him, turning the ridicule to an ovation. Aggie bowed. Mr. Weatherbee bowed to his partner, and the dance began.

"Socks," the woman next to Emma was saying, "with ink in them. Imagine!"

"Strychnine," said Emma as they curtsied to each other.

"She said it was for rats," said the woman. "Imagine!"

Then Emma had to advance to meet Shay for the march down the middle.

"Third guy coming up," said Shay.

"You say words to people," said Emma, "and they talk to you. Oh, you mean the G-man?"

She turned her head to look, saw an ordinary person in a brown suit, medium height, medium size, his only concession to frivolity a red hand-kerchief around his neck.

"Oh no," said Emma.

Another turn, and she was twirling with the ordinary-looking man. Shay was wrong, but she could soon find out; if Strike had an assistant he would certainly know her name.

"I'm Miss Marsh," she said. "Emma Marsh."

"How do you do?" said the man.

Perhaps he was being cagey.

"How are things doing?"

"Fine," said the man. "Lots of fun."

Shay was a dope.

"The true folk spirit," said Emma.

"Yeh?" said the man.

And then Emma found herself with Mr. Albert. Mr. Albert looked surprised too.

"Junior's gained a whole pound since I saw you," she said sweetly.

"Look here—" began Mr. Albert.

Emma left him hurriedly.

When the reel was finished they gathered again around the punch bowl. Aggie was flushed and glowing and almost pretty. Shay asked her for the next set. Sauer appeared, slightly chastened, and claimed Mary. Alvarado collapsed in a chair, and Emma joined Mr. Weatherbee on a bench by the wall.

"That was a nice thing to do," she said.

Mr. Weatherbee said nothing, being engaged in refreshing himself from his private bottle.

He didn't belong in this age, Emma thought; he was a leftover anachronism from the days when a man could do as he liked if he could get away with it. It was a pity to end a life like his in disgrace. It seemed to Emma that there was only one way out for Mr. Weatherbee; perhaps if she hinted at what she knew he would take it.

"Day before yesterday," she began, "I took a walk up behind the old cemetery."

"So?" Mr. Weatherbee's comment was mild.

"I found it," Emma emphasized her words, "very interesting."

"Never been up there. Too many folks I used to know. Sockless, Pete, Bert Estis—"

"And all those opera singers." Emma allowed herself to be sidetracked for a moment in local history. "He married one, didn't he? Mr. Estis? It says on her tombstone: 'Otille, dearly beloved of Bertram Estis, born in Baden—' "

"Say that again!" Mr. Weatherbee was interested now.

" 'Otille,' " Emma quoted obediently, " 'dearly beloved of Bertram Estis—' "

"Why, the ornery bastard," Mr. Weatherbee broke in, "the lying, thieving, double-dyed, double-crossing son of a gun." He elaborated on the character of the late Mr. Estis for a paragraph without repeating himself and then he laughed, long and appreciatively. "The cute old cuss," he finished admiringly, "to have the last laugh."

"I don't get it," said Emma.

"No," said Mr. Weatherbee. "The others swore they'd never tell, and I'm the only feller left to know he caught on. I bet he's laughing in hell this minute, the mule-faced old devil." He took another long drink from his bottle. "Here's to you, Bert."

"Tell me more," Emma urged. "Was it something you did?"

"Me and four other guys," Mr. Weatherbee chuckled, "Stoney Madison, Harlow Burgess, and Putty Commenti—Harlow got to be a Supreme Court justice—my, my, we did a lot of devilment first and last, but this time . . .

"Well, like you said, Bert fell in love with this opera singer and got the notion he wanted to marry her. The idea was agreeable to the lady, but she held out for being married by a preacher from her own church—some kind of Lutheran, I think it was. So, being as Bert was an old friend, we said we'd take care of the matter for him. Down in the Majestic Bar, we was, and Bert was telling us who he'd invited and what a bang-up shindig the wedding was going to be, only he couldn't find this preacher, when Putty said he'd heard of a Lutheran over in Rabbit Gulch.

" 'So long as he's a Lutheran,' says Bert, 'it'll be all right.'

"Putty began to cry and said it was the least we could do for a fellow member that we was losing to the bonds of holy matrimony, and Bert began to cry and said he'd remember it to his dying day. And I guess he did." Mr. Weatherbee paused for another chuckle.

"Go on," said Emma. "So they got married . . ."

"Oh yes," said Mr. Weatherbee, "they got married. At least they thought they did; so did everybody else but us, and we paid the feller a thousand dollars, Mex, to get out of this part of the country."

"Oh," said Emma. "Oh, you mean he really wasn't a preacher?"

"He was a Lutheran, though," Mr. Weatherbee insisted. "Putty made sure of that. That was what give him the idea, Bert's saying anybody, so long as he was a Lutheran. Putty wouldn't have double-crossed a friend."

"Oh no," said Emma, "I can see that. All I think is that Mr. Estis should have known better."

Mr. Weatherbee nodded. "Bert was in on some tricks, too, but this time he had his mind on other things; I'd sure like to know, though, how he found out."

"Promenade!"

As the music stopped there was again the sound of shots and a prolonged cry of "Yipp-ee."

Mr. Weatherbee sniffed the air. " 'Scuse me. Sounds like I ought to take care of Sol."

He left hurriedly. Sauer and Mary came up, panting.

"Fun. . . ."

". . . worn to a nub . . ."

"Why weren't you dancing?"

Shay appeared without Aggie.

"Boy," he said, "I need a drink. That woman is nuts."

"You're telling us?"

Emma thought of asking him where he had been all day and if he had found out anything about Mr. Weatherbee's visit to the professor, but Mary and Sauer were there, and it really didn't matter, now that Strike had taken over.

They went back to the hotel, to the second cold bottle, and Sauer to his whiskey chasers. It was after twelve, and the departure of the train had thinned out the crowd somewhat, but the diehards who remained were doubling their drinks and their noise. They had become one vast, happy family and they welcomed Emma and Mary with enthusiasm. Shay didn't need a welcome; he was right at home.

Mary loved it. A stout blond woman in jeans and a plaid shirt told her that she was marvelous, and Mary loved it. A fat, bald trombone player from the orchestra asked Emma if she ever got to Boston. Emma said practically never. The trombone player asked her if she knew that the street in front of the hotel had once been paved with silver. Emma said she had heard it was the whole block. Someone wheeled the piano in from the patio, and Mary sang the Maypole song. When the song was finished Sauer kissed Mary and shoved away Emma's friend of the war bonnet who had tried to do the same. It wasn't a hard push, and the man laughed, but Shay caught Emma's eye and worked his way over to her.

"What makes?"

"I dunno," said Emma cautiously. "What do you mean?"

"Between Sauer and our little nightingale?"

Emma laughed merrily. "Don't be silly."

"Oh, yeah? All evening I've been watching him and he's been watching her. Next guy that touches her he's going to take a pop at, unless I can pass him out and get him to bed."

"Oh, would you? Then Mary wouldn't have to. Pass out, I mean, not put him to bed."

"Silly, eh?" said Shay, but he moved purposefully toward Sauer.

The man of the war bonnet came up to Emma. "How about a little drink?"

"It's being done."

The man leaned forward confidentially. "Did anyone ever tell you—"

Emma preened herself slightly; Mary didn't need all the attention.

"—that the street out there was paved with silver?"

"No!" said Emma.

"Fact. Clear to the railroad station."

Emma thought that the paving would reach to Denver by morning, but the conversation was interrupted by a noisy commotion outside, where Mr. Weatherbee and Sol Faber seemed to be involved in a heated argument.

"You darned old fool," shouted Mr. Weatherbee, "it was, too, gold."

"I ain't gold, you old fool," roared Mr. Faber.

It looked as though they would come to blows, but instead they flung their arms about each other's necks and swayed through the doorway.

"Yipp-ee," yelled Mr. Faber.

"Drinks on the house," bawled his companion; "bring on the girls."

The bartenders sprang into action, partly because, as Emma noticed with some trepidation, Mr. Weatherbee as well as Mr. Faber now carried a gun, and roaring was the word for the way they were drunk. She climbed quickly onto a stool for fear that Mr. Faber would feel moved to command another performance of dancing.

"You want a drink, Sol?"

"Never touch the stuff."

"He lies," Mr. Weatherbee announced; "biggest liar in Gilpin County."

"Sure am," Mr. Faber boasted, "since you moved out."

They both cackled with glee, and the crowd surged about them.

"You don't need to be nervous," Emma overheard a man say. "There's nothing but blanks in the guns."

"You can bet me," Emma muttered, remembering the rope so neatly parted earlier in the evening.

"What?" said the man with Emma. "That's DeLoss Weatherbee. He's worth millions and he's a real old-timer, not somebody dressed up in fancy clothes for the heck of it."

Then it all happened quickly. Sauer had lurched forward, holding his bottle. "Did I ever tell you about my father—?"

"Why, no," Mr. Faber caught him up. "Did you have one?"

The crowd gasped a little and drew back; Sauer rocked on his heels, his face purpling, raised his bottle to strike, and lunged toward Mr. Faber. A shot cracked, and Sauer fell to the floor amid the sound of tinkling glass.

Over the pandemonium that broke loose Emma could hear Mary screaming. She tried to get to her, but half the crowd was trying to get out of the room; the other half was trying to get to Sauer's body.

Had Mr. Faber actually shot Sauer in self-defense, or had Mr. Weatherbee shot him for some reason that was not yet clear?

A table went over with a crash, momentarily halting the milling crowd, letting Emma through just as Mary and Shay bent over Sauer. Mary was sobbing wildly. Shay rolled Sauer over gently; Sauer was still breathing, breathing loud and noisily. There was no blood, not even a scratch from the shattered whiskey bottle on which he had fallen.

"Humph," said Shay. "He's not dead; he's just passed out."

"Old Sol never misses a bottle," said Mr. Weatherbee, but he looked sheepishly at Mary, who was still undecided whether to laugh or cry.

Shay got help to carry Sauer upstairs, and Emma put her arm around Mary.

"Come on," she said. "Let's go home before they start playing William Tell."

CHAPTER ELEVEN

EMMA awoke suddenly. Her room was pitch-dark and quiet as the grave, but she lay still and rigid because something had frightened her awake and she was still frightened. Nothing moved; there was no sound; the black shadow that she was watching resolved itself into the darker darkness between the two windows. Emma decided that she must have been dreaming of Mr. Weatherbee and his gun and was about to roll over when she heard a faint click to her left, from the direction of the wardrobe.

Pack rats?

She knew it wasn't; she had shut the wardrobe doors enough to recognize the sound, and she knew what was in the suitcase. But why, in the name of common sense, hadn't whoever it was done his rummaging during the time that she had been absent? There was an answer for that. When she and Mary had left she had locked the door of Mary's room; her own door had not been unlocked, but on their return they had entered by their own doors. She had carefully locked hers behind her, but Mary probably hadn't. Emma considered leaping from the bed, dashing through the double doors, and out through Mary's door, locking it behind her. That had, of course, the disadvantage of leaving Mary at the mercy of the prowler, but what really kept Emma motionless was the thought of the accuracy with which Mr. Faber had shot the bottle from Sauer's hand. He might only intend to wing, but in the dark . . .

Emma lay very still because she felt that someone was looking at her. She let her jaw sag open and breathed lightly. Or did one breathe deeply when one was asleep? That was a silly thing not to know, a silly bit of knowledge that might stand between one and death, because Emma knew that the person waiting beside her wasn't fooling. She felt sure that someone was bending closer; then she heard a quick, harsh breath, had felt the tension relax. He was moving away; she heard a soft sound at the foot of the bed and dared to open one eye. There was a whiteness there that wasn't a window, that was dark when it moved in front of the window, a pale whiteness that floated above the floor. Emma opened her other eye in an effort to see more clearly and then shut them again because the figure had stopped. Emma knew that the figure couldn't see any better than she could, but she felt safer with her eyes closed. When she dared to open them again the whiteness was gone; she continued to lie still because the double doors were at the head of her bed, to the right. After a time there was a sound that might have been the closing of Mary's door; then Emma took a deep breath.

Now that it was over she was furious with herself for not having done something to discover the identity of her visitor. There was no light switch within reach, but the figure had been so close to her that she could have reached out and touched it; she could have carried out her projected dash to Mary's room and turned on the light. She could have done something, but she knew very well that the reason she hadn't was because she had been too scared. Perhaps she wasn't cut out for a life of crime after all. Still, she consoled herself, grappling with a real and visible adversary was one thing, and provoking the unknown was another. She hadn't the faintest idea who or what had been in her room. It could have been Mr. Weatherbee, or Aggie, Sauer, or even Mrs. Danforth, hunting for the evidence against Aggie; size meant nothing, because the white blur was small—three or four feet long, she guessed—but so vague as to be indeterminate. And why white? Anyone with a lick of sense would have worn black. Then Emma remembered that the top third of Aggie's costume had been white; the lower part—the red and the blue—would have been dark, wouldn't have been visible, and Aggie was the one person who wouldn't have thought that the white part would show.

Somehow, deciding that her visitor had been Aggie made Emma feel better. Aggie wouldn't have hurt her; she could have sat up in bed and said: "Aggie, what are you doing in my room?" and the poor soul would have burst into tears.

The professor should have tried it.

When her windows were gray with the coming morning Emma fell asleep and when she woke again it was bright and sunny. There were calls and the sound of hammering from the opera house; the boys with the iron hoop were at it again, and the things in her room were comfortably plain and real. There were the bureau and the washstand; there was the carved foot of her bed. There was—and Emma cringed to see it—her white woolly coat hanging over the back of the rocker, swaying gently in the breeze.

"Nuts," said Emma, and got up and brushed her teeth.

Mary was still asleep, but Emma, feeling the need for food, dressed and let herself out quietly. She was glad that she did not see Aggie; she would have been ashamed to look her in the face.

There was a truck backed up to the opera house, and two men in jeans that were work clothes and not costumes were arguing heatedly as to whether one heavy load or two light ones would be easiest on the tires. The "Closed for the Season" sign was already leaning against the door. Time had slipped through her fingers, Emma felt, time and Horsack and the professor; Central City's past was closing in on them, and soon they would be one with the ghosts, mentioned as casually as the others who had lived and died in the world's richest square mile.

Emma decided that she had imagined everything. Horsack had fallen and hit his head; the professor himself had administered the strychnine; Aggie was a harmless idiot; and Mr. Weatherbee was a pillar of society. Then Emma entered the hotel dining room and saw Mr. Weatherbee seated at a table between Mr. Strike and the ordinary man in the brown suit. Mr. Weatherbee looked up.

"They got me, pal," he said sadly.

At least, Emma thought, she hadn't imagined the radio station! But she was sorry for Mr. Weatherbee. He should have followed the professor's example and joined the ghosts. She was sorry for her own part in exposing him, though she knew she shouldn't be. Perhaps Strike hadn't told him. She looked at Strike. He was grinning broadly. So was Mr. Weatherbee. The man in the brown suit was the only one who felt as she did.

"Make you acquainted with Mr. Fox," said the old man, "of the Department of Justice, and my grandson Strike, who is about to go to jail for impersonating an officer."

"I did not," said Strike Weatherbee. "Miss Marsh is my witness that I never once claimed to be what she thought me, and I got in touch with Fox that same night."

Mr. Fox nodded gloomily, as though regretting the whole affair.

"Why, you did so," Emma insisted. "You must have." Light was breaking slowly. "Do you mean to tell me—?"

She sat down quickly and glared at Mr. Weatherbee. "Do you mean he wasn't a G-man at all, but just another of your tricks?"

"Not even a junior G-man."

Mr. Fox moved uneasily, but Mr. Weatherbee looked unashamedly pleased with himself.

"I guessed where you were heading. Burkhardt saw you coming away from the mine, and I knew you were all hell and determined to stir up a stink about Horsack before the opera was over. Burkhardt didn't figure you knew who he was; I didn't either, but I found out later you did because you left this in the car." He drew from his pocket the now well-worn copy of *Time*. "How'd you happen onto that?"

"Look"—Emma was still miles behind—"you saw me with the phone book and made a smart guess. You telephoned to your grandson ahead of me, but I called the FBI."

Mr. Fox cleared his throat, but Strike spoke. "I got there firstest. I was waiting in the lobby of the Brown. The old man told me what you had on, but I had to wait for you to make your call so that you'd think I was the feller you wanted. Fox was right on our heels; he tried several other bars. You remember that we moved?"

"I went back to the Brown," said Mr. Fox. "You weren't registered there."

"No." Emma looked at Strike. "It was suggested that I stay elsewhere. But"—she turned triumphantly on Mr. Weatherbee—"it didn't do any good, all your smartness. Mr. Fox caught up with you, or he wouldn't be here. How did you find out"—she turned to Fox—"about the radio station?"

"My dear young lady"—Mr. Fox smiled gently—"that station was established with the full knowledge and consent of the Federal Communications Commission."

The ground fell away beneath Emma's feet; she snatched for support. "Burkhardt," she said feebly, "the professor? Wasn't he a spy?"

Mr. Fox spoke kindly and finally, as though to a child. "We were thoroughly acquainted with the man Burkhardt."

It was Mr. Weatherbee who explained. "He was all right, the professor; he resigned from his school because he couldn't lecture any more." His hand went to the side of his throat, avoiding the word cancer. "The papers played up his book and his decoration, so he came up here. Then he got this idea for a listening post and I sort of helped him out. But don't feel bad," he added consolingly. "I don't blame you a bit for figuring things the way you did. I don't blame you for being mad at me either. Crimenently!" he broke off. "Ain't you up yet?"

Shay was approaching them, disheveled and wan. He tottered to the table and sank into a chair. "You"—he pointed an unsteady finger at Mr. Weatherbee—"have no business to be alive."

"Shucks," said Mr. Weatherbee modestly, "just a little fun."

Shay groaned.

"Never took a drink," Mr. Weatherbee informed him, "until I was thirty-five. Got my constitution built up to stand the strain. Trouble with you folks nowadays, no constitution. You're supposed to be up at the station relieving the kid Albert sent up to spell you last night." So Mr. Albert had known about the station too; Shay had known it; everyone had known it. Emma sat very still and small, kicking herself mentally for having been a fool.

Mr. Fox got up, withdrawing himself from the sociableness of the group, but not too noticeably. There was not even an implied criticism of Shay in his voice as he said: "Let me know if you replace the professor permanently." His bow included the whole group; it might even have been said to include Emma, but Emma didn't think so. She was not, she was sure, in Mr. Fox's eyes, even a meddling female. Shay, to make matters worse, was looking through her as though she were an unmaterialized ghost.

Mr. Weatherbee waited until Mr. Fox was well out of earshot before he sniffed. " 'Replace the professor,' " he mimicked. "Now will you tell me what fun he gets out of acting like that?"

Strike eyed his grandfather tolerantly. "The activities of G-men are hardly motivated by pleasure."

"Then what the Sam Hill does he do it for? Don't tell me. Git on back to the ranch, out of my way."

Strike got up. Emma thought now she might have guessed his identity. He had a dignity and assurance that was like his grandfather's, and he took his leave with a casualness that implied that he would have been going anyhow.

He extended his hand to Emma. "Good-by," he said. "Let me know if the old man gets shot."

"Why you?" asked his grandfather. "Why not the undertaker?" But

Strike was halfway to the door and ignored him.

Shay stirred and came partially out of his coma. "What was that G-man doing down here anyway?"

"Oh," said Mr. Weatherbee airily, "he's trailing some spy or other."

"I might have known it," Emma shouted. She half rose from her chair, having some idea of rushing after Mr. Fox. "I might have known that you'd get around him somehow, pretending that that station and the professor were all right. Well, maybe they were, but if they were, then the spy he's after is the one that killed the professor. You're so smart, saying he died of cancer! Well, he didn't; he's full of strychnine, and I can—"

Shay had risen also; now he put his big hand over Emma's mouth and forced her down in her chair.

"Hush," said Mr. Weatherbee, "somebody'll hear you."

Emma squirmed and wriggled; she tried to bite Shay's hand.

Shay shook her. "Behave yourself."

Then, to Emma's further rage, tears of mortification and frustration welled from her eyes.

"Aw, baby," said Shay, removing his hand, "don't get sore."

"I'm not." Emma struggled for control. "But he—" She choked, pointed at Mr. Weatherbee, and began again: "This thing goes around and around, getting nowhere, because he blocks it. It breaks out in a new place and then he blocks it again. Now he's sent Fox away—"

"This," Mr. Weatherbee cut in, "isn't any of Fox' business, but if he heard you blabbing that strychnine stuff he might think it was, because the professor was sort of unofficially working for the government."

"There," Emma appealed wearily to Shay, "you see? We mustn't hint that anybody was murdered, because somebody might do something about it."

"Jesus-menders," said Mr. Weatherbee, "do you want Aggie arrested for murder?"

Emma stopped in the middle of blowing her nose, then wiped it hurriedly and sat silent. She had been so sure that she was the only one to suspect Aggie that she was completely at a loss for words.

"Where was your ears last night?" the old man went on. "The place was buzzing with how Aggie had bought strychnine or rat poison, and wasn't it funny that the professor died so suddenly, and all the damn-fool gossip women think up in just their spare time. You want Fox to get a load of that? How'd you know?" He switched abruptly: "He had it in him."

"Did he?"

"Sure, autopsy showed it . . . ."

"But Mr. Faber said—"

"If Sol's learned anything in seventy years, it must be not to tell all he knows, though I'm surprised to hear it. So you was around pumping Sol and he wouldn't give. How did you find out?"

Emma sat mulishly silent. She wasn't going to give herself away. Maybe there hadn't been an autopsy; maybe he was just pretending, to find out what she knew. He needn't think he could get it out of her!

Mr. Weatherbee reached for a toothpick and chewed it placidly.

"Well," he said, "I expect you and Miss Pinzi'll be leaving most any time now?"

Emma glared at him. "It's a free country, isn't it? Or do you think you can run me out?"

"Oh no." Mr. Weatherbee looked meek and mild. "Only the hotel closes up tomorrow, and there ain't much doing. Lizzie Danforth might keep you on, but she don't like to have regular boarders, and it begins to get mighty cold."

He had her, Emma realized. There was no excuse for her to stay. Mary would want to go. This little old man had outplayed her on every move. He was stronger than the law; he was even stronger than the government.

"All right," she said. "I give up. I'll go as soon as I can get out of here, but before I do I want you to know that I know that Horsack was murdered. You said there was blood on the doorknob, but there wasn't any when I found him!"

"Ah yes," said Mr. Weatherbee, "so you said, to my grandson Strike."

"The things you say"—Shay was reproving—"to strange men."

Shay knew about that blood too. They all knew everything, all the bits she had tried to keep to herself, because what she had thought that she told the FBI in confidence Strike had promptly relayed to his grandfather.

"So if you don't want to get out," Mr. Weatherbee was going on, "if you ain't scared, why, stick around to see the finish."

"You—you mean," Emma stammered, "that you're really trying to find out who did them? The murders?"

"I am not," said Mr. Weatherbee, "so totally devoid of my responsibility as a citizen as I have led you to think." His eyes twinkled at her. "When," he asked slyly, "did you first suspect me?"

"Of course I never did, really." Emma tried to save herself, but Shay's and Mr. Weatherbee's hoots of laughter told her it was no use. She was ambushed, surrounded, and out of ammunition. If she surrendered they might not scalp her.

"I guess," she said humbly, "I was just a plain damn fool." She went on, because there was no dissenting opinion: "I thought you were up to something from the first day I was here, because you came out on the balcony and told Chew that all hell was liable to break loose—"

"My granddaughter," said Mr. Weatherbee, "was trying to have another party for Horsack. Her mother, who has some sense, not being a Weatherbee, didn't like the idea in the first place, and I had a hunch we were going to be late and that would make her mad, and that Horsack would try to bring Miss Pinzi and that would make Susan mad. It was a kind of family hell I'd seen before."

"Makes sense to me," said Shay.

"But after I'd found Horsack's body," Emma explained meekly, "I thought you said it because you knew the reason Horsack missed his cue was because he was dead."

"He'd missed cues before. He was the star, and up here he got a little big for his boots. He had Alvarado flying off the handle every few days." Mr. Weatherbee sighed the sigh of one who had been through considerable.

"You could have explained things to me," said Emma. "You could have called the police instead of making me think you and Mr. Faber were crazy."

"At that time," said Mr. Weatherbee, "I only thought that you were a very attractive young lady who was awful easy taken in."

"What he means," said Shay, "and is too polite to tell you, is that he had his hands full trying to make this Festival go, and he didn't think it was any of your business butting in."

"Oh no!" said Mr. Weatherbee. "But Miss Marsh was so sure murder had been done that she was hell-bent to get a posse out right then. First I had to be sure Horsack was dead and not just passed out somewhere, and then—well," he admitted, "there ain't been a killing up here for a long time, and Sol and I had a mind to try our hands at solving it."

"Humph!" said Emma.

"You don't need to be snippy," said Shay. "They did all the spadework; they found out that Mary and Sauer were the only ones in the company who didn't have alibis for the time of Horsack's death."

"Oh," said Emma. Then: "Oh, but Mary didn't do it!"

" 'Round and round,' " Mr. Weatherbee quoted reminiscently. " 'Mary didn't do it.' Every time I asked you a question that was all I got. And I knew you was scared to death for fear she had."

"She didn't do it," Emma repeated. "But I was." She wrinkled her eyebrows. "But you said it was an accident. You told everybody it was an accident. If you thought it was, why did you bother to check the alibis?"

Shay raised his hand. "No prompting, please. Shall I repeat the question?"

Emma looked at Mr. Weatherbee. Mr. Weatherbee looked at Emma.

"Oh," said Emma finally. "How could I be so simpleminded? But what made you think it was murder? You didn't know about the blood then."

"Before we get to that. There was another reason for keeping the accident idea going besides not letting folks think we was suspicious. Sol and I may be old, but we don't hanker to be called fools. We kept telling ourselves that it was too much of a coincidence for this feller to die when so many people wanted to kill him; then we'd remind ourselves that fellers had made a strike just by sticking a pick in the ground. We went round and round a good bit, too, but as I said, there hasn't been a killing for quite a while, and we thought we might as well try to find out what all we could. We checked the alibis and found out that Miss Pinzi had gone to Horsack's room at the hotel *after* she had found the body. But it would have helped if we had known about the blood. Did you catch it right away?"

"No," Emma admitted; "I would have told you right at first, but by the time I remembered it I thought you had put it there."

"Could have," said Mr. Weatherbee. "Maybe I did."

"Cut it out," said Emma, "if you want me to stay on your side."

"Habit," said Mr. Weatherbee.

"And another thing I've remembered," said Emma accusingly. "You went to see the professor, not Mrs. Danforth, the night he was killed."

"Died," said Mr. Weatherbee, "for the time being, died. And I said I made a call on Lizzie, and I did. Burkhardt"—he hesitated, as though loath to go on with anything so prosaic as the unvarnished truth—"well, Burkhardt came here to tell me he'd seen you at the mine. He said there was something he wanted to talk about, but there were people around, and he said to come to his room later. It was pretty late when I got there, and Aggie said he was asleep. Lizzie heard her. Does that clear me?"

"You. But not Aggie. It was Aggie's crayon that was under Horsack. Aggie took up the professor's tray. And now I don't think it was my coat that I saw either." She told them of the visitor to her room and of the tray and the plate and the glass and sipper hidden in her suitcase. "And that," she finished, "is how I knew about the strychnine."

"You've got to get out of that house," said Shay. "That Aggie would have killed you if you'd moved. She poisoned the professor and planted the stuff on you."

"No," said Mr. Weatherbee. "Burkhardt took the poison, and Aggie got scared and hid the dishes."

"Phooey," said Emma. "Mrs. Danforth did it because the professor ate crackers in bed."

"She did it," said Mr. Weatherbee, "but I'll be blessed if I know why."

"Now you're joking again," Emma reproved him. "There was a time when I thought Sauer did it." She paused, remembering what had happened to Sauer the night before.

"Why," Emma asked, "was he suddenly so touchy about his father? He'd done nothing but brag about him all evening. First he was a jockey, then a general, and finally a doctor."

"He wasn't bragging," Shay said. "His father was a major in the last war. He was also a doctor, and the day the Nazis marched into Vienna he jumped out of his office window."

"Oh," said Emma. "Oh, then of course he wouldn't have killed Horsack."

"On the contrary," said Shay. "Being brothers in suffering makes no difference; the Austrians just plain don't like the Czechs."

"Why?"

Shay shrugged. "After the war the Czechs profited at the expense of Austria. The Czechs got richer and the Austrians poorer. But that's only one man's opinion."

"But you don't think he did it."

Shay looked at Emma. "Don't I?" he asked mildly.

"Which brings us," said Mr. Weatherbee, "back to Miss Pinzi."

Before Emma could put in her routine protest a stentorian voice bellowed from the direction of the kitchen: "Are those folks going to sit there all day?"

"Yes!" Mr. Weatherbee bellowed right back. "Bring me another plate of ham and eggs."

"Make it two," Shay echoed him. "You know," he added in a surprised voice, "I feel better. In fact, I think I'll live."

"Maybe we ought to go," Emma demurred. "Maybe they want to clean up."

"Take her cool," said Mr. Weatherbee; "for munitions-plant wages we ought to get the overtime."

"Well, I could do with another cup of coffee."

Alvarado came in, bland and beaming, now that his troubles were over. He shook hands with Mr. Weatherbee, with Shay, and with Emma. All the scenery had gone; all the costumes. He had been paid in full, and as far as the rest of the company was concerned, he didn't care; he was going fishing. Mr. Weatherbee, he said, was a hero, a magician, and the soul of honor. He shook hands all around again and departed.

He was, Mr. Weatherbee informed them, the kind of fellow who worked fine—with a cast-iron contract.

It was not Mr. Weatherbee's nature to make disparaging remarks. "I take it," said Emma, "that you don't approve of contracts?"

Mr. Weatherbee mopped up the remains of his egg neatly with a piece of bread. "You got to have 'em now'days. Things get so complicated that a feller can forget what he promised, but in the old days a feller was either honest or he wasn't, and you took your chances."

Mr. Weatherbee crossed his knife and fork upon his plate.

"You get stung much?" Shay wanted to know.

"Not much. I had four partners once on a little bricklaying job. The bricks disappeared, but nobody bothered to accuse anyone else. We'd done it for a joke, and we figured that if four of us was hornswoggled into paying for it that was all right too."

"It sounds to me," said Emma, "like some more of your devilment."

"They're all dead now," said Mr. Weatherbee, " 'cept me. So I guess it don't make no difference. You ever hear about the time the street out in front here was paved with silver?"

"No!" said Emma.

"Sir," said Shay, "that has become part of the indestructible folklore of America, along with the one about the miner who ordered forty dollars' worth of ham and eggs at Rector's." He glanced at Mr. Weatherbee's plate. "It must have been you. And the dowdy woman who wanted the best diamond necklace at Tiffany's, and the poker game in which the feller bet the state of New Mexico—"

Emma interrupted him: "And that Empire bureaus are always worth a hundred dollars and that chorus girls really live with their mothers—"

"That last has been thrown out," Shay corrected her. "It was a temporary phenomenon of the depression, but three of a kind still beat two pair, and a drunk never catches pneumonia, and Harvard indifference and the Los Angeles city limits—to those eternal verities"—Shay pointed his finger solemnly at Mr. Weatherbee— "has been added the fact that the streets of this fair city were paved with silver."

"As a matter of fact," said Mr. Weatherbee, "it was gold, but we washed it over with silver. . . ."

"Quite right," Shay assured him. "Gold would have been much too ostentatious."

"Where's Rho?" Mary had come up to them, pretty as a magazine cover, but the effect of the blue plaid suit that made her blue eyes bluer was lost on Shay and Mr. Weatherbee. They ceased their joking and became tense and cautious. Mr. Weatherbee pulled out a black wallet with multitudinous clasps and busied himself with its contents.

"Sauer," said Shay, "isn't feeling so well."

Mary shot a vindictive look at Mr. Weatherbee. "He's really all right, isn't he? He'll be ready to leave this noon?"

Mr. Weatherbee clinked a handful of silver dollars, and Shay shook his head. "I very much doubt if he'll be able to raise his head by noon."

If he did, Emma thought, they'd tie him down. It was no part of Mr. Weatherbee's plan, she could see, for Sauer to leave. The rest of the company had alibis, but not Sauer or Mary. Still and all, if Sauer couldn't leave, Mary wouldn't, and that gave Emma an excuse for staying. It worked out very well, as so many of Mr. Weatherbee's plans seemed to. It also, as Mary ought to have sense enough to see, postponed Mary's day of reckoning with Sauer.

Perhaps Mary did see, for she sat down and beckoned the long-suffering waitress.

Mr. Weatherbee cleared his throat and spoke politely. "Very profitable season, thanks to you and that young man."

Mary relented a little. "You certainly did everything . . . . The whole company enjoyed being here . . . ."

"Except Horsack," said Shay bluntly.

Emma could have kicked him; there was no excuse for saying a thing like that when everyone else was trying to be tactful and smooth.

Mary's voice tightened up, but she went on talking to the waitress: ". . . and coffee and ham, I guess."

"We're out of ham," said the waitress triumphantly.

"Oh, bacon, eggs—I don't care."

When the waitress had gone Mary looked full at Shay and asked with studied casualness, "Now that it's all over, why bring him up?"

"Just my native blundering." Shay rolled his napkin into a ball and stood up. "Come on," he said to Emma, "and help me pack."

Emma got up because Shay and Mr. Weatherbee seemed to be operating according to some plan, and she was still sufficiently meek to be cooperative.

Shay steered her through the piled-up bags and boxes in the lobby, through the scurry and commotion of a wholesale departure, and did not speak until they were out on the sidewalk.

"Think of something," he said, "that'll let your landlady give me a room."

"Why?" asked Emma.

"Because"—Shay was reasonable— "I can't stay at the hotel."

"Sauer's staying at the hotel," said Emma. "I'm perfectly well able to look after myself."

"The exact words," Shay added affably, "with which Horsack and the professor met their doom. Sauer isn't staying on at the hotel. When he knows anything he'll find that he's staying with Faber."

"In custody?"

"Under supervision, anyway."

"But he couldn't have killed the professor," Emma began. She was thinking that he had been in Denver with Mary, but she remembered that the professor might have been killed early in the evening, and she didn't want to tell Shay about Mary and Sauer. "Anyhow," she said, "he didn't buy the strychnine. Aggie did."

"If Aggie could, why not Sauer? Oh, I don't know that he did, but he went to Denver a lot, and the old boy is trying to check. I don't know what motive he had for killing the professor, but jealousy is a plenty good motive for killing Horsack, and it's the only one we've unearthed yet. I'm just a passenger; your old friend is running the show, and he told me to get into Mrs. D.'s house and stay there. I got a stack of plates and I'm going to photograph war bonnets." He stopped and felt in the pocket of his jacket. "I got the pictures of the house too; that'll get me in the front door."

Mr. Weatherbee, Emma was thinking, was just plain perverse. Aggie was the one who had done the murders, not Sauer, but for some reason Mr. Weatherbee refused to consider her as a suspect. Sauer couldn't have done them; Mary wasn't entitled to such persistent bad luck in her men; it violated the laws of probability. Emma could hear Jeff's voice saying: "Some nights you can't win. . . ." But a dissolute Italian, Horsack the sadist, and finally a murderer would surely be the result of stacked cards. But there were times, she admitted—last night, for example—when she had almost liked Sauer.

Mrs. Danforth, a neat apron tied over a neat house dress, was pinning sheets over the chairs in the gold room when they entered.

Shay approached her, beaming. "Got something for you."

At the sight of the pictures Mrs. Danforth smiled, though her first expression on seeing Shay had been one of distaste. She winced only slightly as Shay brushed back the bric-a-brac on the center table to spread the prints out.

"Pretty nice, eh? Detail shows up good. This was in here; light was just right, not so good in the dining room." Shay babbled on. His technical comments were Greek to Mrs. Danforth, but the pictures were good; without caricature, they caught the grandiose spirit of the house, and because Shay knew his business they showed full use of lights and contrasts. In one picture the meat hooks cast gigantic shadows of themselves on the alley wall; Mrs. Danforth preferred the glittering one of the chandelier.

"Take 'em all," Shay said. "They're all for you. I've got others. And I've got to take some more of the town for the Historical Society, and I wondered if you could fix me up with a room—any old room. You see, the hotel's closing—"

Mrs. Danforth drew back from the pictures, but she kept her eyes on them. "I'm afraid I haven't a room."

Shay patted her arm. "I know how you feel," he said, "but I'm a tough guy. I wouldn't mind having the professor's room, and you've got to start letting it sometime."

Mrs. Danforth seemed unimpressed. Emma tried to think of something.

"Miss Dolan and I," she piped up, "want to stay a few more days. The weather's so beautiful now. It would make it nice to have a man in the house."

Shay gave Emma a look that said she wasn't saying the right thing, and Emma subsided.

Shay pulled a wad of money from his pocket. "Strikes me," he said, "it ought to be worth a little more to stay in a room like that. What do you say—six, seven dollars a day?"

It was an outrageous price; Emma was sure that Mrs. Danforth would suspect that she was being coerced, but she knew that Mrs. Danforth needed money.

"Well"—Mrs. Danforth was weakening—"it won't be very convenient without a telephone. I have the telephone disconnected after the season."

"I can't think," said Shay, "of a single person I want to talk to."

Well, really, Emma thought, Shay was laying it on with a trowel. She cupped her hand to receive the ash from her cigarette and looked around for a place to deposit both the ash and the stub with the helpless feeling of a smoker in a nonsmoking household. There was nothing within range that resembled an ashtray, and not for worlds would she have desecrated the scrubbed marble hearth. She went out into the hall and nobly restrained herself from dumping her burdens among the canes and umbrellas in the cast-iron base of the hall tree. It was bad enough, according to Emma's rules, to dump cigarette ashes on the floor; it was inexcusable to hide them under cushions, behind radiators, or in umbrella stands. There was an ashtray in her room—cigar bands under glass—and it seemed easier to go up there than to hunt further. She went upstairs quickly, because the butt was burning its way down to her fingers, and then went in Mary's door because it was open. Her own was locked, and she would have had to drop her bag, ash, or cigarette to unlock it, but still she was annoyed with Mary for her repeated forgetfulness. She kicked the door to with her heel, and then with a feeling of great accomplishment she unloaded ash into Mary's souvenir of Pikes Peak. As she started for her own room she looked up and saw that Aggie had been watching her. Aggie in a pale blue smock that was almost white. Emma told herself that Shay was downstairs, that all she had to do was yell, but she wished as she moved forward in answer to Aggie's slowly beckoning finger that she hadn't shut the door.

Aggie stood by Emma's commode.

Thick walls and heavy doors could deaden sound. . . .

There was an expression of urgent desperation on Aggie's face. . . .

The carpet was thick; it would muffle a fall. . . .

Emma dragged her feet across it.

Aggie had something clutched in the hand that she extended as Emma drew close.

Downstairs a door slammed and Shay went whistling down the walk.

"Take this," Aggie whispered, "and get me a brown crayon."

She thrust something into Emma's hand and ran to answer Mrs. Danforth, who was calling her from the hall.

Through the now-open door Emma heard Mrs. Danforth instructing Aggie to get out clean linen for the professor's room, and she let her emotions sink back to normal before she looked at what Aggie had given her.

A neatly rolled crisp ten-dollar bill. Ten dollars for a brown crayon. How very like Aggie! But where had Aggie come by ten dollars? New ten dollars fresh from the bank? Emma had gathered that Mrs. Danforth doled out the money, and she doubted that it came ten dollars at a time.

Aggie had been standing by the commode.

Acting on pure impulse, Emma opened the lower section of the commode and saw the Dresden pot with the crocheted silencer on its cover and began to giggle. It was crazy. Aggie was crazy. And she was as crazy as Aggie.

Nevertheless, she lifted the cover of the pot, and then she knew that she was crazy, for there in the pot was a sheaf of crisp new ten-dollar bills. Setting down the lid, Emma counted them: nine, and one made ten.

Aggie had a hundred dollars hidden in the thunder mug!

Emma broke off in the middle of another giggle. If it was crazy for Aggie to have ten dollars, what was it for her to have a hundred? Lunacy? Or sanity? Somebody had paid Aggie. Paid for her silence or cooperation. That made sense. But Aggie had hidden her money in a pot and wanted only a brown crayon. That was crazy.

But not entirely so. Emma realized that her room was as safe a place as Aggie could find, and only the chance that Aggie had been standing by the commode had led Emma to look into it. Aggie wasn't so dumb. And the dishes hidden among the dirty clothes. Only the buying of the tea set had led to Emma's discovery of that. The tea set!

Emma put the cover back and closed the commode door quietly, busily putting two and two together. She had paid a hundred dollars in new ten-dollar bills for the tea set. Aggie was now in possession of one hundred dollars. Aggie had stolen the money; Aggie had stolen the tea set. Or—Emma conceded that this might be true—the tea set belonged to Aggie, not, as Emma had assumed, to Mrs. Danforth.

What did Aggie want with one hundred dollars? To buy a brown crayon and strychnine. For Emma's money, the case against Aggie was plain. At this point the law should be called upon and an arrest made. That was the way Hank did things, but she wasn't Hank, and the resemblance between Mr. Faber and the Boston police force was far farfetched. And between Mr. Faber and an arrest stood Mr. Weatherbee and his stubborn refusal to consider Aggie guilty. He and Shay seemed to have settled on Sauer as their culprit, a choice that Emma felt was decidedly wrong, though of course *she* wasn't being stubborn about it.

Shay came stumbling and whistling upstairs, rattling the banisters with the corner of his suitcase. Shay's blundering was a comfort, Emma thought. With him around any well-laid plan of murder and sabotage was sure to go awry, because Shay would stumble into the middle of it.

Emma went out into the hall in time to hear Shay's words to Aggie.

"And now, sweetheart," he was saying, "I need another table to spread this stuff out on, and if I catch you touching these cameras I'll cut your arm off."

The words were those Shay would have used to Emma or anyone else, and the tone was no more harried than usual, but the expression on Aggie's face as she went out carrying an armful of magazines was ecstatic.

Good lord, Emma thought, if Aggie had developed a yen for Horsack, Shay's particular variety of brutal blandishment would set her poor thwarted soul to yearning for Shay. She ought to warn Shay that it was not safe to encourage Aggie's affections.

She stepped forward, but Shay caught sight of her and with a derisive waggle of his fingers shut the door in her face.

"All right for you, smarty," said Emma, but Shay was whistling loudly in order not to hear her.

Emma wondered why she didn't go home. No one appreciated her. Shay didn't want her; Mr. Weatherbee had politely invited her to stay, but he hadn't taken her into his confidence; Mary was completely oblivious of any need for help. It would be a good joke on all of them if she packed her bags and took the noon train.

And it would be a good joke on her if Mr. Weatherbee had her stopped in Denver. That is, Mr. Weatherbee would think it a good joke.

At the present moment there was only one person who had asked for her assistance, and that was Aggie.

Who could tell? If she got Aggie a brown crayon, perhaps Aggie would content herself with drawing pictures and not murder Shay. It was worth a chance. Emma went back, got her bag, locked the doors, and proceeded down the street to the Great Mercantile and Dry Goods Supply Company.

"No," said the clerk in answer to Emma's inquiry, "you tell Aggie that I told her we wouldn't have no more crayons till we get the school supplies in. She don't remember so long as your arm, but I guess you found that out."

Emma, used to the anonymity of a large city, was becoming accustomed to local knowledge of her person and her whereabouts.

"I'll tell her I couldn't get any," she said meekly, and then added, "You aren't as busy as you were yesterday."

"Was you in here yesterday?" The clerk seemed surprised to have missed her.

"I came in with Miss Pinzi."

"Then Mrs. Willis waited on you. There was such a jam I couldn't see everybody, but Mrs. Willis said she waited on Miss Pinzi. She's awful pretty; is it true that Sauer is a spy?"

"I don't know," Emma said. "I don't think so." Then, before she could be asked another question, she fired one of her own: "Is it true that Aggie bought strychnine?"

The girl nodded. "Rat poison. My cousin works in at the drugstore. She said Mrs. Danforth sent her for it, but that don't mean anything. Did she really poison the professor?"

Emma caught herself just in time. Maybe Aggie had poisoned the professor, but Emma and Mr. Weatherbee and Shay were the only ones supposed to know it.

"Where did you hear that?" she asked sharply.

Too sharply, perhaps, for the girl just shrugged her shoulders. "I just thought she might. She poisoned a dog once that was running around with his nose full of porcupine quills."

A woman with two children came in, and Emma, abandoned for their wants, went on down the street, pondering the additional motive that the girl had given her. If Aggie had poisoned a suffering dog, might she not have poisoned the professor because of his ailment?

Sure, if she knew about it. But, being Aggie, she might equally well have done it for no reason at all.

"Phooey," said Emma to the window of the dingy antique shop.

But the clerk had given Emma more than one hint. She had presented the possibilities of the direct question. Emma had never, being a New Englander, made an unqualified statement, and she avoided the direct question for the same reason. Only cops, in Emma's experience, asked direct questions.

"Did you kill Mr. X?" a cop would say, but who was ever silly enough to say yes?

Emma allowed herself to be sidetracked in the mental creation of a case in which all the suspects said yes instead of no. Probably there was a law against it.

But out here, in God's and Mr. Weatherbee's country, people, if they hadn't already found out all about you, just up and asked. Emma walked into the antique shop, swallowed hard, and addressed the proprietress.

"Did that tea set belong to Agatha Estis?"

"Yes," said the woman, "and I gave her the money."

Slightly floored at the success of her new system, Emma mumbled that she had thought it belonged to Mrs. Danforth.

The woman sniffed. *"She* wouldn't sell anything, but the tea set belonged to Aggie; her brother had it made."

"Things may be different next year." Emma was thinking that the absence of roomers might force Mrs. Danforth into selling.

"She don't need the money. She's got stingy in the last six-seven years, that's all. She used to buy her clothes in Denver—the Great Mercantile wasn't good enough for her—but now she buys them up here."

"Has Aggie always been the way she is?"

"Ever since I been here, but that's only sixteen years next March. We come up here from Kansas for my husband's chest, but he died fourteen years ago in November, and I never went back. It's awful cold here in winter, but it's awful hot in Kansas in the summer and, anyway, we sold the farm to my brother, and I never could get along with his wife."

When Emma could escape from the recital of family quarrels she went back to the hotel; it was almost train time, and the lobby was a flurried chaos of last-minute changes, mislaid bundles, and lost tickets. Nella, the woman with the mole, was there, standing guard as the desk clerk marked an address on a cardboard carton with a piece of brown crayon. Emma walked over, with the crayon in mind.

"Hello," she said, "or rather, it's good-by, isn't it?"

"I, e, you fool," said Nella, "not y." She glared at Emma as though she couldn't spell either.

Nella was going, and with her Mary's peace of mind, Emma thought. Maybe a quick one would work here.

"Is Count Galeazzo," she asked, "really alive?"

But the dark woman was not caught off guard. Her eyes did not shift as she said nastily: "Don't you wish that you knew?" Then she picked up her box and elbowed herself away.

"That's good riddance," said the clerk; "not so much as a nickel . . . ."

"Never mind," Emma soothed him, "I'll give you a quarter for that crayon."

CHAPTER TWELVE

IF EMMA hadn't given the clerk the quarter he might not have run so fast with the telegram. It was sent merely to Central City, and the local operator, being thoroughly conversant with Emma's habits, had called the hotel, because Mrs. Danforth's telephone was disconnected. Emma had just given Aggie the crayon when the scrawled slip of paper was thrust under her nose.

"Meet tubercular friend one-twenty Denver," she read. The message was signed "Hank."

"Who's Hank?" asked the clerk. "You'll have to hurry."

"What?" asked Emma. "He's crazy. He's a friend of mine. Of all the idiots . . . Shay!"

"You'll have to hurry," the clerk insisted, "to catch the train."

"Oh, my gosh." Emma started upstairs, came back, and thrust the wire into Aggie's hands. "Give this to Mr. Horrigan and tell Mrs. Danforth—"

Hatless, Emma tore out of the house, down to the station, and flung herself on the train just as it gave its final toot.

What, in the name of heaven, she asked herself, was she supposed to do with a tubercular friend? The climate might be good for him, but Hank certainly had his nerve, expecting her to look after him——or her. It might be a woman. That would be dandy! A female invalid was certainly going to be a help when she was busy solving murders. Of course Hank didn't know about the murders, but he might have guessed, if he had any imagination.

Emma fumed all the trip down the mountain and almost missed seeing Fox get off the train with Nella. If they hadn't been so close together she might not have noticed, but she looked again and saw the handcuffs. There was no expression on either of their faces; Fox's was as unconcerned as Nella's was wooden; there was no disturbance as they walked through the crowd jostling toward the bus. Because of Nella's lack of popularity, none of the company hailed her or asked her for help in carrying a bag. No one seemed to notice that she got into a waiting car instead of the bus.

Nella had been Fox's spy!

Her eyes goggling, Emma took a taxi because she had only ten minutes left and sat bolt upright on the edge of the seat in her excitement. She had to hand it to Fox; he had been smooth as silk and sudden as a thunder-clap. When had he put on the handcuffs? She wished she had seen that. Had he stuck a gun in Nella's ribs as she got off the train and said: "Come quietly"? Had he slipped into a seat beside her and had the bracelets on before he flashed his badge? Had Nella been mute from the moment she knew her number was up? Emma felt that she had been cheated, but she was ready to admit that the Hoover boys had something.

And Nella was a spy. That was odd, in a way, because she looked too much like a sinister character to be one. Probably Nella had killed Horsack and the professor. But Mr. Weatherbee didn't think so; he had said that everyone had an alibi but Mary and Sauer.

Emma paid the taxi driver too much because her head was whirling, got a redcap, and found that her train was already in the yards. She got a wheelchair, because an invalid would probably need one, and permission to go through the gate to the platform. She wondered if she should call an ambulance. The patient might come on a stretcher. Nella might have had an alibi for the time Horsack was killed, but how about the professor? Would an ambulance go clear to Central City? The whole thing was absurd.

The train slid in beside her, making her stomach go in waves, as trains always did; the conductors and the porters swung off, and then came the people. There were soldiers and sailors and women with sleek luggage and more soldiers and sailors and other women with bundles, but no tottering wreck or stretcher-borne body. Instead, Hank was suddenly in front of her, tall and grinning and, miraculously, standing up straight in his uniform.

"What," said Emma, "are you doing here?"

"Settling my affairs, and since I only have one—"

"Darling," said Emma. "Angel. . . ."

Hank kissed her. "That's better. For a moment the fervidness of your welcome had me fooled. Do you travel in this?"

He pointed to the wheelchair and the grinning redcap.

"You said 'tubercular friend,' but I should have known, except that I was so upset about the murders, and now Nella is a spy and, goodness, but I'm glad you've come."

Hank had picked up his bag. "I just got off to say hello; I find I have urgent business in Boston."

"Don't be a dope. You know you have no intention of going; you'll love it in the mountains, and Mr. Weatherbee is worth every nickel of the admission, only—" She stopped. "Go on away," she said. "Mr. Weatherbee and I sort of wanted to finish this ourselves, anyway. Well, aren't you going?"

Hank flung his bag in the wheelchair. "No," he said, "I just remembered, 'a member of the armed forces is not supposed to practice his profession for pay,' and you never heard of me working for nothing. Any chance of a little fishing?"

"Sure," said Emma. "I'll be too busy to go, but Mr. Weatherbee will know about it. Come on, I don't even know if the train runs back any more."

As they fell into step down the ramp Hank took her arm. "Would this Mr. Weatherbee be, by any chance, the reason I have had only one post card from you?"

"Why, Henry Fairbanks"—Emma sounded pleased—"don't tell me that you're jealous? I thought you had gone off somewhere where mail wouldn't get you." Actually, Emma had known that if she wrote, her letters would be full of murders, and she had hated to admit that she was involved in another. "Seriously"—she changed the subject— "how did you get leave so soon?"

"Rule number one," Hank answered her, "applicable anywhere, at any time: Don't ask how or why. All the fellows that had hurry-up orders promptly got ten days' leave. And don't ask why, because I don't know that either, but not being one to peer at the molars of a gift horse— Who is this Weatherbee, anyhow?"

"He's marvelous," said Emma, enjoying herself. "He owns half of Colorado and he's terribly clever . . . ."

"Mm," said Hank. "How's Mary?"

"Marvelous; she's married, only she's not sure—"

"While she was drunk, I suppose. I told her to be careful."

"Idiot! She thought he was dead, but now she's not sure, and the FBI has got the only person that knows, and Mr. Weatherbee's thinking Sauer did it really is a blessing because they can't live together until she finds out."

"I love you," said Hank, "the way you are, but for the purposes of clarity you might be a little more definite. You mentioned a couple of murders, but all the information I've been able to gather on that is from my own observation that you are not in the hands of the law."

"I supposed," said Emma, "that Shay was sending you a daily report. Did you send him up here?"

"Mm. I may have mentioned it. Shay can't write; he's left-handed."

"I know it, and so was Horsack. That's one of the odd things. We'll have to take a taxi."

In the taxi they kissed again and did not speak for a time of murders or sudden death.

The little train was running, though Hank professed surprise that it

could, and as they settled down for the trip up the canyon Emma began:
"Well, the first day I got here . . ."

Except for groans and ejaculations, Hank did not interrupt Emma's story. Once when the train was teetering on a narrow ledge far up on the wall of the canyon he moved over to an inside seat, as Emma had done before him, and he reached across the narrow aisle to hold Emma's hand as she described her vigil in the mine shaft. Emma's tale had no chronological order, because as she went along she was always reminding herself of something that she had left out of the earlier part of her narrative. But Hank could find out the sequence of events for himself. What he liked about Emma's mind was the way it picked up little oddments of fact, it being, in that respect, not unlike the pack rat of her story. The shiny, odd-shaped pebbles of information that Emma treasured might be merely curiosa, but sometimes they turned out to be the missing pieces of the picture. He was picking up these scraps now, tabulating them in his mind—the fact that Horsack had been left-handed, that Aggie drew pictures that made sense, even if she didn't, that Mrs. Danforth was stingy, that Sauer was obsessed with his father, that Nella had been in the house on the day on which the professor died, that the streets of Central City had been paved with silver, and that Mr. Weatherbee wore high heels.

Hank had rather a poor picture of Mr. Weatherbee; he rather imagined him as a middle-aged four-flusher, a jack-of-all-trades who wore built-up heels to increase his importance, but this was because Emma had rather slighted Mr. Weatherbee in her narrative for purposes of her own.

At Blackhawk the train jerked to a stop, then gathered itself for the final climb to Central City.

As Hank and Emma got off the train Hank drew a deep breath.

"Well," asked Emma, "do you smell it?"

"What?"

"The smell of crime, the creeping, horrible suggestion of death and treachery in the air that leaves you gasping and waiting for the appearance of Colonel Primrose?"

"Oh," Hank laughed, "you mean the sense of evil unfolding like a loathsome flower, each petal black as sin but streaked blood-red?"

"That's it!"

"No. All I smell is fresh air, and you have to breathe twice to get that."

"It's the altitude," said Emma with the callousness of an old hand. "You'll get used to it, but don't walk too fast."

"Have I ever?"

They smiled at each other with the pleasure of understanding, of being together again.

Hank looked around at the narrow rutted streets, the ramshackle build-ings, the barren hills, and the towering piles of scrap beside the station.

"Not a pretty place," he announced, "but I see the Boy Scouts are hard at it."

"Mr. Weatherbee," said Emma, "and a derrick. That's machinery from abandoned mines and shops. Old Number 6 hauls it down when it's not hauling tourists. Mr. Weatherbee," she added slyly, "owns the railroad too."

Hank ignored her. "I've never seen a gold mine; it might be inter-esting."

Emma sniffed. "There are a few of them working, but it's poor stuff; if it assays two dollars to the ton they can make money."

"Where'd you learn so much? From your friend Weatherbee?"

Emma positively pranced. "Darling, you're enchanting when you're jealous."

Several people nodded to Emma as they passed and stared at Hank's uniform. An old man said, "Hello, soldier," and was promptly corrected by two overalled boys.

"Chummy crowd, aren't they?" Hank spoke a little stiffly.

"They're friendly, but frank," Emma explained. "You have to get used to it."

In front of the hotel Emma paused. "I don't exactly know"—she wrinkled her forehead—"what to do with you."

"Of course, if I'm not wanted—"

"Angel-face," said Emma, "it's only that we've just got Shay into the only available room at Mrs. Danforth's and the hotel is closing . . . ."

The bar door was open, and Emma looked in.

"Come on," she said, "we'll go in here."

For Mr. Weatherbee and Shay were at the bar, and Emma was with them before Hank could protest.

Shay glanced up from his drink.

"Well, dress me up and call me baby, if it ain't the admiral himself come to take over. Hiya, Hank!"

"You two have met, I believe," said Emma demurely, "but Mr. Weatherbee, this is Mr. Fairbanks."

"Pleased to make your acquaintance." Mr. Weatherbee extended a hard hand that Hank shook with enthusiasm.

"Sir," said Hank fervently, "from the stories of your exploits I had imagined a much younger man."

Mr. Weatherbee did not look at Emma; he merely said: "A man's as old as he feels, I guess. Have a drink?"

"He will," said Shay. "No man has ever been able to stop him."

"Shay Horrigan," Emma expostulated, "you never cease to amaze me. Here it is only in the middle of the forenoon—"

"It's not," said Shay. "It's after lunch, and I'm going to drink with the sailor home from the sea."

"Don't kid me," said Hank. "I tried."

Emma looked relieved. "I wondered why I was hungry."

"Chew," bellowed Mr. Weatherbee, "get something for the lady, but mix the drinks first."

Chew grinned at them from behind the bar. He was capable, Emma thought, of running the entire place himself.

Hank looked around the bar. "Cozy," he said. "Sir"—to Mr. Weatherbee—"do you live here all alone?"

"Just temporarily."

"We have to put Hank somewhere," said Emma. "He's really a detective, and he might be some use to us."

"If we needed a detective." Shay was looking smug. "You missed the shooting. Case's all over, all washed up. Meet Sherlock Weatherbee and Watson Horrigan."

"What?" said Emma. "Who? Oh, I think you're mean to do it without me!"

"It's a man's world," said Shay loftily. "Sauer's the baby."

Emma thought of Mary and tore up all her own suspicions of Sauer and threw them out the window. "Oh, you're wrong. I know you're wrong. This'll kill Mary! She didn't even know that Horsack's death wasn't an accident. I hadn't told her."

"She knows it now," Shay interrupted her. "After we got Sauer moved we searched his room and we found this, all neatly tucked in the Gideon Bible."

"Gideon Bible?" said Emma, watching as Shay unfolded a map.

It was a tourist map of the Denver Mountain Parks Area, procurable in any filling station, but around the towns of Leadville and Climax circles were hastily scratched with a brown crayon. There were other lines, straight, and all converging on the city of Denver.

"It's a map," said Emma, "of trips he meant to take and places he meant to go."

"No," said Mr. Weatherbee. "Those lines indicate the route of the Denver water supply, and Climax isn't a ghost town. It is the country's largest producer of molybdenum. For steel," he added, "for ships," as Emma looked blank.

"Oh," said Emma.

"Now your chum Sauer might conceivably want to visit Climax, but what would he want with the Denver water supply, except to blow it up?"

"But he's not the spy," Emma insisted. "Nella's the spy. The FBI got her as she got off the train. You knew that too." She turned accusingly on Mr. Weatherbee, who nodded.

"Fox was real agreeable about not picking her up here."

"You'll go to any length," Emma exploded, "to keep things from upsetting your old opera season, but the minute it's over you dash out and arrest a poor boy—"

She was interrupted by Mr. Faber, who looked slightly upset.

"He's hitched," he announced. "He's handcuffed to the bedpost. He can move the bed, but he can't get it out the door. Whew!" Mr. Faber reached for the bottle and poured himself a stiff drink.

"Where's Mary?"

"She's a-holding his other hand, and ain't she a little wildcat when she gets loose?"

Emma gathered that Mr. Faber's perturbation had to do with Mary rather than the securing of the still-groggy Sauer.

Mr. Faber poured himself another drink and, because this one was for sociability and not to quiet his nerves, added a little water.

"Well," he said, "it looks as though we got him. He had the motive and no alibi; this Horsack was a Czech, and the professor was doing a job for his country, and Sauer was a spy."

Emma waited for Hank to speak, to protest that they had no real proof.

Mr. Weatherbee also deferred to Hank. "Have you any opinion?"

"Leave me out," Hank protested. "All I know is what Miss Marsh told me coming up on the train."

"Then," said Mr. Weatherbee, "you probably know more than I do right this minute."

"All I know is that I'll have to try to help this Sauer, because Mary's an old friend, and if she's married to him—" Hank broke off because Emma was making faces at him while the rest were silent with interest.

"That," said Emma in a small voice, "wasn't supposed to be mentioned."

"So," said Faber, "he goes and gets himself married, because she likely knows he done it."

"No," Emma insisted, "he's in love with her and she loves him and she's there all alone, wherever he is. Hank, you go with Mr. Faber and talk to her. Tell her they've arrested Rho just for a blind, that they don't really think he did it. It won't make any difference," she silenced Mr. Faber's protest, "because if he is a spy Mary'll have to get over him, but if he isn't it'll make her feel better. Darling, please go."

Hank went because he wanted to see Mary and because, if Emma was up to her old tricks of withholding information, it would be better if he kept his mouth shut until he could have a private conference with her. He thought he had broken her of that trick. He smiled wryly to himself as he followed a silent Faber. He had thought that he would have a peaceful leave with Emma, walking, doing a little fishing, perhaps, but here he was, thrown into the customary turmoil. Murders, even spies. Maps hidden in Bibles. So Horsack had been telephoning when he was killed. . . .

Hank caught himself reconstructing the scene of the crime and smiled again, this time at himself.

Back in the bar Shay was surveying his drink gloomily.

"Married," he said sadly. "All the best beetles are married."

Emma bit into the fried-egg sandwich supplied by Chew and said nothing.

"Married," said Mr. Weatherbee, only he was referring to Sauer, "to the girl who might know why Horsack was trying to call the FBI when he was killed. He couldn't be sure that Horsack hadn't told her that he and the woman were working together, so he marries her to kill that testimony."

Well, if they weren't married, Emma thought to herself, that settled that. But still she said nothing. There was no point in airing Mary's matrimonial difficulties before these two men.

"Ain't there ways," Mr. Weatherbee went on hopefully, "of making a person talk?"

"Ways," Shay agreed; "only some of 'em'll die first."

And Emma, remembering Nella's dark, grim face, felt that she was one of those.

"The Indians," said Mr. Weatherbee reminiscently, "used to take slivers of pine—"

"The Japanese," Shay began, "have an engaging trick—"

"Hush, both of you," said Emma. "Has her room been searched or has the housekeeper cleaned it up?"

"Fox," said Mr. Weatherbee, "sealed it. He'll be back. I locked Sauer's."

Emma changed the subject again: "Why are you so dead set against it having been Aggie?"

Mr. Weatherbee put on his most childlike look. "Am I?"

"I thought we were through playing games." Emma was cross. "You've brushed me off every time I've mentioned Aggie, but it was her crayon that you found under Horsack; she bought the strychnine and carried the tray, and don't forget that somebody put that tray in my closet."

Mr. Weatherbee looked shrunken and old, but Emma refused to let herself be deceived; he could put on that look at will; he was still faking in spite of his pretense of coming out in the open and joining forces.

Emma was annoyed that Hank and Mary came in then, interrupting whatever answer Mr. Weatherbee might have made.

"Sauer's asleep," said Hank. "The booze should have worn off by now. What did you give him? Knockout drops?"

"Just a sedative," said Shay. "In polite circles it's called a sedative."

"I'll have some," said Hank. "Just a little sedative and water. And Mary tells me that Horsack must have been on the right track. She says he claimed to have spotted a spy."

"Well, for heaven's sake!" Emma turned on Mary. "Why didn't you say so? Who was it? Nella?"

Mr. Weatherbee was watching Mary, searching her face, almost hopefully, it seemed, but Mary said no more; she was on the defensive, as though Hank had not entirely convinced her that Sauer's arrest was only a blind. She sat down beside Emma and did not touch the glass Chew set in front of her, but she could not, in the face of the things she had not told Emma, berate her for not having revealed that the two deaths were murder.

Hank looked at his glass and looked across at Shay, who was grinning at him. "Just a moment," he said, turning to Mr. Weatherbee. "This matter, I take it, is now in the hands of the FBI?"

Mr. Weatherbee nodded.

"The rooms are locked?"

"The rooms are locked."

"The smart boys are coming back?"

Mr. Weatherbee nodded again.

Hank raised his glass. "Then what are we waiting for?

"Of course," he added after a sizable swallow, "I have no connection with this case anyhow." He winked at Emma, who could have slapped him.

"Down the hatch," said Shay, "if I may borrow a nautical expression."

"It has become," Hank assured him, "part of the vernacular."

Mr. Weatherbee, after what seemed like a last appealing glance at Mary, joined them.

Hank looked around at the high corniced ceilings, at the dark woodwork. "This place reminds me of my great-aunt's house in Dorchester."

"What'd she do," Shay wanted to know, "run a gin mill?"

"She ran the W.C.T.U., but her decor was similar."

"Temperance feller came up here to speak once," Mr. Weatherbee chimed in. "No platform for him to speak from, so the boys made one out of whiskey kegs."

"Cooperation," said Shay. "The association of persons for their common benefit. Chew!" he yelled. "How about a little cooperation? Any of you gentlemen ready to cooperate?"

The vote was unanimous.

"You know," said Hank, "the picture is fairly clear."

"The altitude's getting him," Emma muttered to Mary.

"Horsack," Hank continued, "was onto the woman, Nella. She knew it and was watching him. You say she has an alibi for when he went to telephone, so she must have sent Sauer after him, and Sauer killed him. Perfectly simple. Fine example of cooperation."

"He didn't," Mary broke out. "He didn't; he was with me. I—I'd started for the hotel. Rho thought I was going after Paul and found me taking the letters—"

Shay, whistling softly, looked at the ceiling; Mr. Weatherbee looked at Emma and then dropped his eyes.

"The yard was empty," Mary protested into the silence, "but someone must have seen us."

"Pardon me." Hank applied himself to his sedative. "I forgot, I don't even work here."

"You should have thought of that sooner." Shay spoke to Mary. "Now that you're married to him the cooperation is null and void: no good."

"But I'm not—" Mary broke off because Emma had given her a smart kick on the shin. She turned on Emma, her eyes flashing. "I'm not going to sit here and let them pretend that Rho did it. Hank told me his arrest was just a blind."

"I forgot." Hank looked sorrowful. "I clean forgot, not having this case really on my mind. Anybody read any good books lately?"

"Henry Fairbanks," said Emma, "someday I shall strike you. You're just baiting her, and you know it. That was Nella's map. She planted it on Sauer. A child could figure that out. In a Gideon Bible!"

"A Gideon Bible!" Hank's face lit up. "Bless your little addlepated mind! I knew I'd forgotten something; I have to send a wire."

He got up and, following Mr. Weatherbee's pointing finger, disappeared into the lobby.

"I give up," said Emma. "I thought he would be some use, but I almost wish he hadn't come."

A man in the striped overalls and peaked cap of the railroad came in to see about the loading of the scrap, and Mr. Weatherbee left with him reluctantly. He paused in the doorway. "Come back here and eat," he said. "Chew'll find something. And your young man," he addressed Emma, "can stay here."

Mary wanted to go back to see Sauer and persuaded Emma to go with her, leaving Shay to tell Hank of their whereabouts.

Mr. Faber let them into the back room that was his own sleeping quarters and left them. Sauer, wearing shirt and pants, was stretched out on the bed; his face was flushed and he was breathing heavily. Mary went over to him and smoothed back his hair. Her face was soft now and tender, and if Emma had had any doubts about the depth of Mary's feelings, they vanished at the sound of her words.

"Darling," she said gently, "you didn't do it; I won't let them hurt you."

She sat down on the side of the rumpled bed, cradling Sauer's free hand in both her own. Emma shoved a soiled shirt onto the floor and made a place for herself on the room's one chair.

"There must be some way," Mary went on speaking, "of finding out that Galeazzo is still alive. Maybe Hank will know. I hope he is, because then they'll have to let me testify that Rho was with me."

"Good heavens"—Emma was startled, but she kept her voice low—"you don't want all that mess to come out. What will Rho think?"

Mary looked at her scornfully. "That doesn't make any difference, compared to the trouble Rho's in. I tried to tell them, but you kicked me."

In the face of Mary's ready sacrifice Emma felt ashamed. "You can tell Hank," she conceded meekly. "I didn't think there was any use in broadcasting it."

"It doesn't make any difference," Mary repeated, "about me. Hank might be able to get a sworn affidavit from her if she thought I didn't want him to be alive. Br-rr, I'm glad she's gone, though; she gave me the creeps."

"Was she the one Horsack was suspicious about?" Now that they were alone Emma felt free to press the question. "I wish you had told me."

Mary shivered. "It was bad enough in Rome. Sonny—Galeazzo—was a member of the Fascist secret police. After you've been through a thing like that you don't go around calling people spies." She paused and then burst out, "Paul said it was Rho! That's why I didn't tell you. I didn't believe him; I thought he was saying it to torment me, but I couldn't accuse anyone else. I never thought of Nella."

"I wonder;" Emma mused, "if her alibi is really all right."

"It is." Mary spoke glumly. "I heard her get half a dozen to confirm it. And they were people who would have been glad to cut her up if they could. I've been such a dolt," she went on. "After Paul died—was killed—I was so relieved that I swallowed that story of its being an accident. Are you really sure it wasn't?"

"Not unless Mr. Weatherbee is lying about the blood on the door-knob, and I don't think that because I think he'd have liked to have had it an accident."

"He's a funny old man." Mary smoothed the hand that she held. "They say that once he was engaged to Aggie."

"No!" Who says so?" Emma's exclamation was so loud that Mary shushed her.

"It was just gossip. Don't be so noisy. Who cares now?"

"I care, for one, because it explains why he's blind at everything that points to Aggie: the crayon, the sipper—" She had to explain these things to Mary, along with her theory that Aggie, out of thwarted love, had killed both Horsack and the professor.

"You were awfully busy and you didn't tell me much," Mary chided, "but," she went on hopefully, "it does make sense. There was one of her pictures in with the letters that I took from Paul's room. A picture of Paul, signed 'from an admirer.' I think I burned it up."

"Yes," said Emma, "I think you did."

Mary was thinking in terms of Sauer and did not notice Emma's tone. "That straightens everything out, doesn't it? If Aggie did the murders? Because of course Rho isn't a spy. Darling, you're too, too clever."

Emma, being comparatively modest, didn't think it was quite so simple as that, but if it cheered Mary up she was willing to let it stand.

She got up. "I want to see Hank; maybe he can get some action out of the facts. You don't need to stay here."

"I think I will. He might wake up. I'll see you at dinner."

CHAPTER THIRTEEN

EMMA hurried back to the hotel.

Imagine Mr. Weatherbee engaged to Aggie!

It didn't alter the facts any; it merely altered her confidence in herself. Before, she had thought that Mr. Weatherbee's refusal to see things her way meant that her deductions were somehow faulty; now she knew it for a vestigial, romantic loyalty. Hank would know how to convince him of his duty, or, failing that, how to go over his head to the police. Hank would not be overawed by Mr. Weatherbee's assumption of authority.

The bar entrance was closed and locked. Squinting through the glass panes of the door, Emma could see that neither Hank nor Shay was at the table. She looked again. They weren't under it either, which was some comfort, though it did seem that Hank would sort of stick around on the first day of his visit. Though of course there was no reason to suppose that being in the service would make him change his cavalier ways. She wished that someone would talk to her, would feel about her as Mary felt about Sauer. She wished that she had gone home, hadn't accepted Mr. Weatherbee's challenge to stay, had let the murders pass into oblivion. But that wouldn't have kept them from suspecting Sauer.

Was he really a murderer and a spy, as Horsack had suspected, or was he a pleasant, rather childish person, as he had seemed the day of the celebration? Perhaps Horsack had really suspected Nella and had only said Sauer, as Mary thought, to bedevil her. But Horsack had been killed and Nella had an alibi. Emma wished she could tell about people. She knew she was too given to accepting those who talked her language, liked the things she liked, passing over the eternal verities of honesty and steadfastness for a ready wit and good taste in shoes.

She went on up the street.

Imagine Mr. Weatherbee engaged to Aggie! There it was again. Imagine tough-as-nails old Weatherbee preserving a long-ago soft spot!

Emma climbed the steps to Mrs. Danforth's and opened the front door tentatively. If Aggie were really the murderer it would be well to keep an eye out. Only somehow she couldn't seem to be seriously afraid of Aggie, except for the time she had seen Aggie watching her from beside the commode. She still had Aggie's money, too, because she had paid for the crayon with her own quarter. There was no sign of anyone in the hall, and Emma stepped rather quickly through the late-afternoon gloom up the stairs. Shay's door was open, and so, confoundedly, was Mary's. Obstinately Emma took out her key and let herself in, walked to the bureau, and threw down the key. What was the use? Aggie could get in any time if Mary persisted in leaving her door unlocked. And Aggie had been there. There was a new picture on the bureau. The picture was new, but merely a new variation on an old theme. Aggie's conscience must be after her. Again she had drawn Horsack fallen in the hall by the telephone; again there was the costume in detail, the leather breeches, the alpine hat, but this time Aggie had sketched the telephone in in black and for contrast had made the wall to the left yellow. Or because she didn't have a brown crayon.

Emma turned around sharply, but it was only Mrs. Danforth standing in the doorway. She looked across at Shay's room and smiled.

"I told Aggie to bring you hot water. I thought perhaps—with Mr. Horrigan using the bathroom—"

Ladylike, she left the rest of the sentence unfinished, crossed the room, and rested her hand on the Dresden pitcher.

"I see she remembered, but you know she often forgets." She was looking at the picture that Emma held. "Another one?" She held out her hand. "I'll burn it for you."

Emma gave her the picture. She wanted to ask if Mrs. Danforth thought Aggie had killed Horsack, but she couldn't. Mrs. Danforth had cared for Aggie and protected her; if it had to come out that Aggie had killed, let Mr. Weatherbee be the one to tell.

"She likes costumes, doesn't she?" Emma asked.

Mrs. Danforth, looking at the picture, nodded slowly.

"Under other circumstances," Emma went on, "she might have been an artist, a designer. Has she"—she spoke softly—"always been like this?"

"Always," said Mrs. Danforth.

Shay came up the stairs, whistling, went into the bathroom, and turned the water on loudly

With a discreet I-told-you-so glance Mrs. Danforth went away, and Emma poured water into the washbowl.

Emma had changed her dress and was dimming the polish on her nose when she heard Hank's hail from outside. Without looking out she rushed down and for a moment thought she had been mistaken.

Then Hank's voice came through the twilight. "It's me. Don't I look nice?"

In place of his uniform Hank wore jeans and a scarlet shirt piped in white.

"Good land above," said Emma. "You've gone native pretty quick. I thought you weren't supposed to be out of uniform."

"Authorized exercise." Hank slapped the holster that hung from his hip.

"Don't tell me that thing's loaded?"

"Not yet, but that's the exercise. Mr. Faber's going to teach me to shoot."

"You'll kill somebody. Which reminds me, I want to talk to you."

"You catch me without my earmuffs. Talk away."

"Not here."

Emma led him around the opera house, up the steps to the balcony exit, where, it seemed sure, there would be privacy.

"We can see Shay from here," she said, "when he goes to dinner."

"I don't want to see any more of that Irishman. This is very romantic, and you look cute as a bug's ear."

"Hush. I just found out that Mr. Weatherbee used to be engaged to Aggie. That explains why he won't listen—"

"Engaged?" Hank interrupted her. "Are we engaged? I never can remember."

"Are you tight?" Emma asked suspiciously.

"Now whatever made you think that?"

"The company you keep, and those clothes, to say nothing of the way you talk."

"Do I mumble? I could kiss you without stuttering. I think I will."

He did.

"Ouch," said Emma, because the gun stuck in her ribs.

Hank sighed and shifted the gun, but Emma had moved away from him. An hour ago she had wanted his affection; now she wanted to talk.

"Viewing the evidence," she began, "you know it has to be Aggie—"

"Don't forget," Hank interrupted her, "that I view the evidence from a distance and through rose-colored glasses. For instance, I have to take Weatherbee's word about the alibis, and even if no one crossed him up there, what about the thousand-odd people who were in town that day? Was any effort made to check them? Anyone who had it in for Horsack could have slipped into town and out again."

"They wouldn't have known the precise instant he was going to be at Mrs. Danforth's telephone."

"They, or he, would have, if they were watching him. Suppose that our Mr. Unknown is seen and recognized by Horsack. Mr. Unknown knows that the first thing Horsack will do is rush to a telephone to denounce him. He stations himself out here in the garden to watch which way Horsack will go, and then, bingo!"

"Oh, gosh." He seemed so reasonable that he might have been right. "Gosh," said Emma, "you spoil everything." Then she remembered the professor. "And I suppose," she went on, "that Mr. Unknown bought strychnine and slipped into Mrs. Danforth's and doctored the food and nobody noticed him."

"All right"—Hank shrugged—"have it your way. Which narrows the list of culprits down to a cozy few. I don't think you did it. You don't think Mary did it. Weatherbee doesn't think Aggie did it. That leaves Shay and Sauer."

"Shay wasn't here, and Mary doesn't think Sauer did it."

"What does that leave us? Mrs. Danforth?"

"She didn't do it. She's kind; she looks after Aggie."

"It boils down to the Gremlins."

"It's Aggie, all right." Emma persistently went back to that line. "Except for one funny thing—"

Hank stopped watching the stars come out because what seemed to Emma peculiar often was. "What's that?"

"She put me onto the professor with her funny picture that pointed to the magazine. Why would she do that if she were going to kill him? Identify him, call attention to him, I mean?"

"Probably felt that she had to justify herself to you. She thought he was a spy and wanted you to know it. What are her pictures like? I've never seen any."

"Literal, vivid. I just had one, but Mrs. Danforth took it. People eating or dying—this one was of Horsack in the entry; she'd done one like that before."

"He must prey on her mind. That's literal enough, but that clock number sounded more in the fanciful vein."

"But you see, when you took it literally it told me where to look. She told me about the radio station, too, only I thought her conception of ether waves looked more like lightning."

"She's told you a lot; now if she will just do a self-portrait in the act of murder."

They heard Shay clattering down the steps that led from Mrs. Danforth's and Shay's voice raised in song.

"I—ain't got no—motive," Shay was caroling into the darkness; "they—can't pin—this—on—me."

"A crazy person doesn't need a motive," said Emma. "Come on, I'm hungry."

"If you want some real advice," said Hank, "watch out for the lies."

They ate in the bar, where Chew had set a table and waited on their several needs. To Emma's great annoyance no one seemed the least bit interested in theorizing or discussing the murders. Hank and Shay, still continuing their convivial reunion, ran through the roster of mutual friends. This one was still in Boston; that one was a Jap prisoner; so-and-so was a private, while such-and-such, the old so-and-so, was a lieutenant colonel. It was all very well, while Mary was there, to avoid the topic of murder, but Mary ate quietly and went back to Sauer, and still the review of what had happened since Shay had been away went on. Finally, while Shay and Hank were comparing the relative merits of German and Italian fliers, Emma managed to get Mr. Weatherbee's attention.

"I hear"—she had decided on a flanking attack—"that Aggie used to be very pretty."

"Dern tooting," Mr. Weatherbee confirmed the report. "All pink, like-like apple blossoms—and plenty smart too. At least I used to think so, as you may have heard." He turned back to Shay. "What was that about Chennault again?"

Emma didn't care if Chennault had personally turned into a tiger; very likely he did. It was no more unlikely than the idea that had just now come to her.

"Watch out for the lies," Hank had said. And she had found the first lie, though as yet her mind refused to pick it up, as though it were a burning thing, too hot, too evil to touch. It was unbelievable; it was preposterous; it was impossible. They would laugh at her if she told them. It was such a silly, useless lie.

Mr. Faber came in and told them that Sauer was awake. The conversation stopped; they all looked at Mr. Weatherbee, disliking what was to come, waiting for him to give the word.

"Bring him over," said Mr. Weatherbee. "We'll ask him what he has to say and then show him the map. It's upstairs. Better bring him upstairs." He glanced around at the table, the glasses. "This is a little festive for the inquisition."

They followed Mr. Weatherbee upstairs.

Sauer must clear himself, Emma was thinking. If he didn't she would have to speak, have to make a fool of herself, because there wasn't any motive. If she had a little more time she would find the motive; there was something, something else that she ought to remember, something about Aggie's brown crayon. The idea, hotly pursued, refused to be caught. Emma tried to think about something else so that her mind would relax and she could creep up on the idea unexpectedly.

Mr. Weatherbee's room. Emma had imagined that Mr. Weatherbee would have had the presidential suite, would assume that his personal due as befitting his position of grandeur. But though the room into which they were ushered overlooked the garden and would have a fine view of the opera house when the moon came up, the white iron bedstead that it contained was hardly magnificent, and the couch on which Emma settled herself was pure Grand Rapids.

Mr. Weatherbee had fooled her all along, but not for the reason she had thought.

Shay took up his position by the window and fiddled with the shade cord. Still no one spoke. Now they could hear steps on the stairs, then Mr. Faber's voice: "Right in here, please."

Mary entered with Sauer, who still looked dazed and blinked at them with puffy lids, pausing just inside the room, uncertain. Mary stood beside him and held his hand. She did not face them arrogantly now or defensively; companionably, protectively, she led Sauer to the couch on which Emma sat and sat down herself beside him. Mr. Weatherbee was watching her face, and this time he seemed satisfied with what he saw. They were all waiting for him to speak, but he continued to look at Mary.

When Emma could stand the silence no longer, she burst out, "Aggie brought me another picture this afternoon."

She was talking to Mary, telling her that she was on her side, not lined up with the silent roomful against her. She wished she hadn't started talking about the picture; she was a fine one for tact, bringing up a picture of Horsack. "A picture of the entry," she went on into the silence; "you know, the entry over at Mrs. Danforth's." She was getting in deeper. "She put in the telephone—and a very good telephone it was, too—only she made the wall yellow instead of brown. I guess that was for contrast." Why didn't somebody else say something? "Or because she didn't have a brown crayon—

"That's funny; that's very funny." She turned, and her eyes sought out Hank's, because this was important; this was what she had been trying to remember. "She had a brown crayon. I bought her a brown crayon this morning, so why would she make the entry yellow?"

Mr. Weatherbee was walking across the floor to her; it was Mr. Weatherbee who spoke.

The cord that Shay was twitching broke loose, and the curtain snapped to the top of the window, revealing the round yellow moon rising from behind the mountains.

"The walls," Mr. Weatherbee was asking, "were they all yellow or only part?"

"Part. The wall to the left of the phone. Not the one that the phone was on, the one to the left, the outside wall. And only part way up, the part that should be brown, sort of brown-painted tile."

"I know." Mr. Weatherbee spoke irritably. "There used to be a hanging hatrack there. Right where I've hung my hat God's own number of times."

He left her abruptly and walked to the window and for what seemed a long time stood gazing out at the opera house, or possibly at the house beyond it. Then he went to the bureau, took out the map, tore it across, and dropped the pieces carelessly into the wastebasket.

"I'm getting old," he said. "And I can't hold my likker the way I should."

He looked at Emma, who could only look back at him blankly. When he acted this way she no longer thought he was senile; right now she didn't know what to think. The left wall, her mind kept repeating. And Horsack was left-handed.

Mr. Weatherbee turned to the others. "She gave it to me the other night. Only I was too drunk to get it." He walked to the door and bellowed, "Chew, bring me a bottle!"

"I take it," said Shay, "that the inquisition is adjourned?"

Then everybody started talking at once.

". . . is he talking about?"

"Where is this picture?"

"Who did do it?"

"What's the point of a yellow wall?"

Hank came over to Emma. "Well, baby," he said, "it looks as though you had rung the bell."

"I haven't the faintest idea," said Emma, "what he's talking about. It must be the same thing, and yet I don't see how it can be."

"The same thing as what?" Hank, who had had noble intentions about keeping his fingers out of Emma's pie, now felt slightly miffed at the thought that she had been holding out on him again.

Mr. Weatherbee whispered something to Sol Faber, who nodded, though he, too, still looked baffled.

Chew, who had taken Mr. Weatherbee's order liberally rather than literally, came in with a tray of drinks. Emma took one and said, no less to him than to Mary, "It has something to do with the cemetery."

Chew nodded and grinned politely, but Mary made no pretense of understanding.

"What are you babbling about? He tore up the map. Does it mean you don't suspect Rho any more?"

"Oh, I never did."

"Sometimes you didn't like me." It seemed difficult for Sauer to speak. "I could tell. But I never saw the map."

"Hush," said Mary. "Everything's going to be all right."

"Hush, please," said Emma, "I'm trying to think."

Mr. Weatherbee raised his glass. "Here's to you, Bert. A joke's a joke, and I never had no kick coming. Old Bert died sudden," he added, as though that explained everything, "but he had to tell someone because a joke's no good unless the other fellow catches on. The trouble with women is, they can't take a joke." He did not look at Emma, but he amended his statement: "At least most of 'em can't.

"You have to understand about Bert's telling. He was a friend of mine. He was honest. He wouldn't leave a thing like that. He'd rigged the tombstone, only none of us ever went to the cemetery. And none of us was around when he took sick. I was in Mexico; Harlow was in Washington, and the rest was here and there, but he didn't die so sudden but what he told somebody." He looked around belligerently, as though daring them to deny it.

"Mrs. Danforth," said Emma softly, "was illegitimate."

"She doesn't look it," said Mary.

Perhaps Mr. Weatherbee hadn't heard Emma. He looked around slyly but proudly. "There isn't one of you," he said, "except Sol, who has any tarnal notion what I'm talking about." He shot a quick glance at Emma, took a long drink, and began again.

"I'm a sentimental old fool."

"You ain't old," Faber responded automatically.

"I kind of like this place. I've had some hifalutin old times here. I had good friends. Most of us had too much money, too young or too quick, and some of us lost it—"

"But not you, you old buzzard," Shay muttered from the window.

"Too much money is bad for kids. I've got a granddaughter." Mr. Weatherbee looked around at the listening faces. "You're nice folks," he said. "I liked the way Miss Marsh stood up for Miss Dolan. I thought she'd killed Horsack, but all I cared about was keeping the thing from ruining the opera. You know how it is with friends. You stand up for them because you like them; you abuse them and expect them to put up with it. Like when a feller nails your shoes to the floor on a hunting trip, you know he's got no reason to be mad when you set his mattress afire. And that's the way practical jokes progress. You do something to a feller, and then he has to do something worse back to you, and so on ad infinitum."

He looked at Emma almost impatiently.

"But I started talking about friends as kind of an apology for being so willing to think that Miss Dolan or Sauer had done the murders. I didn't want it to be anybody I knew, anybody up here. After I got to know Miss Dolan I didn't want to accuse her; Sauer looked guilty, and I wasn't sure until tonight that Miss Dolan loved him. It is so easy to blame the Nazis for everything these days."

"I am not—" Sauer began, but Mr. Weatherbee waved him to silence.

Hank looked slightly shocked. The old man was completely indifferent to law or legal justice; he would probably have sacrificed Sauer without batting an eye, just to protect the village peace. Hank wasn't trying to figure out what the old man was driving at, but he knew that Emma was; he could see her mind working fifteen to the dozen.

Mr. Weatherbee moistened his throat with another drink. "As I was saying, we used to have some high old times. There was four or five of us, and their names wouldn't mean anything to you, except that Bert Estis was one of them."

"Aggie's brother," Mary whispered to Sauer.

"I've told Miss Marsh about the phony wedding we rigged for Bert. And I never knew Bert caught on until Miss Marsh told me he'd left the word 'wife' off the tombstone. That explained a lot. Bert wasn't a man to take a thing like that lying down.

"We did a little bricklaying job once, and the bricks disappeared. Nobody asked any questions. We divvied up the loss. Somebody else could have taken them, but only the five of us knew the bricks were—"

"Gold!"

Emma shouted the word as Mr. Weatherbee spoke it.

"Gold," she repeated. "Not yellow. Aggie was trying to tell me that the wall was gold!"

Mr. Weatherbee crossed the room and shook her by the hand.

"Jesus-menders," he said, "I've talked myself hoarse waiting for you to get it."

The rest of them, all but Sol Faber, still looked blank. Hank looked at Shay, trying to fit the pieces together, but Shay had turned to throw his cigarette out of the window and was staring, fixed, as though he were seeing a ghost.

"What's the matter?" Hank's voice was sharp.

Shay could only point.

Hank rushed to the window, the others crowding around. The moonlight was white and bright now. They could see the deserted garden and the stiff, unadorned rear of the opera house, but it was not there that Shay pointed. They were high enough up to be able to look into the courtyard behind the Estis house. The moon shone there, too, on the litter of boards, the empty coalbin, and on the great meat hooks. A figure in white was standing there, and as they looked the figure threw a rope over a hook and mounted a chair.

"Run!" Mr. Weatherbee's voice commanded. "Run! For God's sake, you can run!"

Hank and Shay were gone before he had finished speaking, with Sauer close behind them. Emma tried to keep up, couldn't, and fell back with Mary. Behind her she could hear Mr. Weatherbee steadily cursing Sol Faber and Chew for holding him back.

"Who is it?" Mary caught at her arm, but Emma didn't answer her; she clattered up the steps and ran as hard as she could to the rear of the house, where Hank and Shay were holding Aggie. Above their heads dangled a noose.

"She told me to do it," Aggie was saying. "She told me to do it. She said that I had made a mistake and got the poison in the professor's food and that they would arrest me because I had bought the poison. She said I might as well kill myself. She put on the ghost shirt and told me to kill myself."

When she caught sight of Emma she began to cry. "You don't believe me. You thought I did it. You were afraid of me."

"Why, Aggie," Emma began, "I didn't either." For the second time that night she found herself denying her suspicions and blushed for them and for herself.

It was Mary who put her arms around Aggie and said: "Agatha Estis, stop your crying; you'll ruin your eyes."

"You're good to me," said Aggie. "You gave me the beads."

Those damn beads, Emma thought. First she had suspected Aggie of stealing them, and then she had sunk so low as to think that Mary had used them as a bribe.

Mr. Weatherbee and Mr. Faber went straight to the back door. It was locked, and the entry was dark, but beyond the entry a light burned in the kitchen. They could all see the kitchen stove, with a coffeepot upon it, a chair, and a corner of the cupboard. Viewed through the darkness of the entry, it was like a stage, ready and waiting for action.

Curtain, thought Emma. *The curtain rises, revealing an empty set.*

They watched, quiet and anticipatory as any audience in the dark.

Enter an old woman, well dressed, carrying a cup.

With a growing feeling of tension they saw Mrs. Danforth cross left and pour coffee from the pot on the stove. Her air of complete detachment, of being oblivious of any audience, heightened the theatrical effect, kept them motionless.

Mrs. Danforth moved to the cupboard, opened a door, and sugared her coffee with a white crystalline substance from a glass jar. Then, still moving slowly, deliberately, she turned, seated herself in the chair, and drained the cup.

Hank broke the spell. He dashed forward, pushed Mr. Faber aside, and threw himself against the door. Mr. Faber, recovering from the surprise attack, resumed his position, in time to prevent a second assault.

"Young man," he said, "you smash that door and I'll arrest you for forcing an entry."

"Good God"—Hank was aghast —"you can't stand there and let the woman die."

Mr. Faber drew his gun, and the moonlight glinted on its barrel as he twisted it on his finger. "I'm the sheriff of Gilpin County," he said, "and I'll administer the law as I see fit. You ain't going to break into that house. And nobody else ain't either." He cast a wary eye at Shay.

"Take the womenfolks back to the hotel," Mr. Weatherbee put in. "I saw a feller die of strychnine once, and it ain't a pretty sight."

Emma went willingly; she was shivering in the thin, cold air, shivering and sick, but filled with a horrified admiration at the way the woman in the kitchen had played her part, played it to the hilt, and rung down the final curtain with her own hands. Mrs. Danforth, the wise, the kindly, the benevolent, had killed Horsack while the tourists were laughing at her gilt chairs, had poisoned the professor because in some way he had found out, and had almost driven Aggie to suicide after she had seen Aggie's picture of the gold wall.

They moved slowly back to the hotel. Aggie, half a head taller, cowering incongruously against Mary, helped down the flight of steps by the bewildered Sauer; Hank following reluctantly after Shay, who, for once, was speechless. The figure of Chew scuttled past them and when they reached the hotel had the bar ablaze with light and drinks already poured.

Emma took hers neat and felt the liquor relax somewhat the knot that was in her stomach. Shay took two in quick succession and found his voice.

"You could telephone the state police," he offered.

"She'll be dead before they could get here." Hank plucked at a raveling on his shirt and resigned himself to the flouting of all his principles of law and order. "It may be better this way."

"She told me to do it," Aggie whimpered. "She'll be mad at me." It was a shock to them to realize that Aggie either had not seen or had not realized the significance of what had happened in the kitchen.

"Hush," said Mary. "She's going away. You won't have to see her again."

Believing, with a sigh, Aggie dropped her head on Mary's shoulder and fell asleep.

"Golly," said Shay, "she's still nuts."

It was so. Emma realized that she had expected Aggie to arise now, phoenix-like, sane and normal, from the ashes of her experience; Emma's incurable romanticism had even envisioned a reunion, after all these years, between Aggie and Mr. Weatherbee, but Aggie was too old; she had been too long crushed and cowed; only between her hand and brain was there still established a link of intelligence.

"You were right." Emma spoke to Hank. "All along she was trying to tell me with the pictures."

"What was the first one? Do you remember the first one?" It was better to talk; anything was better than to think about what was happening up there in the kitchen.

"It was Horsack. In the entry. Lying there with his hat off and an alpine stock beside him."

"That alpine stock," said Sauer. "He used to hook you with it, on the leg, anywhere—"

Mary nodded.

Emma could see Horsack standing, impatient, by the phone, prodding, poking with the alpine stock in his left hand.

"That's it," she cried excitedly. "That's how he found out. He was poking and scraping and the paint came off. Only how did she see him through the door?"

"And why didn't you or Weatherbee see the scratches? Gold ought to show up on that brown."

"The brown crayon!" Emma was getting it. "She used the brown crayon to cover the scratches up later, when she put the blood on the knob, and she was hurrying and a piece broke off and rolled under Horsack and Mr. Weatherbee found it. You'll see; there'll be the marks, and we'll go up there and work it out. Tomorrow," she added, remembering.

"With that imagination," Shay broke in, "aren't you ever afraid of her?"

"A little ghoulish"—Hank smiled at Emma—"but nice."

"Mr. Weatherbee was really very fair," Emma went on; "he gave me the piece of crayon, but I thought it pointed to her"—she gestured toward

Aggie—"and I thought it was just another of Mr. Weatherbee's stories when he said the street was paved with gold."

"Gold!" Sauer was still behind the others in picking up the threads. "You mean she had a wall of gold?"

They nodded.

"Then why," Sauer asked simply, "did she take roomers?"

"The government," Hank explained, "called in all the gold in 1933. Seven years ago. If she turned in all that gold she had to account for it, had to admit that it was there, and she knew that Mr. Weatherbee, at least, would know that it wasn't hers."

"She was always talking about her father," Emma put in; "she wouldn't have thought it a joke that he had taken it."

Sauer nodded; he could understand that.

"It is mine." Aggie had opened her eyes. "It isn't hers; it is mine. Bert and that dancer weren't married." Her lids drooped and she dozed off again.

"She gives me the creeps." Shay prepared himself against further shock.

"It makes me so mad!" Emma exclaimed. "It was all there. I had every bit of it. I knew her father and mother weren't married; I knew she had a father fixation; why, I even knew she was mean to Aggie. I caught her at it once over some spilled water, but she buttered me up with that 'poor-Aggie' business. Poor Aggie nothing. Part of whatever Bert Estis left belonged to Aggie, not to her, but she wasn't going to lose control, so she frightened Aggie with stories of disgrace and blackening her father's name—"

"Whoa," Hank interrupted, "you're running off into fields of fancy, though you're probably right."

"Of course I'm right," Emma snapped at him, "but I was a fool not to have caught on. I should have known the minute I found out she wouldn't let anyone in the house who was left-handed—she made everybody register."

"She let me in," Shay reminded her.

"Not at first, smarty; not until she had had the phone disconnected. Then I should have guessed." Emma beat her brow in punishment for its lack of perspicacity.

"If it's any comfort to you," Hank assured her, "you told me everything, and I didn't get it either. The scent of Nazi red herring was too strong."

They had no idea how long they had talked; they were surprised when Mr. Faber and Emma's acquaintance from the antique shop came in from the street door.

" 'Loss's gone to bed," said Mr. Faber. "He had Chew fix up some rooms for you upstairs, but Minnie here'll take care of Aggie."

He didn't mention Mrs. Danforth; he didn't say how long ago Mr. Weatherbee had gone to bed. He made it all at some indefinite past time.

Mr. Weatherbee had known, Emma thought, that they would look at him and say: "It is over now." In this way they knew it was over, but they were spared the definite, shocking now.

Minnie wore a coat over her nightdress, and her hair was pulled back tight in a bun. Aggie woke with a start at her touch but went with her willingly, dazedly. Mr. Faber followed them out silently, shut off from those he left behind by the answers he did not wish to give to the questions they had no wish to ask.

They stood silent for a long time, and then Sauer took Mary's arm, as though to lead her upstairs. Emma wished she and Hank were married; tonight was the night, if there ever was one, for the closeness of bodily comfort. But Mary wasn't going; she had taken Sauer's hand from her arm and was speaking.

"Good heaven's above!" said Emma.

". . . have to tell you—" Mary was as simple and direct as she had been with Aggie; there was no trace of the theatrical left in her manner. Sauer was a fool, Emma thought, should he be angry.

"—that I may be married to a Count Galeazzo. I thought he was dead, but Nella said not. Believe me, I didn't know."

"To who?" asked Shay, setting down his glass.

"Count Gabriel Galeazzo," said Mary wearily; "you wouldn't know him."

"No," said Shay, "but I saw him. What was left of him. He was shot down in Africa."

Mary was looking as though the sun had risen in her face. "Are you sure? It couldn't be a mistake?"

"They scraped up something to go with the identification tag," said Shay brutally, "but it wasn't much."

But only the assurance of his words had any meaning for Mary. "I think," she said, "that you are the most wonderful man I ever saw."

"And with that remark," said Shay when Mary and Sauer had gone, "I am supposed to comfort myself?"

CHAPTER FOURTEEN

"LIKE THIS," Emma was saying. She and Hank, Shay and Mr. Weatherbee and Sol Faber stood in the Estis house side hall, between the cases of Indian relics.

"That crowd that Albert had up here were completely out of hand. She came in here to herd one of the strays back on to the regular route and heard someone talking on the phone. Through there"—Emma pointed to one of the convex cuttings that ornamented the frosted-glass panel of the door—"she could see Horsack plain as day, could see him doodling with that alpine stock, stop and examine the scratch he had made, and then—"

Emma took the stone tomahawk from the wall beside her, quietly opened the door. . . .

"Bingo!" said Shay.

Emma handed the weapon to Mr. Faber. "You can have it examined."

Mr. Faber put it back on the wall.

"Wouldn't it be funny," Shay said suddenly, "if that wall wasn't gold?"

Quickly they all crowded into the entry. The wall in front of them, the side to the left of the phone, looked no different from the rest. For perhaps five feet from the floor it was plastered, marked off in oblongs roughly six by three inches, to represent brick or tile, and painted an ugly dark brown. Emma peered at the innocuous surface.

"There," she cried, pointing to a faintly visible smear. She scraped with her fingernail, removing a peeling of brown wax, exactly the color of the paint.

"I still don't see any gold," Shay protested.

"The point of the alpine stock was sharp," Hank reminded him.

Mr. Weatherbee took a clasp knife from his pocket and drew it heavily across another brick; the paint chipped away in several layers; he drew the knife again, and through the thin wash of plaster came a sharp bright gleam.

"A strike, by God," said Mr. Faber.

They pressed closer, the magic of the metal exciting them more than the confirmation of their theories.

"A telephone booth," said Shay, "lined with gold bricks! From now on I'll believe anything."

Mr. Weatherbee worked across the wall, his knife testing brick after brick, until an area roughly five feet by three was proven. At the bottom, near the floor, there was a row of common brick, neatly fitted and covered with several layers of paint, but lacking plaster.

"She had to repaint"—Mr. Faber was practical—"every time she took out a brick to live on."

"I bet she made Aggie do it," said Emma. "How much is a brick worth?"

"It varied," said Mr. Weatherbee. "Thirty-five dollars an ounce right now. Four hundred ounces to the brick equals fourteen thousand dollars."

He ran a practiced eye over the wall, counting bricks. "There's better'n a million dollars' worth here."

Shay whistled. "That ain't lettuce."

"I make it a million, a hundred and ninety-six thousand," said Mr. Faber.

"A pretty big joke," said Hank, "to laugh off lightly."

"Gold," said Mr. Weatherbee modestly, "wasn't worth that much when we got these here bricks from the mint. Gold wasn't worth hardly nothing. Why, it took a whole hatful of gold to buy a quart of whiskey and a darn sight more to buy a loaf of bread. All that gripes me"—Mr. Weatherbee was getting back his spark—"is the number of times I've hung my hat right over the danged stuff."

"Good morning, all!"

Mary and Sauer were coming up the steps, bright and happy, and worlds removed from tragedy.

Shay, after one look at their shining faces, turned aside.

"Go away," he said. "You make me sick."

"Love," said Hank, "is a wonderful thing. They look good to me."

"Look who's talking," said Emma.

"It's a beautiful day." Mary beamed on them all. "We ought to take a walk or go on a picnic."

"Let me out of here," said Shay. "I can't stand it."

"Celebration," said Mr. Weatherbee. "We'd really ought to celebrate."

"You little lovebirds run along"—Emma detected a general tendency to stray from the path of righteousness—"but be back for lunch. We found gold," she couldn't help adding, "just as we thought. Only about a million dollars' worth."

"Oh, really?" said Mary. "How nice for Aggie."

They all turned to Mr. Weatherbee, accusingly, hostilely. Mrs. Danforth had done murder to keep the knowledge of this gold from Mr. Weatherbee. They had spoken of it as Aggie's, but really it was no more Aggie's than it had been her brother's.

Mr. Weatherbee looked up at them with his blandest expression, and Emma was sure that for a moment he toyed with the idea of pretending that he was going to keep it, but the moment passed.

"Why, sure," he said. "It's got to be turned over to the mint, but the money's Aggie's."

Emma wanted to kiss him, but instead she squeezed Hank's arm, and somewhat to her amazement he returned the pressure.

"Let's get out of here," said Hank.

"Shame on you," said Emma. "There's still a lot to do. We've got to get the tray and things out of my suitcase and talk to Aggie, and Fox is coming up to go over Nella's room."

"But look." Hank found himself talking to Shay, who wore a broad grin. "Oh, shut up," said Hank.

Emma was already on her way upstairs.

"Dog-foot it." Mr. Weatherbee gave up his attempt to use the disconnected phone and, opening the outside door, bellowed for Chew.

"Get some lunch," he addressed the head that popped from a hotel window.

"Get a good lunch. Get some champagne."

Emma came down bearing the tray, and on it the plate and glass. She looked, Hank thought, like a terrier that had finally brought the right slippers.

"The sipper's in the laboratory in Denver," she said. "What'll we do with these?"

"Put 'em back in the kitchen," said Mr. Weatherbee; then he read Emma's crestfallen face. "You don't need 'em to find out whether she or Aggie hid them. Put 'em in the dining room and let's go see if Fox has showed up."

"Hadn't somebody," Shay wanted to know, "ought to stay here, to sort of keep an eye on all this?"

"Not you," said Hank.

"What's the use?" said Mr. Weatherbee. "Nobody'd steal anything up here."

Fox was there, utterly noncommittal. She would never again, Emma was sure, make the mistake of confusing a person of Strike's loquacity with anyone of the FBI.

Fox did not even give them the satisfaction of knowing whether or not Nella had talked, but he did not mention Sauer. Neither did anyone else. Their faces were blank when Mr. Weatherbee handed over the marked map with the comment that it had been found in a trash can. Fox accepted the map but excluded them from his examination of the room.

Hank, who had been called to the phone by Chew, came back in time to follow Fox outside and talked earnestly with him for a few minutes. When he came in again he wore a very pleased expression. "So you finally gave him the grip," said Shay. "Did she have an accomplice, and was there a booby trap under the bed?"

"Oh," said Hank, "he didn't say. I told him that I'd just got a wire confirming my hunch that a Gideon Bible would break the book code the agents have been using."

"What did you tell him for?" Emma wanted to know.

"If you'll come outside"—Hank took her hand—"I'll explain everything."

"Not now," said Emma. "It's lunch time."

Again Shay laughed.

Mr. Faber brought Aggie back to the hotel. Minnie had told her that Mrs. Danforth had taken poison and Aggie, after a first startled refusal to believe, had accepted it as the Lord's will.

"The wicked have perished," she announced as she came in.

Emma caught Shay looking from Aggie to the champagne bottles, avid for experimental research, and shook her head at him.

"Hello, Aggie," said Mr. Weatherbee. "We're waiting for Miss Dolan and Sauer. They've got married, and this is a kind of celebration."

"Why, how nice." A troubled expression crossed Aggie's face. "Mr. Horsack was handsomer."

"Mr. Sauer is taller," said Emma. "I like tall men, don't you?"

Hank drew himself up another inch but failed to get any attention. Emma was completely concerned with the problem of questioning Aggie.

"How—?" Emma began.

"What made you—?" asked Mr. Weatherbee.

Then they both waited politely for each other.

"They want to know"—Hank stepped into the silence—"what made you suspect Mrs. Danforth?"

Aggie looked at him with puzzled eyes. "Why, who else would have done it?"

In the light of subsequent events her logic was irrefutable.

"And the professor?" Hank seemed anxious to get the questioning over with.

A cunning gleam came into Aggie's eyes, and she said nothing.

"Agatha Estis," Emma demanded, "did you hide that tray in my suitcase?"

Aggie's face puckered up as though she were going to cry, but she glanced quickly around, as if to assure herself that Mrs. Danforth was not lurking in some corner, and nodded her head. "I thought she would blame me."

"But you knew about the professor," Emma persisted; "you drew that picture of the clock and put the magazines in my room—" She broke off, because Aggie was shaking her head in bewilderment.

"Well, I am a dummy," said Emma. "I thought that business was too—er—complicated for Aggie." She was speaking to the others. "She did it—Mrs. Danforth. She was trying to throw suspicion on the professor, to give me a reason for thinking he killed Horsack, to provide a reason for his suicide."

"That's what she said." Aggie nodded vigorously. "At first she said he had taken the wrong medicine, because he always took something through that tube before he ate. For his stomach. And then she said I did it. She said I had put the rat poison in his milk instead of sugar. She said he was dead when DeLoss came to call, that they wouldn't believe I thought he was asleep when I knocked on the door. She said I did it and they would lock me up and take away my pictures—"

Her voice was rising higher and higher; Mr. Weatherbee put a firm hand on her shoulder. "She isn't here any more. Did the professor try to get her to talk about Bert? He was kind of interested in the early days, wasn't he? He used to talk to me about what went on up here"—his voice was soothing—"him being a history professor."

Aggie forgot her fear and smiled. "It was really laughable," she agreed, "the way he went on about that silver. It even made her laugh, because we knew it was gold instead. Bert told us to tell you about it"—for a moment her voice took on a vigor remembered from a saner time—"but after he died she wouldn't let me. She said it was the disgrace, but she was a greedy woman. He kept asking her"—she, had wandered back to the professor now—"if the silver wasn't buried somewhere—"

"—asked his friend: 'Going to take a bridal tour?' "

"A gentleman," said Shay, "is one who says he hasn't heard it, but I'm no gentleman."

"Look at Aggie looking at Mary," Emma whispered to Hank. "Poor thing, she's so romantic."

"Whereas you—" The rest of Hank's remark was lost in a burst of laughter.

"Oh, dear," Emma reproached him, "I didn't hear the end of the story."

Shay stood up. "To the bride and groom!"

Hank leaned over and whispered in Emma's ear.

"What did you say?"

"I said," Hank repeated, "will you marry me?"

"That's what I thought you said. Someday you'll say that once too often."

"This couldn't, by any chance, be the day?"

"Don't be silly. You know there isn't a minister."

"What's that?" A silence had fallen, and Mr. Weatherbee had picked up Emma's words.

"In the presence of witnesses," Hank's voice rang out, "I'm asking her to marry me."

Emma wished he wouldn't try to be funny about it. He was always asking her to marry him at completely impossible times.

"He knows he's safe," she explained a little bitterly; "there isn't any minister."

"Why, bless my buttons," Mr. Weatherbee ejaculated, "I can fix that!"

"No, you don't!" said Emma. "Not you. I know about the kind of ministers you get. When I get married it's got to be legal."

Mr. Weatherbee looked hurt. "Sol, here," he said, "is a justice of the peace. They don't come any legaler."

"When I tie 'em"—Mr. Faber stood up with a flourish—"they stay tied!"

Shay was fervently shaking Hank's hand.

The joke, Emma decided, was on Hank. It would be fun to see him try to get out of this.

THE END

Murder is a Collector's Item by Elizabeth Dean. "(It) froths over with the same effervescent humor as the best Hepburn-Grant films."—Sujata Massey. "Completely enjoyable."—*New York Times.* "Fast and funny."—*The New Yorker.* Twenty-six-year-old Emma Marsh isn't much at spelling or geography and perhaps she butchers the odd literary quotation or two, but she's a keen judge of character and more than able to hold her own when it comes to selling antiques or solving murders. Originally published in 1939, *Murder is a Collector's Item* was the first of three books featuring Emma. Smoothly written and sparkling with dry, sophisticated humor, this milestone combines an intriguing puzzle with an entertaining portrait of a self-possessed young woman on her own at the end of the Great Depression. **0-915230-19-4 $14.00**

Murder is a Serious Business by Elizabeth Dean. It's 1940 and the Thirsty Thirties are over but you couldn't tell it by the gang at J. Graham Antiques, where clerk Emma Marsh, her would-be criminologist boyfriend Hank, and boss Jeff Graham trade barbs in between shots of scotch when they aren't bothered by the rare customer. Trouble starts when Emma and crew head for a weekend at Amos Currier's country estate to inventory the man's antiques collection. It isn't long before the bodies start falling and once again Emma is forced to turn sleuth in order to prove that her boss isn't a killer. "Judging from (this book) it's too bad she didn't write a few more."––Mary Ann Steel, *I Love a Mystery.* **0-915230-28-3 $14.95**

Common or Garden Crime by Sheila Pim. Lucy Bex preferred Jane Austen or Anthony Trollope to the detective stories her brother Linnaeus gulped down but when a neighbor is murdered with monkshood harvested from Lucy's own garden, she's the one who turns detective and spots the crucial clue that prevents the wrong person from going to the gallows. Set in 1943 in the small town of Clonmeen on the outskirts of Dublin, this delightful tale was written by an author who was called "the Irish Angela Thirkell." Published in Britain in 1945, the book makes its first appearance in the United States here. The war in Europe seems very distant in neutral Ireland, though it draws a little nearer when Lucy's nephew, an officer in the British army, comes home on leave. However, most of the residents are more interested in how their gardens grow than what's happening on the Eastern Front or in Africa. It's a death a little closer to home that finally grabs their interest. The Irish Guard is called in to investigate but this time it may take someone with a green thumb to catch the murderer. Pim's detective stories were greeted with great critical acclaim from contemporary reviewers: "Excellent characterization, considerable humour."—*Sphere.* "Humor and shrewd observation of small town Irish life."—*Times Literary Supplement.* "Wit and gaiety, ease and charm."—*Illustrated London News.* "A truthful, humorous, and affectionate picture of life in an Irish town."—*Daily Herald.* **0-915230-36-4 $14.00**

A Hive of Suspects by Sheila Pim. Jason Prendergast built his fortune taking minerals from the earth near the Irish town of Drumclash, but bees became the real passion of his life once the mines gave up the last of their riches. When he dies after dining on honey from one of his own hives, village beekeepers suspect local bees are feasting on poisonous plants and infecting hives with deadly nectar. Prendergast's solicitor, Edward Gildea, consults his fellow beekeepers, who think rhododendrons the most likely source of the poison. But why is it that only Jason Prendergast's hives were infected? And why should bees suddenly take a liking to this particular plant? The Civic Guard prefers to look for a human hand and suspicion falls upon those locals who stand to benefit from the old man's death, including several servants and an aged distant cousin who deliberately hacks her own rhododendron plants to bits in a crazed frenzy. The chief suspect, however, is Phoebe Prendergast, a niece who gave up a promising career on the stage to look after the old man. Gildea can't believe in Phoebe's guilt and conceals from the police the fact that Prendergast was about to add a codicil to his will disinheriting her should she return to the stage—even after his death. Nor does the Phoebe's odd behavior following the old man's death bode well for her innocence in this 1952 novel. **0-915230-38-0 $14.00**

Black Paw by Constance & Gwenyth Little. Thanks to some overly indulgent parents, Callie Drake was "brought up soft" and doesn't know the first thing about doing housework, which makes it a bit of a stretch for her to pretend to be a maid in the Barton household. She's there dressed in the skimpiest maid's outfit this side of Paris to snatch some compromising love letters written by her friend Selma, who's afraid that her brute of an estranged husband just might use these adulterous missives to lower her alimony. Altruism isn't a big part of Callie's makeup and she agrees to the scheme only after Selma offers to hand over the keys to her hot little roadster in exchange for this bit of petty larceny. But when murder erupts in the Barton mansion, the police think it's a little odd that the bodies started falling only hours after Callie's arrival. Even worse, Selma's soon-to-be-ex is on to Callie and seems to take perverse enjoyment in forcing this spoiled debutante to continue her domestic chores. In between long hot baths and countless cigarette breaks, Callie stumbles across mysterious pawprints in a house without animals and comes upon rocking chairs that move even when there's no one in the room. It's enough to make this golddigger start digging for clues in this 1941 charmer. **0-915230-37-2, $14.00** Other Little books available from The Rue Morgue Press: *The Black Gloves* **(0-915230-20-8),** *The Black Honeymoon* **(0-915230-21-6),** *Black Corridors* **(0-915230-33-X),** *The Black Stocking* **(0-915230-30-5),** *Black-Headed Pins* **(0-915230-25-9),** *Great Black Kanba* **(0-915230-22-4),** and *The Grey Mist Murders* **(0-915230-26-7) ($14.00 each).**

Brief Candles by Manning Coles. From Topper to Aunt Dimity, mystery readers have embraced the cozy ghost story. Four of the best were written by Manning Coles, the creator of the witty Tommy Hambledon spy novels. First published in 1954, *Brief Candles* is likely to produce more laughs than chills as a young couple vacationing in France run into two gentlemen with decidedly old-world manners. What they don't know is that James and Charles Latimer are ancestors of theirs who shuffled off this mortal coil some 80 years earlier when, emboldened by strong drink and with only a pet monkey and an aged waiter as allies, the two made a valiant, foolish and quite fatal attempt to halt a German advance during the Franco-Prussian War of 1870. Now these two ectoplasmic gentlemen and their spectral pet monkey Ulysses have been summoned from their unmarked graves because their visiting relatives are in serious trouble. But before they can solve the younger Latimers' problems, the three benevolent spirits light brief candles of insanity for a tipsy policeman, a recalcitrant banker, a convocation of English ghostbusters, and a card-playing rogue who's wanted for murder. "As felicitously foolish as a collaboration of (P.G.) Wodehouse and Thorne Smith."— Anthony Boucher. "For those who like something out of the ordinary. Lighthearted, very funny."—*The Sunday Times*. "A gay, most readable story."—*The Daily Telegraph.* **0-915230-24-0 $14.00**

Happy Returns by Manning Coles. The ghostly Latimers and their pet spectral monkey Ulysses return from the grave when Uncle Quentin finds himself in need of their help—it seems the old boy is being pursued by an old flame who won't take no for an answer in her quest to get him to the altar. Along the way, our courteous and honest spooks thwart a couple of bank robbers, unleash a bevy of circus animals on an unsuspecting French town, help out the odd person or two and even "solve" a murder—with the help of the victim. The laughs start practically from the first page and don't stop until Ulysses slides down the bannister, glass of wine in hand, to drink a toast to returning old friends. **0-915230-31-3 $14.00**

Come and Go by Manning Coles. The third and final book featuring the ghostly Latimers finds our heroes saving an ancestor from marriage and murder in a plot straight out of P.G. Wodehouse. **0-915230-34-8 $14.00**

The Far Traveller by Manning Coles. The Herr Graf was a familiar sight to the residents of the Rhineland village of Grauhugel. After all, he'd been walking the halls of the local castle at night and occasionally nodding to the servants ever since he drowned some 86 years ago. No one was the least bit alarmed by the Graf's spectral walks. Indeed, the castle's major domo found it all quite comforting, as the young Graf had been quite popular while he was alive. When the actor hired to play the dead Graf in a movie is felled by an accident, the film's director is overjoyed to come across a talented replacement who seems to have been born to play the part, little realizing that the Graf and his faithful servant—who perished in the same accident—had only recently decided to materialize in public. The Graf isn't stagestruck. He's back among the living to correct an old wrong. Along the way, he adds a bit of realism to a cinematic duel, befuddles a black marketeer, breaks out of jail, and exposes a charlatan spiritualist. In the meantime, his servant wonders if he's pursuing the granddaughters of the village maidens he dallied with eight decades ago.   **0-915230-35-6 $14.00**

The Chinese Chop by Juanita Sheridan. The postwar housing crunch finds Janice Cameron, newly arrived in New York City from Hawaii, without a place to live until she answers an ad for a roommate. It turns out the advertiser is an acquaintance from Hawaii, Lily Wu, whom critic Anthony Boucher (for whom Bouchercon, the World Mystery Convention, is named) described as "the exquisitely blended product of Eastern and Western cultures" and the only female sleuth that he "was devotedly in love with," citing "that odd mixture of respect for her professional skills and delight in her personal charms." First published in 1949, this ground-breaking book was the first of four to feature Lily and be told by her Watson, Janice, a first-time novelist. No sooner do Lily and Janice move into a rooming house in Washington Square than a corpse is found in the basement. In Lily Wu, Sheridan created one of the most believable—and memorable—female sleuths of her day.   **0-915230-32-1 $14.00**

Death on Milestone Buttress by Glyn Carr. Abercrombie ("Filthy") Lewker was looking forward to a fortnight of climbing in Wales after a grueling season touring England with his Shakespearean company. Young Hilary Bourne thought the holiday would be a pleasant change from her dreary job at the bank, as well as a chance to renew her acquaintance with a certain young scientist. Neither one expected this bucolic outing to turn deadly, but when one of their party is killed during what should have been an easy climb on the Milestone Buttress, Filthy and Hilary turn detective. Nearly every member of the climbing party had reason to hate the victim but each one also had an alibi for the time of the murder. Filthy and Hilary retrace the route of the fatal climb before returning to their lodgings where, in the grand tradition of Nero Wolfe, Filthy confronts the suspects and points his finger at the only person who could have committed the crime. Filled with climbing details sure to appeal to expert climbers and armchair mountaineers alike, *Death on Milestone Buttress* was published in England in 1951.   **0-915230-29-1 $14.00**

Murder, Chop Chop by James Norman. "The book has the butter-wouldn't-melt-in-his-mouth cool of Rick in *Casablanca*."—*The Rocky Mountain News*. "Amuses the reader no end."—*Mystery News*. "This long out-of-print masterpiece is intricately plotted, full of eccentric characters and very humorous indeed. Highly recommended."—*Mysteries by Mail*. Meet Gimiendo Hernandez Quinto, a gigantic Mexican who once rode with Pancho Villa and who now trains *guerrilleros* for the Nationalist Chinese government when he isn't solving murders. At his side is a beautiful Eurasian known as Mountain of Virtue, a woman as dangerous to men as she is irresistible. Together they look into the murder of Abe Harrow, an ambulance driver who appears to have died at three different times. There's also a cipher or two to crack, a train with a mind of its own, and Chiang Kai-shek's false teeth, which have gone mysteriously missing. First published in 1942.

0-915230-16-X $13.00

Death at The Dog by Joanna Cannan. "Worthy of being discussed in the same breath with an Agatha Christie or Josephine Tey...anyone who enjoys Golden Age mysteries will surely enjoy this one."—Sally Fellows, *Mystery News*. "Skilled writing and brilliant characterization."—*Times of London*. "An excellent English rural tale."—Jacques Barzun & Wendell Hertig Taylor in *A Catalogue of Crime*. Set in late 1939 during the first anxious months of World War II, *Death at The Dog*, first published in 1941, is a wonderful example of the classic English detective novel that flourished between the two World Wars. Set in a picturesque village filled with thatched-roof cottages, eccentric villagers and genial pubs, it's as well-plotted as a Christie, with clues abundantly and fairly planted, and as deftly written as the best of Sayers or Marsh, filled with quotable lines and perceptive observations on the human condition. **0-915230-23-2, $14.00.** The first book in this series is **They Rang Up the Police** by Joanna Cannan. "Just delightful."—*Sleuth of Baker Street* Pick-of-the-Month. "A brilliantly plotted mystery...splendid character study...don't miss this one, folks. It's a keeper."—Sally Fellows, *Mystery News.* When Delia Cathcart and Major Willoughby disappear from their quiet English village one morning in July 1937, it looks like a simple case of a frustrated spinster running off for a bit of fun with a straying husband. But as the hours turn into days, Inspector Guy Northeast begins to suspect that she may have been the victim of foul play. Never published in the United States, *They Rang Up the Police* appeared in England in 1939. **0-1915230-27-5 $14.00**

Cook Up a Crime by Charlotte Murray Russell. "Perhaps the mother of today's 'cozy' mystery . . . amateur sleuth Jane has a personality guaranteed to entertain the most demanding reader."—Andy Plonka, *The Mystery Reader.* "Some wonderful old time recipes...highly recommended."—*Mysteries by Mail.* Meet Jane Amanda Edwards, a self-styled "full-fashioned" spinster who complains she hasn't looked at herself in a full-length mirror since Helen Hokinson started drawing for *The New Yorker.* But you can always count on Jane to look into other people's affairs, especially when there's a juicy murder case to investigate. In this 1951 title Jane goes searching for recipes (included between chapters) for a cookbook project and finds a body instead. And once again her lily-of-the-field brother Arthur goes looking for love, finds strong drink, and is eventually discovered clutching the murder weapon. **0-915230-18-6 $13.00**

The Man from Tibet by Clyde B. Clason. Locked inside the Tibetan Room of his Chicago apartment, the rich antiquarian was overheard repeating a forbidden occult chant under the watchful eyes of Buddhist gods. When the doors were opened it appeared that he had succumbed to a heart attack. But the elderly Roman historian and sometime amateur sleuth Theocritus Lucius Westborough is convinced that Adam Merriweather's death was anything but natural and that the weapon was an eighth century Tibetan manuscript. **0-915230-17-8 $14.00**

The Mirror by Marlys Millhiser. "Completely enjoyable."—*Library Journal.* "A great deal of fun."—*Publishers Weekly.* How could you not be intrigued by a novel in which "you find the main character marrying her own grandfather and giving birth to her own mother?" Such is the situation in this classic novel, originally published in 1978, of two women who end up living each other's lives. Twenty-year-old Shay Garrett is not aware that she's pregnant and is having second thoughts about marrying Marek Weir when she's suddenly transported back 78 years in time into the body of Brandy McCabe, her own grandmother, who is unwillingly about to be married off to miner Corbin Strock. Shay's in shock but she still recognizes that the picture of her grandfather that hangs in the family home doesn't resemble her husband-to-be. But marry Corbin she does and off she goes to the high mining town of Nederland, where this thoroughly modern young woman has to learn to cope with such things as wood cooking stoves and—to her—old-fashioned attitudes about sex. In the meantime, Brandy McCabe is finding it even harder to cope with life in the Boulder, Colorado, of 1978. **0-915230-15-1 $14.95**

About The Rue Morgue Press

The Rue Morgue Press vintage mystery line is designed to bring back into print those books that were favorites of readers between the turn of the century and the 1960s. The editors welcome suggestions for reprints. To receive our catalog or make suggestions, write The Rue Morgue Press, P.O. Box 4119, Boulder, Colorado 80306 (1-800-699-6214).